THE WALLED GARDEN

Philip Glazebrook was born in 1937. His books include *Journey to Kars,* which describes a lonely journey taking him through the Serbian and Greek provinces of the old Ottoman Empire, and through the ruined classical cities of Asia Minor as far as Turkey's frontier with Russia and the fortress of Kars. These travels furnished the picturesque background for his two most recent novels, *Captain Vinegar's Commission* and *The Gate at the End of the World. The Walled Garden* was originally published as *The Burr Wood,* his third novel and the one which firmly established his reputation as a writer.

The author lives with his family in Dorset.

Philip Glazebrook

THE WALLED GARDEN

Flamingo
Published by Fontana Paperbacks

First published by Victor Gollancz Ltd 1977
under the title *The Burr Wood*
This revised Flamingo edition first published
in 1989 by Fontana Paperbacks
8 Grafton Street, London W1X 3LA

Flamingo is an imprint of
Fontana Paperbacks, part of
William Collins Sons & Co. Ltd, Glasgow

PART ONE

FOR REASONS THAT were not evident, perhaps legendary, perhaps a mistranslation from the Welsh, the pool the boy fished was called Chapel Weir. There were no mill ruins, no ruined chapel; only crags deckled with firs against a wild and hurrying sky, the rapid brown waste of broken water, wet rocks, the smell of spring. And fear.

To fish the pool so that his fly covered the salmons' lies the boy should have waded deeper, cast further. But the bottom was treacherous, his body light in water so heavy and strong; he waded deep, at the limit of what he could endure, balanced between terror and love for what he did, and shot the long uncurling lash of line as far as his strength could propel it. He knew where the fish lay, he imagined them beyond, just beyond where his fly pecked into the snarling current; but to stumble deeper into the river would put him at the mercy of what was merciless, this inchoate force of water which clamoured and bayed not only at his body but at the doors of his mind. It frightened him. And yet he was happy. He didn't think, only waded and cast. Warnings ran in his mind: Never trust your weight to a rocking boulder, never look at your reflection in swift water. He was fifteen, and had not as yet hooked a salmon.

So, expecting a silver smash, a running streak, a screaming reel, he did not at first know what had happened when the fly checked in its sweep. A dark pull. A pause in the current stronger than its swiftness. Louder than the river, sudden silence. In his mind stillness. Suspense. Then he knew. By the rod's tremor the fish communicated its strength. Its strength was to be still in that chaos of water, to impose stillness upon fury, silence upon sound, as frost petrifies the breaking wave.

Very slowly the salmon began to forge against the current, moving steadily—angrily—towards him. It was unafraid, sure of its strength. The boy reeled in till the line sung taut between them. The fish turned; the weight of water on its flank arched the rod; he glimpsed the flash of its side, saw through the swift translucence its grim head slowly shaken, saw its forked tail score the surface. Then the line cut water, the reel ticked, the fish swam steadily away. Captor and captive were held in a tension which made their rôles interchangeable. Now that he had seen the fish the boy's idea of it, though of water, was not watery; his idea was of flux given shape. He waited. He had never felt so utterly alone. He knew that he should act, should fight his way ashore into his own element, should put pressure on the fish. But he waited.

The salmon too waited for a while. Then for no reason that was apparent the line was adrift on the wild brown water. The fish was gone. The clamour of water poured back into the silence, the river surged at his body again, the wind blew and clouds hurried across the sky: what had been suspended flowed on. The fish sank back into the river, redissolved into water, became legendary as the Weir and the Chapel, and was gone.

He floundered ashore and crunched across the shingle. Out of the water his waders looked absurd, clumsy as clown's trousers. He found a dry rabbity bank out of the April wind where he sat down. With hands which shook he examined the fly which had been in the very jaws of the fish, the black hook which had almost caught the shape of flux. But it had not. You cannot draw up Leviathan with a hook. As usual nothing that he could express had happened. Would a fish on the stones beside him have expressed it? He doubted if a dead fish could have expressed what he had felt. There was nothing to tell anyone. Looking about to make sure that he was alone he took a packet of cigarettes out of the top pocket of his tweed jacket and lit one.

A few moments later his father, crying out 'Damnation!'

in surprise, fell down the bank almost on top of him. Reggie Vannick fell over everything, and was always surprised: how he had survived all these years in rivers, or flighting geese at nightfall on sea-marshes, or crossing Piccadilly, was a miracle. But he never thought of the danger, so confident that the earth was flat and made expressly for his delight that he never checked a foothold before throwing his weight gaily forward, every step he took a leap in the dark. He picked himself up. He was lean and tall, a disdainful figure. Knocking soil off the elegant old fishing coat he wore above thigh-waders he addressed his son in his pleasant, sardonic rasp.

'Any luck?'

Kim had had plenty of time to throw his cigarette away. 'No nothing' he replied. 'Have you?'

'Couple of pulls. Had one on for a second.' Against the rapid sky Reggie's beaky head quested about for the next event. 'You've fished the pool out have you?'

'Not quite no.'

'What are you waiting for then?'

'I was just resting. The wading's awfully dangerous.'

'Dangerous fiddlesticks! But I'll stop and watch if you like. Go on, you won't catch anything sitting here, on you go.' He rather hoped the boy would temporize, then he could make an issue of it, tell him to pull himself together: the whole point of this trip to Wales had been to find an opportunity of giving Kim the blowing-up people thought he needed.

But Kim complied. He picked up his rod and tramped away, his wading-staff rattling on the shingle until he entered the water just below the point where he had lost his salmon.

Reggie folded his angular frame into the shelter of the bank and pulled out his cigar case. How was he to make an opportunity for giving Kim a rocket when the boy melted away from every point you brought guns to bear on? Authority was impossible, he thought, impossible except when both sides accept the conventional hierarchy, as they had done in his only experiences of exercising authority: at school and in the army. Kim seemed to harass the hierarchy's right to impose its rule, but to harass it in such general terms that he presented no target for reprisal. He neither fought for ground nor appeared weakened by its loss. Reggie as a boy hadn't known anyone who used these guerrilla tactics against authority, for he and his friends, by virtue of the privileges they co-opted upon one another, had themselves constituted an authority, a ruling caste in the school. With their coloured waistcoats and their interconnections no one had questioned the rightness of their rule. Kim obeyed too, but with a mocking compliance which negated authority. It never seemed to worry his mother. 'Oh, Kim is just the same' she always said when some new charge, some fresh cavil, was laid against him by infuriated masters; 'he is at a difficult stage, but underneath he is just the same'. What did she mean? The same as what?

It was she, apropos of Kim's latest report, who had suggested this trip to Wales. 'Why don't you take him off for a day or two, just the two of you? I am sure it will set your mind at rest.'

She had not even troubled to read the report which lay on the table in her bedroom when he went in to say goodnight to her. She was not interested in the school's opinion of her son. Reggie on the other hand was desperately anxious to learn what schoolteachers and the world in general thought of his two children; he had perused the report off and on all morning in the library at Larkford, staring out of the windows, going back to his desk to check once more a particular phrase. 'A bit of a misfit' one beak had called his son. A bit of a misfit! It wouldn't do. It didn't do. You did yourself no end of damage if you didn't fit in. But how to convince the boy of this, if he hadn't learned by example? Take him off to Wales, his mother suggested: all right he would. Wales had seemed comfortably far off. Something would turn up to do Reggie's work for him.

But nothing had. The atmosphere was not comfortable. Reggie was reminded of the atmosphere in the Scottish lodge which his own father used to take: he felt a reluctance to confront his son identical to the reluctance he had then felt to confront his father. Now, as then, he felt ill-equipped to defend himself against an individual who threw doubt upon the accepted world. What could you say to people who didn't speak the proper language? He felt again the severe bleak glitter of his father's disapproval lighting upon him across the billiard table in that Scottish lodge. Father always chose the billiard room in which to administer reproof, where you were a prisoner with neither escape nor occupation whilst he tramped round the table picking off the hard cold balls like so many butts of his sarcasm. Father (who took his coffee after dinner in a room apart from his family, examining *The Times* fiercely through his pince-nez for signs of mankind's foolishness) would look into the drawing-room later and summon one of his sons: 'Reginald, just step along and give me a game of billiards would you'. He walked off without waiting for an answer. Reggie left the fireside, the talk, his brothers, to follow Father along matchboarded corridors under the lofty gaze of stags' heads. The forbidding elderly back receded ahead of him, leaving open for Reggie to close the doors which cut off retreat, into draughtier and more cheerless extents of the lodge; until Father waited at the billiard room door, which he closed behind Reggie himself. He switched on the lights: at a stroke the free dark hill outside vanished behind blackly-reflecting windows. Reggie helped fold the cover off the table with the feelings of a virgin preparing the bed for her own downfall. Upon the brilliant green rectangle, light pouring upon his silvery head, his father was soon performing whilst Reggie leaned on his cue in the shadows and waited.

'Didn't take to that fellow Taylor' he began, puffing out his moustache as he lined up a shot. 'Didn't care for him at all. Lot of hot air and swagger as far as I could see. He by way of being a particular friend of yours is he?' The black ball shot into a pocket iike Taylor sent packing.

'Tinker's a friend of everyone's, Father. You meet Tinker

everywhere' Reggie protested in defence of the guest who had motored off in his Lagonda that day, lucky beggar. 'He's gone on to stop with the duke' he added rashly, replacing black on the spot.

'You don't say so!' Father was contemptuous of neighbours on principle. 'They may do as they please in that gin-palace, but I don't care for gambling in my house as well you know. Don't care for guests who poach out my salmon with spinners either.' Black was again sent about its business. 'That fine fellow will get into hot water some of these days, you see if he don't.'

'Everyone plays Contract for money now Father.'

'Everyone! Everyone is a friend of Taylor, everyone does this, everyone does that——!' He huffed and puffed, chalking his cue with a fierce screwing action. 'If your only line of defence is "everyone" I may as well talk to the man in the moon. Haven't you an opinion of your own haven't you?' His contemptuous, heavily-lidded eyes glistened at Reggie for a moment before he resumed his break with a cannon so delicate that no one in a rage could have achieved it.

What could Reggie say? It floored him to have the standing of a fellow like Tinker Taylor questioned, a fellow who'd been in Pop and at Trinity with him. How could you set about defending what everyone took for granted? Uneasily, people laughed at Father; made a joke of his having corresponded as a young man with Prince Kropotkin; sniggered at the extravagant Paradise Garden he was creating at Larkford, planting it with exotics which the company's timber ships brought to Bristol from every part of the world; but nobody laughed to his face. 'Your governor's an odd bird' people had been saying to Reggie for years; and oddity wasn't a distinction he cared for.

He wouldn't have an odd bird for a son, Reggie thought as he watched Kim fishing. The line sprang like a bowshot from the long sweet action of the rod, the boy fished as gracefully as his grandfather. But where in the world would that get him? God knows what would have become of Father nowadays. All very well being a misfit then if you had ten thousand a year. Nowadays you had to fit in. Especially as there would be precious little of Father's money left by the time Kim was grown up. Oh—money! He thought of the dismal interviews with Mr Sowerby, his man of business, from which he longed to escape just as he had longed to escape from billiards with Father. He threw away his cigar.

It was cold by the river. Reggie chafed his hands. He couldn't understand why he felt the cold so, nowadays. He never used to, and he didn't feel any older: that is to say, he couldn't believe in himself as being older. It all seemed like a dressing-up game, getting older, having children growing up—he expected another player to unmask him, and then they could all play something else. The war, that had been a game worth playing ... but now no new games seemed to come along, and he had to go on impersonating a middle-aged responsible man. People were not taken in; Kim's housemaster for instance, during conferences in his study, looked out of the window most of the time as if embarrassed by the poorness of Reggie's disguise. 'Kim tells me some rigmarole' the man began 'about you approving his giving up chemistry.' Protuberant fish-eyes gave Reggie a cold scrutiny before turning back to the window. 'I believe we would make a grave mistake in allowing Kim to take the line of least resistance.'

His fish-eyes had not cowed Mrs Vannick. 'Do you mean to tell us that the world would lose a great chemist?' she enquired in her silver tone.

'Perhaps not.' The schoolmaster's fingers were white as chalks, pressed together behind his back. 'But in my opinion —in my experience—it is a mistaken kindness to let—er—to allow, allow a boy with Kim's tendency to ... well let us say "to take the easy route"; a mistake to allow such a boy to give up in the face of a little difficulty.'

He turned and looked severely at Reggie again. Caught unawares—he had been thinking that so bald a man must find it delightful to plunge his head in the bath each morning—Reggie said 'Quite. Quite. Yes.'

But his wife didn't dodge hostility. 'We all know perfectly well that Kim is quite capable of learning chemistry' she said serenely, 'it seems that this particular master isn't able to teach him.'

The tutor's pampered face was solemn. 'He is an excellent teacher I assure you. We have spoken together and come to the decision, the—er—conclusion, that it would be a foolish mistake to let Vannick, Kim, to allow Kim to run away to square leg in the face of a little fast bowling.' A joyless smile thinned his lips. 'But in the nature of things the decision, the —er—final decision, rests with you as his father.'

Through the window had come the voice of a boy calling 'You bag a court and I'll bring a pill'. Reggie longed for a game of racquets with a boy his own age.

Kim was waiting for them in the street outside, his overcoat turned up round his thin, hawkish face, his shoes scuffed and broken-laced. Reggie remembered the splendid figure he had himself cut at this school (a splendour which only Father had mocked). 'Afraid the decision's gone against you' he said, walking towards the car beside Kim.

'What decision?'

'About the chemistry. You'll have to soldier on I'm afraid.'

'Oh that.' Kim dismissed it. 'I didn't know there'd be such a palaver.'

'Do you need anything darling?' His mother's face looked out from her furs through the car window. 'Anything I can send?'

'I don't think so thanks.'

'You will be home in a month.'

'Yes. Goodbye.'

In the mirror as they drove off Reggie saw him hunch into his coat and slouch away. Guilt, inadequacy, troubled Reggie for a mile or two. Then he treated his wife to a take-off of Kim's tutor and recovered his spirits. He was a good mimic, and she was amused.

Or was she? She, like Kim, seemed to laugh behind her eyes, privately, more amused at the idea of him still doing imitations than by the imitations themselves. So, in the pub last night, Kim had laughed. Reggie, thinking that claret would loosen the boy's tongue and create companionship between them, had pushed the bottle towards him: 'Come on, another glass won't hurt you.' 'I'd rather not thanks.' Reggie had finished the bottle and loosened his own tongue into telling stories complete with mimicry; and Kim, watching, had laughed behind those secretive eyes.

Something had to be done. Reggie looked up and down the river for some person or event that would do his work for him. At that moment a salmon showed in the pool. That was it! Let Kim hook a fish and he'd talk. No boy could hook his first salmon without excitement breaking down his reserve, and then would come companionship and understanding between himself and his son.

But Kim didn't hook another fish. At last he came ashore and tramped along the shingle towards his father, the long rod springing on his shoulder.

'Nothing much doing?' Reggie squinted up at him.

'Nothing.'

Kim sat down, his canvas waders crackling. He chose a spot not as close to his father as a friend would have sat. He looked cold and lonely.

On impulse, to offer the nearer ground, Reggie said cheerfully 'Smoke a cigarette if you want. Don't tell Mother I let you though.'

'She doesn't mind me smoking.'

Reggie was handling a stone; its cold hardness reminded him again of playing billiards with Father. 'Well, smoke if you want' he said.

'Not at the moment thanks.'

Reggie was irritated. Irritation gave him the impetus to plunge in, though he had not thought what he would say.

He dropped the stone with a sharp detonation on the shingle and began. 'Your tutor seems to think you're rather losing ground in the house Kim.'

He felt in his pockets for his cigar case. Kim sat tailor-fashion, contemplating the stones, his mop of black hair inclined forward. 'Oh?' he said.

'What do you say to that?' A cigar was clipped.

Kim's long hands drooped on the knees of his waders. 'Depends what he means, losing ground.'

Reggie rattled matches, made a windbreak. 'Well' he said between drawing on the cigar 'not—pulling your weight not —doing yourself justice not——' The charges gusted off his lips thin as cigar-smoke, dissolved. His cigar alight, Kim still silent, he rasped 'Come on now, you must have something to say about it.'

'I was trying to think what he could mean.'

'Oh come along Kim you know very well what he means. You may think it's good enough to ... but your whole attitude is ... well, bloody slack.' His irritation fed him no better word than slack. Beaks never came up with anything specific either, just uneasy cavilling grumbles in their meticulous handwriting. Bloody ushers. 'And quite apart from the beaks' he said, shifting his ground, 'other boys see that kind of thing you know. It doesn't wash.'

Kim continued to stare at the stones. He seemed insulated by the sound of the river like someone listening intently to music.

'I mean to say—' Reggie retreated to old reports for more ammunition '—well, take that do about you shirking training in the winter half. Getting across the Captain of Games, that's the kind of thing I mean.'

'It's so pointless running. I didn't see any point.'

Here was a specific issue. 'It isn't up to you to decide what the point of running is Kim. What would happen if everyone in the place started deciding for themselves what the point is? Lower boys and every Tom Dick and Harry slacking about. Eh? It would be chaos—anarchy. How do you expect the Captain of Games to carry on if everyone disobeys his rules? If everyone thinks like you?'

'Don't worry.' Kim turned his contemptuous long-lidded eyes on his father. 'Everyone doesn't.'

'No, and everyone thinks the less of fellows who go against the grain.'

'I don't think it matters what "everyone" thinks.'

This echo of Father's sarcasm took the wind out of Reggie's sails. How to defend a principle so universally accepted as oligarchy, if the boy didn't see it already? But he would, he must. 'Wait till you're at the top of the school yourself. There has to be authority, you'll see.'

'Maybe. But I don't want to run anything.'

'You will. There has to be authority Kim. Everyone— people I mean, people have to learn to obey so later they're fit to command. That's the system. Am I not right?'

Kim looked away, over the river to the firwoods, the wild hillside and the sky. 'You're right it is the system' he said.

'Of course I am.' Reggie gained confidence. 'Of course I am, it's anarchy else. And fellows who don't go along with the system find themselves out on a limb before you can say Jack Robinson ... and what's more, when the time comes round to think about getting on, getting into Pop and so forth, the awkward squad find it's gone against them, this trying to be superior. They find themselves—' he thought he might as well fire off every missile whilst he was at it '—well, find they're misfits if you like. Do you see what I'm driving at?'

'Yes I see what you're driving at. But I don't think I want to get into Pop much' Kim added.

'Everyone wants to be in Pop.' Reggie paused. 'Why on earth not?'

'It isn't the sort of thing I want. It wouldn't help.'

'It always helps to be successful, popular, call it what you like.'

'Depends what you want to do.'

'And what do you want to do?'

Kim's eyes seemed to measure his father's capacity to understand an answer. Then he looked away. 'I don't know' he said.

The roar of the river came between them, isolating each. Reggie chafed his hands, his cigar in his teeth. I don't mind, I don't know, it doesn't matter: Kim's negativeness baffled him. In looking beyond success, Kim saw disenchantment; beyond action he saw the futility of action. What would become of him? Well, Reggie thought, time enough to worry about the future. He's got his National Service then Cambridge; plenty of time to meet up with a group he wants to be part of. Some chap will come along and dazzle him, give him a style to imitate. Something will turn up.

'I think you'll see things a bit differently when you're nearer the top of the school' he said comfortably. 'You wait till all your friends are getting colours and so on you'll feel differently, see if you don't. Any chance of you being tried for the Eleven next half? Still a bit early I suppose.'

'I don't know, I don't like any of the people who run the cricket.'

'Not like them?' It was a view which had never occurred to Reggie, not to like the people who ran things. To explain its eccentricity to himself he said 'I don't think you'll find it'll pay dividends to try and set yourself up as different from everyone else Kim'.

Kim accepted this, his head bowed.

'You'd find you had a very much easier passage if you joined in a bit more ... fitted in you know. Believe me. It's not just a school thing either: I've found that wherever you go it's best to sink your differences and rub along with all sorts. City, the army—doesn't matter where you go, people'll like you more if you're one of them. It simply does not pay to be the odd man out. Oddities' he said, remembering Father, 'are held against you, make no mistake on that score.'

Kim said 'I wonder what oddities my tutor can mean?'

'Oh I don't say he used the word. I was talking in general terms, nothing specific ... nothing you can't put to rights at any rate. It's—er—just this general tendency to question what has to be accepted and—do you see?' Reggie was terrified that he might lapse without meaning to into his imitation of Kim's tutor.

'It's rather hard to change a general tendency' Kim said. 'I mean if that's what you're like you can't——'

'Good Lord you're only fifteen you know. You're not like anything. But if you want a particular instance take this business about Pop for instance,' Reggie said, 'no reason on earth why you shouldn't get in. But you won't get anywhere if you keep on telling yourself you can't or don't want to or don't like it or something.' In a moment he asked 'What's wrong with Pop anyway? According to you?'

'Oh nothing.' Kim made an unquiet gesture. 'They just —swagger around. I don't know.'

'Of course they swagger around, perfectly natural. So will you. And you have a bike and all that sort of thing. Privileges.'

'It isn't a privilege at home, having a bike.'

Again Reggie feared that his son's context was too wide, his values absolute instead of relative. 'You'll see' he assured himself, if not Kim; 'You'll learn.'

He smoked in silence, listening in his mind to footsteps in the street, cocksure voices below his window, his door flung back and his room exploding in the jolly riot which told him he'd been co-opted into Pop. The archetype of all later delights. He so wanted that for his son. 'Tell you what' he said, 'I'll look out all my old waistcoats sometime and make 'em over to you.'

'But—' Kim laughed '—but they've been in the acting cupboard for years.'

'In the acting cupboard?'

'For when we dressed up when we were children.' Then he saw that his father was crestfallen. 'But I would love to have them though' he said 'for in case I get in.'

'Of course you'll get in if you once set your mind to it.' Reggie's voice warmed with enthusiasm enough for both of them. Ah, he was so heartened—so relieved. 'And don't take all this jawing too much to heart will you? Promised your tutor I'd have a word with you and I have. We'll see an improvement eh? Don't give the ushers too rough a time—!' He stretched out and grasped his son's arm like a companion's. 'They're only trying to set you on the right lines you know.'

He looked earnestly into his son's face. Kim in response, though passive under the hand's pressure on his arm, gave the wonderful smile which he and his mother shared; and Reggie glimpsed, as he had often glimpsed in his wife's smile, that hint of mockery. Something had eluded him: it glinted like a coin twisting away through water. He withdrew his hand. He got to his feet.

'Come on then' he said, pulling a large silk handkerchief out of his top pocket and blowing his beaky nose, 'come on, let's see if you can't get a fish out of Chapel Weir. Wade right out this time, deep as ever you can. I'll stop here, so you'll be quite safe. Right?'

'Yes okay.' Kim picked up his rod.

'I know it seems you'll never hook a salmon' Reggie said, 'but you've just been unlucky with the salmon always.'

'I don't mind much. I just like fishing.'

'Ah, wait till you hook one. Then you'll know all about it. I do so hope you get a fish Kim.'

Kim smiled again. 'I wish I could' he said.

With love now in his mind Reggie watched this only son he had wade out until only head and arms, and the long rod glancing, showed in wild water. A misfit indeed! he wished that pampered tutor could see the boy fishing there. Reggie scrambled up the bank and walked away downstream for his own rod. In his delight he forgot his promise to watch over Kim.

There stepped into his path from amongst the alders a Welshman, an old man in a long macintosh tied with string and a hat knocked shapeless by weather. They spoke. Unsure whether the apparition was poacher or keeper, or neither, Reggie used a bluff tone which served either case. Parting he said, 'I left my son fishing Chapel Weir if you should see him. Ought to be a fish there.'

The old man's finger rubbed stubble on his cheek. 'Pity the lad didn't hold that fish he hooked a bit harder though. Soft on him he was. He'll lose the fish, I said to myself.'

'What fish? He hasn't hooked a fish. A salmon?'

'Yes indeed.' The old man looked for words slowly. 'A big fish too I should say, fought deep you know. Deep he stayed. I shouted to the boy, shouted I did, but he paid me no heed.'

'Well, he won't take anyone's advice.' The harsh rasp was back in Reggie's voice. All that talk, and Kim had told him nothing. He turned away. 'He'll have to learn the hard way that's all. Good day to you.'

2.

'C-C-COAL WAS NO problem in our house in the war,' declared the young exquisite from his easy chair as he struck a light for his cigarette on a silver match-case. Sulphur wreathed him like the smoke-puff in which the Demon King makes his appearance in pantomime. 'If we needed a few Derby Brights my m-m-mama popped into bed with the coalman.'

Kim giggled excitedly. 'So did mine' he claimed. 'Maybe madame Deffin's coalmerchant didn't fancy her do you think?'

Up in Kim's bedroom they were commenting on the conversation begun downstairs in the French house where Kim had been staying since New Year: madame Deffin had been speaking of the shortages and high prices of the war. Sparse meals and low fires kept alive the memory of a war which had never quite ended in her own mind.

'Do you think?' Kim repeated.

But Evelyn Sele had tired of the subject. Stretching out his feet in embroidered slippers he asked 'Do you always go to bed at this hour?' He had only arrived from England that day.

'Depends what time we finish the mot-croisé'

'You sit doing that crossword every evening? And up to bed at ten?'

'Sometimes it's later' said Kim. He stood by the table in his pyjamas, for he had been writing out a poem when Evelyn had strolled into his room. 'There's nothing much else to do,' he added defensively, covering his poem with a book.

His new friend laughed. He unscrewed the top of a silver flask lying in his lap and tipped an inch of whisky into the tooth-mug balanced on the arm of his chair. Then he reclined and contemplated Kim.

Evelyn's own appearance—sheeny black hair smoothed off an alabaster brow, penetrating eyes set deep and rather close, tie loosened in the neck of a silk shirt—had the gloss of manhood. In face of his leisurely gaze Kim pulled a dressing gown over his school pyjamas from which his wrists and ankles gawked.

Evelyn laughed. 'Well' he said 'I daresay we can find a way of cheering things up. Have a snifter?' He held out his flask.

'Oh, thanks, but there isn't another glass' said Kim.

'Fetch one from next door.'

'Annie's next door.' Annie was another pupil.

'She won't b-bite.'

'Yes okay.'

Watching the younger boy saunter with affected nonchalance into the corridor made Evelyn smile. He tapped his teeth and looked round the bedroom. A sliver of moonlight slid between the curtains and he got up and shut them roughly. He did not like the cold white purity of the moon. Then he explored Kim's possessions: clothes, letters, books —there wasn't much. A silk handkerchief he liked the look of and would contrive to procure. On the table a letter from a school in Berkshire signed 'masses of love from Sue'. He moved a book and uncovered a poem written fancifully in green ink. Reading it he was delighted, for he fed upon what people tried to hide. His glittering eyes grinned at their reflection in a glass. Yes, there were possibilities. Wherever there was innocence and moonshine, there was something to destroy. He had been exiled here against his will, and destruction was the only method of retaliation within his power.

When Kim returned he found Evelyn nursing his whisky in the easy chair, the snake-brilliance of his eyes now somnolent again. 'No glass?' he enquired.

'I think she must be asleep.'

'Didn't you go in?'

'No but I knocked and she didn't answer. I don't really want a drink, or not just at the moment.'

'I'll get Annie's glass.'

Evelyn kicked off his slippers and prowled into the passage. When he returned he held up another tooth-mug.

'Here we are.' Pouring whisky into it he said 'Annie sleeps nude sensible girl. Have you had a b-bash at her yet?'

'She's engaged' Kim told him.

Evelyn laughed—a blue vein stood out on his forehead—and handed Kim the mug. 'Then drink destruction to her troth' he cried.

By the time Evelyn went to bed he had captivated Kim. It was the first step in his plans for self-amusement. Parents anxious to have him off their hands had parachuted him again and again into what they hoped was difficult terrain; Evelyn had learned to fall on his feet. At nineteen he prided himself that no one could devise an exile for him so lacking in possibilities that he couldn't either amuse himself or get himself repatriated in disgrace.

When he came downstairs next morning he found that his three companions—Kim, Annie and a jug-eared youth named Swindells—had already finished their breakfast amid the blackened boiserie of the dining room. Guarding their cups they watched him pour himself coffee. 'She might have

23

let us have some of the m-marmalade I brought' he said, buttering his bread.

'Gosh you certainly got in madame's good books bringing marmalade' Annie said.

'Gosh, didn't I just.' He made his eyes glitter at her. She was a slight, blonde girl whose fresh colouring and softness, her haziness of outline, made her pretty.

'Hey!' Annie exclaimed, reaching to stop Swindells pouring himself more coffee. 'It's not your turn for the second cup, is it Kim?'

'She had it two days running last week' muttered Swindells, still struggling to master the pot, 'it's Kim's if it's anyones.'

'Help me Kim' Annie appealed, 'then I'll give you half.'

Kim helped her, but Evelyn noticed that he avoided touching her fingers as if they were Hell fire. 'Why not get some more?' he suggested.

They had not thought of that. Evelyn took the pot into the kitchen. They heard the cook laughing. He brought it back refilled. However, the fresh pot seemed to them to have no savour, as a game played for tokens has no point once currency is introduced.

Madame Deffin taught her pupils for an hour each throughout the morning, reading with them in the French classics and then, for the second half of their period—speaking in thin, excitable tones whilst the hair strayed out of her bun —she trod the scratched parquet from one marble chimney-piece to the other, to and fro on squeaky shoes, passing and repassing the tall windows, the chipped gilt chairs, her pupil at the table, hurrying through centuries of French history until she arrived at their climax, the great days of the war and her own famous deeds in the Résistance. How she had ridden the countryside on her bicycle, setting fire to out-of-the-way woods; how she had refused to black the boots of a German officer billeted upon her; she recounted all this again and again to pupils of exactly the wrong age to be interested.

'God how they go on about the war' said Evelyn to Kim, who was giving him an account of madame Deffin's ways that morning. 'Every one of them might have won the bloody thing single handed instead of the entire lot of them losing it. Not that the English are any better—you should hear the gallant Colonel Sele.'

'My father's just the same' Kim lied. 'But madame isn't a bad old stick really' he added out of loyalty to the inexplicable happiness he had felt—inexplicable now that Evelyn showed him how dull a place it was—in this tranquil French house. 'And I suppose the war was fair hell for them all.'

'They caused it, if I was them I'd shut up about it' Evelyn said.

Kim said nothing, letting this large new thought about his parents' generation, and his teachers' generation, sink into his mind. Caused it; he supposed they had, yes.

Whilst Annie was closeted with madame Deffin he and Evelyn were strolling on the gravel which extended from the grey house to a stream flowing sluggishly amongst reeds. 'So what do you d-do for amusement?' Evelyn asked.

Kim wondered, stared. 'Oh we ... I don't know, talk, and read ... or I read; Annie writes these endless letters to her fiancé. Or we go for walks sometimes and ... It's quite fun. I mean pretty boring but not too bad.' He felt ashamed of such small pleasures.

'Sounds like the first act of *Uncle Vanya*.' Evelyn flipped his cigarette disdainfully into the stream at their feet.

Kim wished he had read *Uncle Vanya*. 'Swindells really is the most frightful fool though' he said, glad to find something positively unpleasant to condemn.

'Why? Seems all right. A nice b-b-bloke, I thought.'

'You can't think so!' Kim couldn't be sure what those staring black eyes really thought. 'Annie can't stand him, she thinks he's going to jump on her, and madame can't stand him either.'

'Unanimity doesn't budge me. He looks a bit of all right to me.'

'Honestly you don't know him. He was at my private and he was called——'

' "At my private" ' mimicked Evelyn in a high childish squeak. 'You're as bad as the old folk harking back to the war. Fuck your private. History is bunk, kiddo. This is all we got—' he made a sweep with his hand at the visible world '—so carpe bloody diem.'

Carpe diem. Kim took in the hazy spring sunlight on the slender trunks of poplars across the water, and the hollowing blue of the sky. He felt life beginning. He couldn't help his soul joyously mounting. From the copse, like an icicle thawing in the sun, dripped a chiff-chaff's song. 'Ah listen!' he said.

Evelyn watched the boy's face turned upward. Clapping his hands to see if the bird would fly away he said ' 'Tis the voice of the lobster I heard him declare, they have baked me too hard for such rustical fare'. Turning back towards the flaky house (and Kim turned too, like a dog on a lead) he said 'So for amusement all you can offer is Annie. Now you assure me she's a v-v-virgin?'

Again Kim stared. 'Oh yes. I mean I suppose. I mean—do you think so?' he appealed, failing to conceal the gleam that the idea lit in his eyes.

An hour later Evelyn was walking with Annie in the garden. Kim had trotted indoors for his lesson and Annie had emerged from the house blinking her large milky-blue eyes in the sunlight, her exercise book under her arm, to find Evelyn idling beneath the plane trees. 'Come and show me the garden' he had called to her.

She looked round for a place to leave her book.

'I'll carry it' he said, detaching his bat-black form from the trees' shade and approaching her across mossy gravel, 'isn't it the first step in c-courting, to c-carry your schoolbooks? "Going courting, oh it sets your senses in a whirl",' he sang in a sudden rumbustious bass.

Annie laughed, which dimpled her cheek. She gave him her book and then, finding empty hands awkward, reached up to pull a twig from the tree and busied her fingers in peeling it as they walked along.

Nearing the kitchen garden wall she said 'We aren't supposed to go in the potager basically.'

'Ah petit chou' he replied 'c'est les fruits interdits qui sont doux.'

She tinkled with laughter. 'There's this funny old jardinier' she told him 'he's super but madame says I'll pick up his accent so I sneak in when she isn't looking.'

'Does he say "P-pop into the potting shed and I'll show you my accent"?' Evelyn watched her face grow doubtful, and went on 'Kim asked me did I think you were a virgin'.

'Kim did?' Now her face had clouded.

'Surprise you?'

'It doesn't sound like Kim.' Behind the childish eyes an older spirit looked out. 'And what did you answer pray?'

He stared her up and down. She ran the peeled twig juicily in and out between her lips. 'How can I tell what you and he have been up to?' he asked.

'Oh honestly! Me and Kim? Anyway I bet he's one.'

'One what?'

'You know. What you said. A virgin.' The colour ran through her cheeks.

'And him with a lady-friend in England?'

'A schoolgirl she is. I know all about her' Annie asserted. 'Kim's terribly young basically.'

'You mean not daredevil enough to go in the kitchen garden?' Evelyn pushed open the green door in the flint wall.

Stepping through it she told him 'I'm in enough trouble already, I just don't want to get in any more that's all.'

He struck a match for his cigarette. The kitchen garden oppressed him, a rectangle of weeds and tottery vegetables, dilapidated glasshouses glittering in the misty sun. He was oppressed by neediness and provinciality. He leaned against the door and smoked.

'Quite enough trouble I'm in' Annie repeated.

Evelyn recollected that these hobbledehoys were the only

amusement he had. 'What sort of trouble m'dear?' he enquired.

'Gosh are those spring onions?' Away she tripped to pull two. As he approached she held one out to him: 'You have to have one too, then it won't matter our breath smelling.'

'Planning to drag me into the lettuces and show me your c-c-curly kale?'

'Oh you've got sex on the brain is your trouble.' She bit crossly into her onion. Yet the subject kept her coquettish.

'What's this spot of bother you're in?' he asked.

'It's frightfully involved.' She wandered ahead, flirting out her skirt.

'Ah, better not tax my poor old loaf with it then.'

She began at once. 'I don't know if anyone's let on—I had to tell Kim—but I'm engaged to this fantastic man, I mean it's not official but—anyway everyone's livid because he's miles older and he's an Australian and I promised Mummy I wouldn't write and then madame found this letter and we don't know if she's told Mummy—so you see it's ghastly.'

She's like the chiff-chaff twittering, Evelyn thought. 'They packed you off here so you're out of range of the b-bounder's boo-boo-boomerang?'

Against her will Annie laughed. 'You're insane' she said. 'Yes they sent me here. Honestly, as if I'd ever forget Charles!'

Evelyn made his voice scornful, his eyes cold: 'And you just let them.'

'Well what——? I mean basically I can't do much can I?'

'You mean you haven't the price of a ticket to wherever the man is?'

'I suppose, but——'

'But bloody nothing. Why the hell not go if you want? Meet a taxi in the village, train to Paris, Christ you could be in bed with him tonight if you want. If you want that is. They can only shut you up if you let them. Authority's a conjuring trick kid, if the audience doesn't believe in it it doesn't work.'

She stared, just as Kim had stared, at the possibilities of freedom. In her blue eyes Evelyn watched these possibilities, which she had not imagined, burgeon like Japanese flowers he had dropped into blue saucers. Then he flicked his cigarette into the cabbages and turned away as if he was tired of her. 'I know why you don't go' he said 'you've got hot knickers for Kim, that's the thing.'

So he began to cast his shadow this way and that, sullying the moonshine.

Days passed. When Evelyn took his turn in the salon his voice, and madame Deffin's sheep-cough laugh, drifted through the windows to Kim or Annie who idled outside for the chance of attaching themselves to Evelyn when he emerged. But they did not wait together: Kim and Annie had become uneasy in each other's company. If one saw the other strolling in the garden both would falter, and turn off under the trees apart. It was as if they had suddenly found in that garden a maze whose paths would not bring them together. The only simple pleasure left from the old days was teasing Swindells; but in this sport Evelyn did not join, and it too began to pall.

In the afternoons Evelyn often took out an old flat-bottomed boat he had found in a garage that the others had never explored, and in this craft, stocked with his flask and an Olympia Press paperback, he punted himself gently away downstream till his voice singing songs from *Seven Brides* —'Sun's getting shinery to spotlight the finery'—faded from the garden. When he had gone Kim and Annie were bored. They could not think what they used to do with their afternoons. Annie confided that she had stopped writing to her fiancé for a bit 'just to see'; but the possibilities which this implied made them turn away from each other more shyly than ever. On separate stone benches each sat imagining how their conversation might have continued.

One day Evelyn asked Kim if he would like to go boating.

'I don't mind' Kim shrugged.

'Don't come if you don't want to.'

'Oh I'll come.'

Kim brought a volume of Descartes, which he was studying with madame Deffin, and Evelyn punted downriver till he moored to a willow and lay back in the strengthening sun. Longing to talk or to argue Kim couldn't bear to see Evelyn close his eyes. 'I do love that matchcase of yours' he said when Evelyn lit a cigarette. 'Is it a family thing? Can I see?'

Evelyn chucked it along the boat. 'Have it if you want. I've got several.'

'Really?' Kim handled the slim silver trinket which seemed the quintessence of Evelyn's elegance. 'Are you really giving it me?'

'In return for anything you've got that'll keep this f-fucking sun out my eyes.'

Kim had in his top pocket the silk handkerchief that Evelyn had noticed before. He gladly gave it to his friend, who spread it over his face and seemed to fall into a doze. Because Evelyn's green paperback lay on top of Descartes Kim riffled through it. Soon he was reading intently. The book so startled him that he could not put it down. He looked up at last to find Evelyn watching him. 'Do you mind me borrowing this?' he asked, holding up the book.

'Haven't you read it?'

'Not this one I don't think?'

'Sad stuff. I only bought it to swat the flies. Give us a light,' he said, cupping his hands to catch the matchcase Kim lobbed down the boat. When he had lit his cigarette the matchcase slipped into his brass-buttoned boating jacket. 'Well, anchors aweigh!' he cried, springing up so that the craft rocked and Kim clutched the gunwhale for safety.

Evelyn poled the boat along, singing, the silk handkerchief knotted piratically around his brow. Kim longed to discuss Annie, or the paperback, but he always felt that subjects that Evelyn did not introduce himself were naive—Evelyn was apt to mock. Nor did he like to ask for the matchcase back in case he had somehow misunderstood something. He wished he had thought of tying his handkerchief around his brow instead of just wearing it in his top pocket like his father. It was the silk handkerchief that now seemed the epitome of Evelyn's style.

In the evenings they no longer did the crossword, and no longer went to bed at ten. Evelyn had brought a backgammon board and he taught Kim the game whilst Annie hung over his shoulder. Provided that they spoke French madame Deffin smiled on anything Evelyn did. About ten she would fold the local paper over which she had muttered and exclaimed since supper, would collect together bag and shawl, would admonish them for using two lights where one would serve, would claw logs off the fire and creak away to bed. It was the lonely lamplight in which Swindells had been snorting over Racine that she had extinguished, and he too crept round the wall and fumbled open the door, grunting 'Bonsoir' like a rustic oath. Kim and Annie were left in the stillness of the salon, books unread in their laps, hoping to start an interesting conversation with Evelyn, who was practising card tricks at the table.

'I must say' Kim began, 'I do think Descartes, I mean his theory, I must say I agree with it, don't you Evelyn?'

Taper fingers were dealing four hands swiftly. 'You agree do you? "I agree therefore I am"—not quite the same as "I think therefore I am" is it? "I agree therefore I don't matter" is the zombie motto seems to me. Now, if one of you folks'll pick up that hand you'll find thirteen spades in it with a bit of luck.'

Annie beat Kim to the hand. 'Gosh fantastic' she said, letting the cards fall. 'Honestly Evelyn, if Swindells doesn't do something about his spots I'm going to go insane.'

'It's because he m-m-masturbates too much' said Evelyn chattily as he restacked the deck. 'I'll lay you odds it's him pinched your knickers.'

'Someone pinched—has someone pinched them?' Kim asked.

'Off the washing line. We're watching the suspects aren't we Annie?'

Annie looked at Kim, looked away. 'Oh honestly!' she giggled.

'But tomorrow' Evelyn continued 'tomorrow I plan to examine their p-p-palms.'

Kim had put his hand over the spot on his chin. Now he hid his hand. 'Why their palms?'

'To find the black hair which sprouts from the masturbator's palm of course. Haven't you read Friedmann? Now, t-take a card one of you.'

Both reached for a card, as eager for the subject of sex to be dropped as they were for it to be raised.

The books which Evelyn had read were ones which no one else had heard of, and he was so contemptuous of 'classics' that a conviction grew in Kim's mind that the course of reading he had set himself in the New Year, on madame Deffin's advice, was too slow and too pedestrian to serve his new purpose. Besides, Swindells had now outpaced him on the same course. Kim needed short-cuts to the heights where Evelyn strolled. He learned the line of Racine which is quoted in the first few pages of Proust, and left the rest of Proust and Racine unread. On Swindells he practised a mocking manner. Finding him bent over Lamartine he said:

'I wouldn't bother reading a man who wrote a line as bad as "Dieu que le son du cor est triste au fond des bois".' To his annoyance the magic line raised prickles on his scalp.

'Lamartine didn't write it' snuffled Swindells.

'No but he might well have done' retorted Kim passing on. From Evelyn he had learned that it is not necessary to be right in order to squash inferiors.

He was thunderstruck when he heard Evelyn ask Swindells if he would like to go boating. That Swindells refused made it worse rather than better.

He went upstairs and watched Evelyn embark below his

window, the silk handkerchief in place around his brow. The plash of the boat receded, the rippled stream grew placid, the vacant afternoon stretched ahead. Bored now with his own books he went softly to Evelyn's room to find if he could the paperback he had read in the punt. There were several similar green books on the table and he opened one. There he stood absorbed, but for some reason increasingly unhappy, until the door opened and Annie came in. They were both embarrassed.

'I was just . . .'

'I only wanted . . .'

Before Kim got himself out of the door he had noticed in Annie's hand too a green paperback. How could a girl read what he had read? How could Evelyn have discussed such books with Annie?—in this house where he thought he knew what was happening? Kim's mind raged with emotions, pain he couldn't categorize. It was to Evelyn that Annie confided now. They talked in the garden. About her knickers being stolen. He remembered Evelyn kicking off his slippers, prowling into the corridor. No doubt they laughed at him whilst he slept. Was humiliation jealousy?

To recover the ivory tower of earlier days Kim looked out the notebook in which he used to write poetry before Evelyn's arrival. Another, a worse shock, made him flush: below the last poem was sketched in his own green ink by a clever hand a naked girl, a vulgar illustration befouling the poem. Kim squirmed like a skinned eel. He read the poem now with Evelyn's mocking eye. He ripped out the pages and shook and shook their fragments in the waste basket until not one scrap could lie next its match. In his mind the lines danced, a string of dead fish, little corpse-words in stiffened skins in place of the shapely images in flowing water which he had tried to catch. Never never again would he attempt to express what he felt, and lay himself open to such humiliation.

Even Swindells was chosen above him to go in the boat.

He decided to write home and tell them that he must be

sent back to England at once. Oh—think what he had said about his mother and the coalman!

'What's your plan when you get back to B-blighty?' asked Evelyn a few days later in the village bar he had taken to visiting for afternoon cognacs since he had tired of the river. He and Kim had come there on bicycles borrowed from the servants.

'I'm going to Cambridge in the autumn' Kim replied. He had not written home after all; into the waste paper basket, along with the poems, he had thrown the person who had tried to write poetry.

'Waste of time Cambridge.'

'God I know.' Kim paused. 'Why do you think so?'

'Three years being pushed around by dusty old buggers in gowns? No thanks.'

'You don't have to work very hard or anything' Kim said mildly.

'Christ then, what's the point going at all if you're just going to skyve like as if you were still at school?' Evelyn banged down his glass and made his eyes glitter at Kim. 'Grow up! You know why oiks are much flier than us?— because they don't go on living in the bloody nursery half their lives like we do. Or like you will: I ducked out of that.'

'You've been sent here' Kim pointed out.

'Okay, but I don't treat the Deffin bag like a fucking head-master like you all do. So I get adult treatment from her.' He cocked up his idlers on the table. His stammer vanished when he spoke in earnest.

Kim asked 'Is she letting you drive us to this party in her car?'

'Of c-course.'

'I see what you mean' Kim said admiringly. Evelyn could manipulate people. He seemed to have such a clear view of things. Kim too tried to sharpen his eyes to pierce into the misty landscape of the future. 'I suppose I needn't go to

Cambridge' he ventured, 'but ... I don't know what I'm going to be you see. And I mean without a degree you aren't much qualified are you?'

'Qualified! If you want the sort of job you need qualifications for I give up. That crap's out of date kiddo. That's like going by train since they invented aeroplanes. Planes are going to drop bombs on us anyway, so we may as well fly in them. Fly and skip the dull parts.'

'Yes but—' Kim limped behind '—but people keep asking what I'm going to be. My father keeps saying things like "Splendid opportunities in banking these days". You know?'

'He didn't grasp them with both hands I notice.'

Kim laughed. It liberated him, the way Evelyn spoke of people's parents as though they were contemporaries. It was indeed like flying over country whose landmarks had seemed imposing at ground level. 'People weren't expected to work then' he said in defence of his father.

'Or that's their story. Still, your old d-dad can't have blued the lot so you'll still have some money.'

'I don't know. A bit I suppose. But now my sister's married this pauper.'

'What pauper?' Evelyn was interested in who exactly was who. Once told he never forgot. He knew whom everyone was related to, how much money they had and where they lived. To Kim and Annie his knowledge was a revelation, the ground plan of a fortress uncovered. He opened their eyes to the significance of their own connections. 'What's his name?' he asked.

'Tom Phelps he's called.'

'Never heard of him. Well' continued Evelyn cheerfully, 'bugger him, you'll still have the readies to look around without b-busting a gut in some office.'

'That's rather what my mother thinks.'

Evelyn smote his forehead. 'Stop quoting the old timers will you? You're on your own kiddo, you get no help except the wrong way. You hustle is how you get on. All there is in the world is two sorts, the pusher and the pushover—you want to push, or get pushed over? Garçon!' he called 'encore deux fines.'

Watching him, watching his bat-wing arms in the loose cashmere signalling at the waiter, thinking how splendidly predatory he looked, Kim made a stab at pushing. 'By the way' he said 'did you mean to take back that matchcase you gave me? Because you did.'

'D-d-did I?' Evelyn felt in his pockets. 'M-must be in my room. Incidentally' he went on, warming the cognac in his pale hands, 'you don't seem to be getting much nearer dipping your w-wick with our Annie.'

'Me?' Kim flushed. 'What about you, it's you lends her dirty books and she tells about her knickers and, and, every thing. I mean who cares but I thought you said you didn't fancy her that's all. I mean who cares.'

'You care for one. So don't get pushed over, push' Evelyn said. 'Push a little, kiddo. I'll help. Treat me as your p-pander.' He gulped down his cognac, squinted at Kim. 'Don't let me foozle confuse or bamboozle you, p-panders choose booze and for food some bamboos'll do. How's that?'

Kim laughed. He made his friend repeat the rhyme. Brandy lit the thought of freedom to come, and delight, in his blood. Evelyn said 'Do give us a rendering of that exquisite poem of yours.'

'You mean——?' Kim was taken aback.

'From the perfumed wreath of pleasure' intoned Evelyn. 'Go on.'

'I have plucked the palest flowers' (Kim mimicked the other's soulful tone) 'In the flame-licked caves of suffering I have lingered fever'd hours, Through the reveries of poets I have glimps'd th'enchaunted land, Have seen the moon's pale fingers touch the towers of Samarcand. That's as far as I've got' he finished uncertainly.

'Beautiful beautiful' murmured Evelyn, lying back with eyes closed. 'Brilliant—it's a brilliant pastiche of those cretins like Dowson. Any more?'

To amuse his friend Kim recited one or two more of his

poems. Aware now of their new value, he would have traded anything in his heart for the glittering coin of Evelyn's laughter. He was only selling what he had once been, not what he now intended to become. Later, wobbling with brandy, they bicycled home through the spring vineyards.

The party to which Kim had referred was to come off in the house of a madame Mohun who took in a few girls of sixteen or seventeen to whom she taught the tricks of the trade. This rival establishment was ten miles off in the town. Madame Deffin did not go herself, nor did she encourage Swindells to go. By Evelyn she felt that her establishment was well represented, and to him she entrusted her car and Kim and Annie. Such was her judgement.

'Off on our whirl of gaiety!' cried Evelyn as he slewed the old Panhard out of the gates, 'pray heaven we return intact.'

As the car bucketed along Annie sat between him and Kim, an arm behind each. 'Honestly I can't think why I'm going' she said brightly. 'Promise me you'll rescue me if I get stuck with some lechy man.'

'Suppose you're a wallflower. Will we t-tango with her Kim?'

Annie was confident these days. 'You haven't seen the Mohun hags. Except you're such a perve you might fancy them darling—Evelyn I mean.' She gave his shoulder a squeeze Kim couldn't see.

Evelyn nudged her towards Kim as if pushing her on-stage. 'Kim fancies one of them' he said.

She gushed scent over Kim. 'You can't be that desperate honestly. Which one love?'

Kim grinned. Ash fell from his cigarette. She brushed it off his trousers, let her hand lie there. Headlights raking, tyres shrieking, Evelyn rushed them through the night, his wolfish smile lit by the dash-light.

Madame Mohun's town house stood on the waterfront facing the river which slid by under the moon. Kim and Annie followed Evelyn through the door like cockleshells bobbing in a speedboat's wash. They were nervous.

Evelyn was patient, his plan unfolding. For the first wretched half hour of the party, in the candlelit room whose parquet shone like a pond where no one dared test the ice—and the gramophone ground out music and the girls sniggered amongst themselves—he established himself on a sofa, stretching his legs comfortably and sipping his ruby-red wine. At first Kim sat beside him; but like a boy refused the share of a man's umbrella he soon wandered away. Evelyn, snug and dry, watched from the shelter of imperme-able self-assurance, and waited.

With a tremendously bright smile Annie had at once greeted the resident girls, admiring dresses, chattering in gusts of enthusiasm, quite ignoring the bristle-headed French boys amongst them. When one of them offered to fetch her a glass of wine she accepted in an off-hand style. Kim moved from the bookshelves to her side. 'But I got you some wine' he said.

'Did you love?' She took the glass the French boy brought her.

Kim scowled. Evelyn called him, drawing him to stand in front of the sofa. 'Which of these f-f-floozies is the one you told me about?' he asked.

'The one in the awful blue dress' said Kim angrily.

Evelyn pushed him aside with the toe of his shoe so that he could examine a coltish girl in blue smoking through a long holder. 'Saucy' he allowed. 'You planning a c-c-coup?'

'God no.'

'She's got her eye on you.'

'She can get stuffed.'

'Annie's watching you too. You're the belle of the ball kiddo.' He watched flattery take effect. 'Annie fancies you you know.'

'Me?' Kim's sullenness was lifting.

'Only she thinks you're so shy.'

'Me shy?' Kim laughed at the notion.

And Evelyn smiled too, swinging his elegant idler. Then he said 'Oh dear, she's off with a F-frog.'

Kim turned. Annie was dancing. He heard the soles of her shoes shuffle drily, saw her skirt twirled round the French boy's legs and his paw on her back. He turned back to Evelyn. But the sofa was empty: Evelyn stood tall and sly amongst madame Mohun's flock, holding out his glass for the girl in blue to fill. His black clothes and hair absorbed the candle-light which glimmered on his alabaster face. Alone, Kim sat down on the chair where Annie had left her bag, to be ready.

When Annie, followed by the French boy shooting his cuffs, walked off the floor it was Evelyn who closed with her before she reached her bag and Kim. 'Point a shoe?' he said, slipping an arm through hers.

Someone had blown out some candles, so that shadows wavered in the room's corners. Dancing in one of these Evelyn undid a button of Annie's shirt. Though she arched her back she didn't complain. They swayed slowly. Presently she mur-mured in his ear 'Honestly isn't this silly?'

'Silly what?'

'Us just dancing.'

'Why?'

'Well I mean. After knowing. You know.'

'Time you danced with the boy' Evelyn told her.

'Must I? You are pushy love. I do love you.'

'Do as I say then. You be pushy. Come on, it'll be a laugh in the car. I'll get the blue c-clothes-horse going. Go on' Evelyn ordered her sharply, giving her a shove towards Kim's chair. She was unsteady on her legs, gazing at Kim out of big unfocused eyes. 'Dance with me love?'

Kim carefully put down her handbag and followed her onto the floor. There he stood in his grey suit which was too small for him, left arm and shoe extended whilst he counted the beat before launching out. When, after several turns, he discovered the button which Evelyn had left undone he inched in his hand as gradually as if tickling a trout. They grounded in a dark corner and ripples of music rocked them.

Both their minds crawled with the books Evelyn had lent them.

Later their mentor himself bumped against them, the girl in blue plastered against his shirt. 'We thought of a sp-pin in the motor' he said. 'You two on?'

Kim opened his eyes and enquired into Annie's.

'Mm, okeydoke' she said.

'What about madame Mohun though?' Kim wondered.

'What about the old sweetie? Want to bring her along?' Evelyn asked.

'Come on love' said Annie, pushing Kim.

The girl in blue drew Evelyn's hand after her through the house, and by a side door into a covered passage which led to the street. 'It's how we always get out at night' she told them.

The air, cold moonlight, chilled Kim. Crinkled window-panes of old houses reflected the moon, gables stood black against the night; chilled, he noticed the beauty of the scene, the river flowing by. He compared in his mind the river to satin, wrinkled where the bridge's piers snagged its flow. But Annie's hand pulled him towards the car. Could he use the image of the satin river in a poem to make Evelyn laugh? He burrowed into the car, into Annie's scent and heat, and forgot the moon on the river.

Evelyn smiled to himself as he drove to a quiet corner of the cathedral square and parked. Before long the heat of his creatures' humiliation misted the windows of the car, and the moonshine was excluded. But he should have used Swindells instead of Kim, he thought. It would have been funnier. Next time he would.

PART TWO

I.

SUNLIGHT TOUCHED LIKE a blessing the closed eyes of Kim's sister resting in a long wicker chair in the rose garden at Larkford. So sequestered was this walled garden amongst its trees that the wind passed over it, and nature, the woods without, broke against its defences as waves break against sea walls. Only rivulets of ivy foamed over the rose-red brick as a spent wave sends its trickles into a rock pool. It was a deep, hidden, peaceful place to be. Clara could hear the trees whispering in the wind, she could hear bees in the lavender and the flutter of a fly-catcher as it darted from its nest against the wall. These sounds made pictures on her closed eyelids; she did not need to open her eyes to see the garden she had known all her life. But she could hear too a continuous low susurration, uneasy as the sound of surf when you did not think that the sea was near, and this made her open her eyes.

'Mother's quite right' she said, 'you hardly can hear the gravel works.'

Her husband Tom threw away the handful of daisies he had been restlessly pulling. The sun greyed his face and deepened its lines. 'That isn't the point' he said, 'the present gravel works is outside our control.'

'She says it's the point. Not to have another closer.'

'Oh Lord. What she says!' He sounded very weary of distinguishing what his mother-in-law said from what she meant. 'If she can stand the noise off her own land where it isn't doing her any good' he said good-humouredly, 'you'd think she could stand it a bit closer where it'll make her some money. Anyway she's getting deafer. Another gravel works wouldn't sound any nearer to her probably.'

'She isn't as deaf as your father you know' his wife said. 'Have you done anything about getting him to see an ear person?' She had closed her eyes again.

'Clara we're here to deal with your mother not my father.' His complaint was patient, if not gentle. 'I haven't much time, I've got to get back to London with Bob Swindells when he comes. So pay attention.' He threw a daisy at her. 'Wake up Clara.'

She turned her head on the bleached cushion so that she could smile at him. She was at peace, unhurried. 'I told you you'd never deal with Mother in a day' she said, 'she isn't like a board-meeting. Anything at Larkford takes a week. Once you're west of Salisbury a day's work takes a week.'

'But I haven't got a week' he protested.

'Nor had I till I got here' she replied. 'Till I got here I never thought of staying on while you're in America.'

'No ... Anyway Clara I'm not trying to do it in a day just, the whole issue's been hanging fire for weeks. Months. It's nearly a year since your father died. And if something isn't decided she'll get herself dug in here all over again. You know I haven't tried to rush her Clara' he appealed.

She stretched out her hand to absolve him. 'Poor Tom with us all' she said. Peace was restored. She closed her eyes again.

'But darling what does she want?' He tried to reagitate her. 'I can't get a straight answer from her. And none of you ever try to get straight answers from each other. In fact' he added, rubbing his eyes with the heels of his palms, 'in fact you're every bit as hopeless as she is when you're at Larkford. God help us if you were like this in London. You're like children when you're here you and Kim.'

'Maybe that's why Mother wants us to stay on here.'

'So she does want to stay then? Has she told you?' He hoped to progress.

'Would you want to leave, if you'd come here as a bride?'

They both looked towards the stone gables and twisted chimneys which rose beyond the walls; Clara towards her home, Tom towards a vast impediment in his path. He despaired of extracting answers, gave his opinion: 'I certainly wouldn't want to rattle about in a barrack that size at her age. Not with servants dying on their feet and no money. No I wouldn't.'

'She ran it on her own during the war remember.'

'Twenty-five years ago Clara! It's the root of the problem, that none of you'll admit that a quarter of a century has made changes. But it has' he asserted.

His vehemence ruffled the air for a moment and was gone. Twenty-five years made no more stir than that in the garden.

'What she really hopes' Clara said presently 'is that Kim will come back from Italy and live here.'

'Well we all thought he would' Tom agreed, 'if he put the thing on an economic footing and ran it properly it was the obvious answer.'

'Yes but she still hopes he will.'

'Hopes!'

'Well, faith then. She believes he will.'

'Clara if she just lives on hopes and faith there isn't going to be any Larkford soon. It'll be too late to save it if the gravel isn't exploited soon, the place'll just collapse into bankruptcy.'

Clara smiled. She couldn't believe that it was money that kept the walls standing and the roses in bloom. In London yes, life was built upon money and was shaky; here surely the greater certainty of the place was founded upon something else—upon her mother's hopes, her trust, perhaps?

'Has anyone heard from Kim?' Tom asked, gloomily contemplating his black shoes amongst the daisies. 'Has your mother?'

'I doubt it. She would have shown me a letter. You know how pleased she always is if he writes.'

'Honestly. Kim——' he shook his head, trapping behind his lips what he thought of his brother-in-law. 'He might at least write to her.'

'They understand each other without writing' said Clara.

'They always have, in a funny sort of way. Like the way they bid when they're partners at Bridge.'

'Well I wish he'd keep his funny ways for Bridge and come back and face life' said Tom hotly. 'It's he who ought to deal with your mother and arrange about selling this place—if it's going to be sold' he added, having let slip his private intention inadvertently.

'It's no use you getting cross with me about it.' Once more she closed her eyes.

'Well I can't get cross with Kim he just vanishes. Look what happened after the funeral.'

'He didn't come to London because he knew you'd bully him.'

The accusation took the wind out of his sails. 'I don't mean to darling. I really don't mean to bully him but ... His attitude's so irresponsible anything I say sounds critical. I mean I can't praise him can I? Nor can you.'

'Between praise and blame there's toleration. Patience. You haven't any patience with the world's wasters' she said. 'It's best just to like Kim if you can and let him go his own way.'

'You can't help liking him' Tom rejoined. But he spoke as though liking or disliking counted for very little. 'The point is, where's his own way going to lead?'

'Does it matter to us?'

'Potentially there's a lot of money in this gravel Clara.'

'Do we need it?'

He stared for a moment. 'Let's get back to Kim' he said, 'two years he's been fooling about in Italy, all the time we've been married he's been playing about at this game completing his education. What for? That's nine years gone Clara, it's bloody ridiculous. First it was France, that was the first mistake, letting him hang about France for two years instead of going in the army——'

'They'd stopped National Service. And he learnt very good French.'

'What use was that? Like his History at Cambridge—

46

what use has he made of it? Now it's Italy—what's it all leading up to?'

'It's led to him being what he is I suppose.' She spoke upward to the sky, not expecting to be understood.

'Exactly. Nothing.'

'Educated, cultivated ...' Running short of epithets she made a sweep with her hand to suggest what more her brother was. 'Anyway I shouldn't worry, Tom.'

'You worry. It worries you.'

'Not here it doesn't' she said simply. 'After all, directions only lead a little way.'

'That's just the sort of utterance your mother comes out with' he said in exasperation. 'Well here's a saying of my father's: "Who willna be ruled by the rudder maun be ruled by the rock".'

When he spoke the dialect one realized that the hard edge in his voice was Scottish. 'Yes' she said 'we're all our parents' children.'

A silence fell between them. Under the soft whisper of the wind in leaves she heard the gravel works a mile away, grating like the stony trace of accent in her husband's voice. Under soil, stone: behind summer, winter.

'Yes but here you——' he began, and stopped.

Interrupting him, announced by the latch of a gate in the wall, there entered a stooped old servant bearing tea. He carried the silver tray between beds of roses taller than himself, past the stone fountain, towards them over the grass, and set it down on the low summerhouse wall by Clara's chair. Tom evidently thought it wrong to continue their conversation in a servant's hearing. Clara however appealed to the old man:

'Apps we were just wondering if you'd heard anything from Kim?'

'Not in a while Miss Clara madam' he replied.

Silence. More he wouldn't say in Tom's hearing. Whilst his hands set out china and silver his lips emitted an almost soundless whistle, as though he was cleaning a horse. When

Clara asked if her mother knew that tea had been brought out he said:

'Off tother end of garden soon as tea's laid her'll go.'

He pottered away, the sun showing up the rubbed seams of his black jacket. So fixed seemed his course between the rose beds that one expected his feet to have worn a track in the grass. When he had gone Clara said:

'I believe Apps misses Father more than any of us. I believe Father was his only friend.'

This idea seemed to make Tom impatient. He paced to and fro bouncing a tennis ball which a dog must have left in the garden. He did not want to have to take into account the ramifications of such ideas as friendship connecting worn out servants to the outworn house. Whilst the tea cooled and Clara dozed he bounced the ball and planned in his mind.

Presently the snip-snip of secateurs could be heard beyond the walls. A murmurous sound pitched between humming and conversation floated into the rose garden. Clara opened her eyes. The humming receded.

'Tea Mother!' she called.

No response. Then at an unexpected door in another wall Mrs Vannick appeared.

'Tea my dears' she said, 'I daresay it will be somewhere about. Apps makes me hunt high and low for my tea.'

Her voice was singularly musical, clear as silver in the hollow garden. Between those tall roses she approached, straight-stemmed and graceful under her flower-twined garden hat, a flat basket of flowers on her arm, and began to pour a thin smoking stream of tea carelessly into the cups from a considerable height, talking as she did so: 'I always think of Kim at tea time, do you remember Clara? "Tea is optional Mother, an optional meal." He always seemed to go fishing just at tea time.'

'You know why' said Clara taking her cup, 'so he wasn't caught for croquet after tea.'

'Why do you suppose he won't play games?' Mrs Vannick wondered, the cream jug poised motionless in her hand.

48

'Won't compete' Tom said, taking a finger of toast from the muffin dish. 'Toast anyone?' he asked before replacing the cover.

'I don't suppose it would do if we were all to be beating each other day in day out' replied Mrs Vannick as she sat down on the low wall. The roof of the summerhouse dripped blue wistaria almost to the flowers in her hat. She lifted the cover of the muffin dish for herself, perhaps because she did not care to accept toast from someone who criticized Kim. The contents of the dish made her sigh. 'Toast again oh dear! Apps poor old soul, still laying out the things Father liked. He might give us bread and butter sometimes now you would think.'

'We were just saying how hard he's taken it' Clara said.

'I know. His trouble is, do you see, he never had to make do without Father' she explained. 'He was Father's servant in the war whilst I looked after the estate and the children on my own' she told Tom. 'Poor old soul. I told you about the bath mat did I?'

Clara only sipped her tea, but Tom cued his mother-in-law: 'Whose bath mat was that?'

'Well, for as many years as I can remember Apps has pottered upstairs each evening and taken the mat off the hot rail in our bathroom and laid it out ready for Father's bath before dinner. You can see for yourself how tired he is looking but of course he is too touchy to be told not to go running upstairs every two minutes, so I began laying down the mat myself so that he should see it and leave off paddling up. Not a bit of it! Beats me to it every day. The wretched mat is hardly off the floor in the morning before he puts it back now. I never saw anything so stupid at his age.'

Again Tom seemed irritated. 'I don't see why you can't tell him to stop.'

'Oh, the old fool must do as he pleases' Mrs Vannick said.

Silence fell, and peace. Like her garden Mrs Vannick possessed the blessing of repose. Her stillness, or her unhurried movements, her soft laughter or musical voice, gave to her

49

presence grace and quiet authority; around her all seemed in order, so that peace could settle as butterflies settled on the lavender beside her. A thrush too dropped from the trees onto the grass, and the world the walls enclosed was at rest.

Yet the very quietness she seemed to diffuse made space for the sly chuckle of the gravel works to insinuate itself into the garden. Its snake's scales slid over the wall. She set down her cup so sharply that the thrush fled.

'Whenever I hear that wretched gravel business' she said, 'and often we don't hear it for weeks you know if the wind is right; but if ever I do it is money boxes I think of. Tin money boxes being rattled at me. That is since you told me how valuable gravel on our land would be Tom. Beastly rattle—do you hear what I mean?' They listened. 'But I don't suppose there is any gravel on our land' she added more comfortably.

'I know there is' Tom said sharply.

'Mother so do you' Clara told her.

'Then why has Mr Sowerby never said so?' Mrs Vannick asked.

'That agent of yours won't consider anything which upsets things, especially upsets the pheasants' Tom said. He sat forward to press the attack. 'Now can we just run through the points could we' he suggested, making ready to count points on his fingers. 'First off we know that the seam runs into the property beyond that sham wood——'

'The Paradise Wood is what it always used to be called' Mrs Vannick corrected him.

'You mean Burr Wood?' Clara asked.

Tom was lost. 'Well we know where it is whatever it's called' he said, 'and the bed lies——'

'Have you ever heard the history of that wood Tom?' asked Mrs Vannick.

He resigned. 'Only that Clara's grandfather planted it' he said.

'He did indeed.' She ignored his crossness, spoke of the

past as if it was sure to interest him: 'It was really the centre of his life latterly that woodland garden ... of course the frame of oaks and beech was always there but everything else he planted himself. All the rarities and especial prizes. It was before my time of course but I've been told, people used to say, that the company's ships were delayed and their voyages altered to collect seeds and exotics from all over the globe. Indeed it was said that there was a to-do of some sort with the shareholders and that was why he resigned. Long before that of course he had planted the shelter, all those ilex and yews and evergreens so as to create the climate for a Paradise Garden—what I believe gardeners now call a microclimate. No frost or wind do you see. "Nor ever wind blows loudly there"' she quoted, musing under her shady hat. 'There is something magnificent about creating a climate I think' she went on, 'beginning at the beginning of all things so to speak. One used to walk down there in midwinter or in an October gale ... still and warm the wood would be. Not that any one ever did go there except Grandfather' she added with a laugh.

'I thought it was open to the public' said Clara, 'I thought Grandfather was this great democrat. Didn't he have that special Russian secretary so he could write to Lenin?'

'To Prince Kropotkin actually, he only cared for aristocratic revolutionaries ... Yes in theory it was open to the public. In theory but—he alarmed people so, the public never quite took to going there. Nor did we. No, nor did we. He would never label any of the plants do you see, so one could never talk to him about them because one didn't know what anything was called. And he had a way of speaking rather contemptuously if one appeared ignorant, which made people uneasy. Awfully uneasy. But your plan Tom' she said sweetly, 'your plan would mean grubbing up the Paradise Wood I take it?'

Clara said 'It's a ruin anyway Mother.'

'A ruin? Overgrown I daresay, wild. I don't think you speak of ruins in nature.'

'But it isn't natural it's artificial. Like Tom says, sham.'

'Once set going there is nothing artificial about it. Once set going it regenerates itself, there is nothing artificial about that. So long as the climate is not upset' she added.

Clara changed her tack. 'Father never went near it' she claimed.

'Your father never liked it. No, he never went there even to shoot. It was very much Grandfather's domain. Even after his death—especially after his death. His ashes were scattered somewhere there as you know. I never knew quite where, I don't think anyone did except Apps' father who did the scattering. Father never cared for the idea.' She thought for a moment, then said more cheerfully 'Did I ever tell you what Grandfather said to the stupid woman who asked him if he liked flowers to have a scent?'

'I like my garden to smell of my own sweat Mrs Parker' Clara supplied. She shared a moment's silence with her mother. Then she said 'But Mother no one's been there for years except Kim. Admit. Be practical. It honestly wouldn't matter if they discovered a coal mine there, you need never go and see it.'

In response to the call to be practical Mrs Vannick revealed her standpoint with full unpractical candour. 'A Paradise Wood is such an awfully nice idea to have at the back of one's mind don't you think?'

Clara recoiled. Tom said 'I'm afraid ideas of that nature are a very costly luxury nowadays. Look I don't want to rush anyone but I'll have to be off to London soon as Bob Swindells gets here and has a look round, so if we could just decide what I'm to tell him. Firstly we know where the seam runs in. Secondly we must decide——'

'Rushing up to London tonight?' asked Mrs Vannick.

'Afraid I must. Plane to catch early.'

'Change your mind Tom dear. Surely they can get along without you for a day or so?'

'Can't I'm afraid. Or I hope they can't' he added smiling. 'But we've time to talk about your plans. Now if——'

'Ah yes there will be time enough in the summer' Mrs Vannick said, her eyes vaguening. 'Clara dear you must let me know your dates. Because I daresay the children will want to be here for a good long stay.'

Tom and Clara looked guiltily at one another, said nothing. Their plans for the future did not include Larkford.

'Clara you don't have to rush off tonight?' Mrs Vannick continued.

'I've told you Mother, I'd love to stay while Tom's in America if you can have me.'

'Of course darling, it's the point of the house that you should all come and go just as you please. As I hope the children will when they are a little older' she said, suggesting a serene future.

'Mother haven't you decided at all what's to be done with Larkford?' Clara appealed, miserable with guilt. 'You must say. This Swindells man will be here in a minute and Tom's got to know what you want.'

Mrs Vannick rose and drew on her gardening gloves. From her fine large eyes sadness looked down on them both. 'My dears' she said 'I want what is best for you all.' She clipped a dead head or two off the roses in the nearest bed, and with her back towards them went on 'What is to be done depends more upon Kim's plans than mine.'

'But Mother Kim never has any plans. Have you ever known him have a proper plan?'

She replied from amongst the roses 'Kim is wise to wait until whatever it is that he really wants to do comes along. Time is what he is buying; what else so precious can money buy you at 26? He will choose in the end. When he has decided what he doesn't want to do' she added.

'What'll happen is he'll just run out of money' Clara said, 'then he'll have to take the first job that's offered. Which he could have done just as easily at eighteen.'

'More easily in fact' Tom said, 'he's getting a bit long in the tooth to start at the bottom and he's not qualified for anywhere but the bottom.'

'He's not that old' said Clara, turning on him, 'he's younger than me.'

Tom was silenced. Within this family the in-law was a welcome ally on neither side. He looked at his watch, impatient for the arrival of the outsider: the outsider who would smash through their niceties as his bulldozer would smash through their Paradise Wood.

'Father always took rather the view that what you want turns up in the end' Mrs Vannick told them, 'and it always seemed to for him. Even death' she added, a remark, like many she made, which gave the impression that The Four Last Things were never far from her mind.

'But Father always had millions of influential friends' Clara objected, 'whereas Kim's friends are disasters. Look at that Sele creature he brought to stay who ended up in prison in Madagascar.'

'I never understood him liking that boy' Kim's mother said. 'What do you suppose he saw in him that we all missed?'

Clara lay back in her chair and closed her eyes, irritated that her mother attributed perspicuity to Kim and blindness to the rest of them.

Snip-snip clipped the secateurs. Having scattered Tom's points to the four winds and met Clara's pressure with imperturbable calm, Mrs Vannick dead-headed her way through the garden until she came to the gate in the wall. From there she spoke again in her clear tone:

'In any event my dears we can do nothing till Kim knows his own mind. I am sure it seems awfully stupid to you Tom to delay, but I believe that the only way to convince Kim that he has responsibility is not to take it away from him. He is very much more important than Larkford. At any rate Tom your gravel won't run away. If there is gravel under the Paradise Wood after all' she added, lifting the gate-latch.

She was gone. Tom and Clara's thoughts struck the wall and rebounded. They had got nowhere.

Presently Clara spoke. 'I wish to goodness everything could

go on just the same. I hate the idea of change, when I'm here.'

He said 'You know if we get this Hampshire house we'll never come here Clara.'

'Hush.' She looked round as though the garden heard her treachery. They had decided to buy a country house of their own. 'We haven't got it yet' she said.

'We've talked it over till we're blue in the face. You know it's logical Clara.'

'London logic. Money logic. It seems so ungrateful when I'm here' she said unhappily.

'That's a pressure you have to shut your mind to Clara' he said. 'The pressure one generation puts on another is unfair.'

'You don't know pressure like that. You don't owe things, in your family.'

'Which is precisely why I see it for what it is in yours, counter-productive to both sides. Unhelpful. Giving in to it you only encourage her to carry on living in never-never land. In an artificial climate like that wood. Look, whatever we do she can't go on here. This place can't survive, you can't keep reality out forever just by hoping. It's beginning to fall down as it is, have you looked at the kitchen-garden wall?' He jerked his thumb at the larger walled enclosure beyond the rose garden. She shook her head stubbornly. 'Cracked from top to bottom' he told her 'the very next hard frost and it'll come tumbling down. And what about Apps? What happens when he packs up? Can't think how she puts up with him anyway, rigmaroles like that stuff about the bath mat.'

'Don't you see?' Clara appealed, 'they're lonely, they're playing with each other.'

'It's too late for games Clara.'

The sinking sun cast long shadows. Clara was no longer warm enough in her wicker chair. Evening had come. She got up.

'This place limping on' he continued, 'it only helps Kim make believe he needn't bother. Needn't be responsible for your mother or money or anything. It isn't a joke Clara' he warned his wife who had laughed.

'I know it isn't' she said, putting the tea cups onto the tray. 'It just sounds funny to talk about Kim being responsible. So long as I'm here it's Mother I think of in charge. Even in charge of me.'

'Precisely. It's an artificial climate and the sooner some fresh air is let in the better.'

There came between them the silence which divides husband and wife when the stronger, or better armed, knows that he will have his way, and the weaker knows it too but will not submit.

Again the gate-latch announced an arrival. Behind Apps, who cast him loose like a tug casting off its tow, Bob Swindells steamed through the wall.

'Hullo there Tom' he called confidently in a voice made sonorous by the hollow garden.

'Ah Bob good to see you!' Tom's voice too filled out in welcome.

They approached one another. In his blue suit Tom alone had looked singularly out of place in the rose garden, like a solitary policeman in the countryside; but now two men in the uniform of business suggested more, suggested a search, the house surrounded, the Force at the door. It was the rose garden which now looked out of place, so delicately can the relation of figures to ground be readjusted. The plumpish blue figures met. Clara was introduced.

She at once disliked the egg-smooth face, too large, too fleshy. The eyes beady, the mouth thin as a hairpin. No, she didn't like him.

'Your brother and I have been pals a long time' he said, crushing her hand. 'Prep school, France, you name it we been through it together old Kim and me.'

'You saw Kim in Italy Tom says' she replied coldly.

'Did indeed. Had to run up to Florence to see a pal, one of these principes as they call themselves, and Kim came along so we could talk things over.'

There was something in this which was obviously not true. Whether the man's manner or his matter was false she could not tell. But he lied. Nor could he and Kim ever have been friends, she knew that at once.

'Nice old property you got here' Swindells was saying, 'have to see what we can do for you.'

'Or what we can do for you' she said.

'Come along.' Tom stepping between them took her arm. 'Let's have a look round.' As they left the walled garden, and Apps whistling to himself over the tea tray like a wintry little bird, he said 'What about footwear if we're going down the wood? Any gumboots we can borrow darling?'

'Kim's are probably in the gunroom, Father's too' she replied.

'Right, we'll get into those Bob.'

'Hang on a tick' he said, 'we'll have a dekko round the grounds first, I got a hunch the bed could run this way.' His hand sliced down as though chopping through the garden.

Clara turned on her husband. 'You never said anything about the garden Tom. The wood's one thing, the house and the garden's another.'

'We're talking about the whole estate darling not a corner here and there.'

'A company the size of Rhinehart's' Swindells said, 'we can't gear down for your piecemeal operation I'm afraid.' He sucked his teeth, looked glum. 'No way madam.'

Clara stopped. 'You know where the boots are Tom.'

'You not coming?'

'What's the point? What's the point of any of us coming with you? You'll do what's best.' She expelled the last word bitterly.

'I know just how you feel' Swindells commiserated. 'Come from a similar sort of old place myself.'

His dishonesty and his malice were so apparent that even Tom protested: 'I daresay the house probably has a preservation order hasn't it darling? Isn't it scheduled?'

'We can usually get round the preservation johnnies for you' Swindells said, his glance disparaging the stone front of the house which could now be seen through garden trees.

'Official preservationists yes' Tom admitted 'you probably can but ... I wonder where your mother is darling?' he asked.

'I have no idea.' She left them and walked towards the front of the house alone.

She knew that her mother would be upstairs in her own sitting room, that matrix within a matrix to which she retreated beyond reach of anyone save Clara or Kim. But approaching the house Clara hesitated: how could she go to her mother, whose side she was no longer on? Where could she go? The contending forces could all retreat or advance, except Clara. What made her miserable was that the conflict was within herself, between one loyalty which was inborn and another which was acquired by marriage. She could neither retreat with her mother nor advance with her husband. She wandered unhappily away towards other parts of the garden. In the windows of the old house the evening light flashed like the spark of life in determined old eyes.

Behind one of those mullioned windows, looking out, Mrs Vannick decided to go to Italy. When Clara thought that her mother had retreated she had underestimated the resolution of Mrs Vannick's will.

2.

AT FIRST ETTIE didn't notice the irritation in Kim's voice when he spoke of his mother coming to Rome. Of tones and reactions, unless she was their direct cause, Ettie was not observant: people, even the man she was living with, were to her opaque surfaces in which she looked only for reflections of her own actions. Her world was in consequence at once lonely and crowded, like a hall of mirrors.

'My mother is coming next week.'

'Oh. What for?'

'To bother me of course' Kim said. They spoke French, for Ettie was French.

It was his own business, how his mother's arrival affected him, and her mind didn't penetrate other people's business. How did it affect herself? She thought it would be an improvement, she would be free to go out with someone else for a change. Change, movement, she craved: in the pool into which she had dived to live with Kim the ripples of her plunge had died away. Secret, silent, he lay like a fish on the fin sensing currents she didn't perceive in depths she did not want to plumb. She let it be known that she would be free, looking for amusement, whilst Kim's mother was in Rome, for she dreaded an hour alone with herself as if she was her own most boring acquaintance. A dualism in her nature made her own company like that of a duenna. Her own self, in the hall of mirrors, was a person to be tricked and evaded.

On the day Mrs Vannick was to arrive Kim said to Ettie as they were getting up for lunch 'I have to go and meet my mother at five'. He was lying in bed watching her make up her face.

She liked to be watched, spectators made any chore worthwhile. 'Shall I move out while she's in Rome?'

'Where to?' No reply. 'No need, I'll keep her away from here.'

'She'll want to inspect where you live won't she?' That Kim had a mother made him somehow childish, a dependant, not the free agent she believed herself to be.

He didn't answer, only turned on his face in the pillows. She watched him in the looking glass: she loved his black tangle of hair in the morning before he brushed it flat, and his long slim back barred with gold by sunlight through the shutter slats. She loved him but—she sighed—he was always there. It was getting harder to inveigle him into going to parties, or even to the sea for the weekends. Nowadays they often came home after dinner without dropping in on a nightclub. She felt time and life passing by like a lighted train seen from a cottage window, speed and flare streaming through the night, passing her by.

Presently he asked 'What will you do for dinner tonight?'

She leaned towards the glass to draw a line under her eye. 'Oh, something or other' she replied.

A little bolt of excitement discharged in her heart: someone Kim didn't know, a film man called Jack Peel whom she had met with Marco Roccaleone on Via Veneto, had invited her to dinner. It was only for a change. She was surprised that Kim had asked, he was usually so incurious and secretive himself.

That evening Kim came into the apartment when he had dropped his mother at her hotel: came in cursing the traffic, and pitched Ettie's clothes off their bed. She was in the bath. When she got out he made love to her violently, as if it was a punishment. She lay beside him hurt and disrupted. Yet she would not accept that sex could hurt; she had so confused her mind by identifying her supreme goal, pleasure, wholly with sex that the question of enjoyment did not enter into it. Pleasure, whether or not she enjoyed it, ruled her life. She lay waiting for Kim to go out again. He lounged about the room drinking whisky and dressing. She did not like to have another bath, or prepare herself for Jack Peel, whilst he was there. 'You can't wear this' he said, holding up a flimsy dress she had laid out.

'Why not?'

'Because I hate you in it. You look awful.'

'As you won't be there it doesn't matter.'

'Yes it does' he said, 'yes it does it matters to you, you let yourself down wearing that. Or give yourself away' he added, narrowing his eyes.

She wouldn't dispute, she only waited for him to go. When at last he dragged himself off to dine with his mother he called from the door:

'I shan't be late.'

This she recognized as the nearest he could bring himself to entreating her to be back early herself. Even the shadow of an entreaty she interpreted as contributing to her own strength. She poured a second bath and lay soaking in it, as if to soak Kim out of herself and so free herself for the evening ahead.

But her thoughts strayed after him towards the mother and the English background she knew nothing about. She could not picture Kim's mother because she had never thought of him having one; none of her friends in Rome, the foreigners, forestieri, struck her as the possessors of mothers, homes, childhoods. To the mothers of her Roman friends she was not introduced. All of them, Romans and foreigners, might have sprung to life fully armed as she saw them, fully armed as she thought herself to be. Nor could she picture Kim in England. In France learning French, at which moment his French-speaking persona (which was all she knew of him) had been conceived, was the first picture of Kim she could form clearly in her mind. Now she learned that he was related to a wider context, and in their usual circle her thoughts returned to herself: where did she fit into that context? Its width diminished her.

She pulled the plug of her bath and impatiently stepped out. Thought trammels freedom. She met her image in the mirror, admired the glister of water beading her skin, admired the naked blade of selfhood whose sharpness no longer seemed to slice through Kim. It was high time she went out with someone else. She pulled over her head the dress Kim had said he hated her in. It was another skin, a disguise. She had chosen it because she thought that Jack Peel would like the sort of girl who was in, or partly in, such a dress. She hadn't thought What shall I wear? but Who shall I be? Like all her clothes it was a disguise. The dress would please, and in the fact of pleasing she existed. She lived only for pleasure, so she thought, but Ettie had somewhere confused being an object of pleasure with pleasure itself; as, too, in the hall of mirrors she had lost sight of her real self amongst the images.

Though her outing with Jack Peel was to end in tears it began exactly as she hoped. She had walked to her friend Marietta's flat because she didn't want Jack to know—nor did she want to start from the premise herself—that she lived with Kim. The chauffered car stopped beneath the windows. Up the stairs leaped Jack like a golf ball bouncing on stone.

'Quite a car!' she exclaimed as he handed her into the gleaming machine.

'Like it?' Smoothly the limousine drew away through the streets. Lounged against the fawn leather Jack smiled at her. His grin tightened his lips into a predatory line. 'Any city we're in we try and get the same kind of car' he told her, 'that way it don't feel we moved.'

'We?'

'The bunch of us making the picture.'

Purpose, energy; she felt the thrust of the car in her back like excitement. 'Are you American?' she asked. Although she didn't talk English with Kim she spoke it fairly fluently. 'I can never know with accents. I thought you were an English man are you?'

'I forget' he said. 'You know how many towns we been in the last year?' She listened while he counted the far-off cities. Travel left a residue of exoticism clinging to the traveller which was incense in her nostrils. She uncrossed her long legs, feeling his eyes lick them. When the car stopped outside a restaurant the driver spoke to Jack over his shoulder, and Jack said to her:

'The place is closed up. It closed up.'

He announced it like a catastrophe. He wouldn't be comforted by her suggestions of other restaurants nearby.

'No I know the place we'll go' he said 'but Christ, what they want to go and close up here for? Never mind, relax sweetheart I can guess where they might have gone.'

'They?'

'The bunch of us making the picture' he repeated.

Until the car reached the next restaurant there was a lacuna. Jack sleeked his hair, glossy as black paint which leaked sideburns down his cheekbones. Ettie clasped her hands in her lap. The journey was like a bridging scene inserted in his script which he hadn't got around to writing any dialogue for. Evidently he counted on things running smooth.

As soon as they stepped into the restaurant his driving-force came back; following him between the tables she felt taken care of. As a change from Kim's indecision, nowhere more apparent than in choosing a restaurant or what to eat when he got there, she loved to be seated and her food swiftly ordered. To please him she said 'I always wanted to come in this place.'

He was twitching grissini out of a packet and snapping them into dust, looking around the other tables. 'It's some-place you can relax' he said distractedly, 'but I wonder where the hell Sol got to.'

'Sol?'

'Sol Wenkel?' He looked amazed that she didn't know. 'Never mind I'll call the hotel we can catch up on them later. Let's us eat you and me.'

As if by shelving a problem he found himself with an unexpected holiday, he relaxed and focused his attention on her. Instead of being the representative of someone else he sketched in himself in the seat opposite her. But he talked about this group-identity he belonged to. Listening, hearing about Sol Wenkel and his friends, Ettie had the impression of a sleek and powerful locomotive whistling arrow straight through the night with its linked lighted coaches streaming like a comet's tail. She too belonged to a group in Rome, but it only revolved, a merry-go-round. Besides, by taking up with Kim she had stepped outside its centripetal pull. This group of Jack's was travelling. She had a ticket, she sat back in her seat. The destination she didn't know, but she was travelling. If it was only the rush of the pendulum swinging from what she knew into what she didn't, still it was speed and felt like freedom. When their coffee came she put a Gauloise in her mouth.

'You spare me one of those?' he asked.

'Oh please——' she was delighted: he had seemed so complete without anything she could offer. Shaking cigarettes out of the pack she said 'Take how many you want'.

Looking at her through steel eyes, a smile clipping his lips thin, he pushed a couple into his crocodile case. Her skin shivered under the cat's paws of his smile. Across the table his physical presence swelled like a doubled fist. Confused she said 'What a lovely cigarette case'.

'Have it if you want.' He pushed it into the middle of the table.

She didn't take it at once: she felt as if she had reached for his hand and found it come away from his arm, a piece broken off. She was used to possessions being intrinsic to their owners, and he came apart. He could spare bits of himself and remain undamaged. Opposite her was not himself but an assemblage of bits and pieces he had chosen to put together.

Still, the crocodile case was a trophy she would have collected had not Jack, who continued to take cigarettes from it as they talked, slipped it back in his pocket as they stood up to leave. Perhaps he didn't think. She should have taken it at once. She followed the crisp silk suit, which cut out of the air the silhouette he chose to present, to the chauffered car outside. He said:

'Listen I just need to take a look at a couple of spots for a location we might use, you mind?' He told the driver where to go.

She didn't mind. He told her they had some spoiled footage of a town in Venezuela which they meant to replace with film shot in Rome. The interchangeability of Rome for Venezuela didn't seem surprising in the silent car gliding through streets which themselves looked remote, unreal as back-projection, through tinted windows. The Rome she knew dissolved into a dim city flickering by. Any city. Only inside the car was real. She understood what he had said, 'Any city we're in we try and get the same kind of car, that way it don't feel we moved'.

Across the river he had the driver stop in a flaky piazzetta whilst he compared the scene with a sheaf of stills laid on the jump-seats. He touched a button and the window buzzed open: into the car flooded the smell and noise of this spot, this moment, as if he had chosen to create it out of flux. Jack rubbed his jaw and smoked and stared and shuffled the stills and stared again. Ettie said nothing, unsure whether she had been taken on this trip or left behind. At last he caused his window on the world to close, and sat back beside her.

'Sorry sweetheart' he said, patting her hand. 'Now I just ought to tell Sol we can fake it here, okay? To the hotel will you' he told the driver. The car swept them away, and set the flux of dimmed streets rushing by outside once more.

Like the window to its electric impulse she responded to his touch. His physical presence flooded in upon her, pattered over the selfhood under her clothes. She felt meek, steered into the hotel, into the bar, by his hand on her elbow. She didn't think What next? Here I am, she felt.

In the bar a small, fat, famous actor slid off his stool like a penguin down a chute. When his feet hit the floor he waddled over as if he'd been waiting for them. And Jack apologized for missing him at the restaurant. And Jack introduced her by her Christian name only. An alarm bell rang in Ettie's head.

'While I run up and tell Sol his fairy story' Jack said, 'you two keep each other happy will you.'

He was gone. She knew he wasn't coming back. Smooth as runners exchanging a baton the actor's hand replaced Jack's on her elbow.

'Here we go doll, let's head for some quiet.'

She found herself impelled towards the foyer, the elevators. She looked at the man beside her. In his mouth a red tongue licked like a flame in a boiler-hole. She shook her arm free. She made a dash for what beckoned like freedom, the street, Rome outside, the world she knew.

She was across the street in the chatter of the Café de Paris before her mind caught up with her legs. She bolted herself in a cloakroom cubicle and leaned her forehead against the wall. Like scattered chickens into their coop thoughts crept back into her head. She felt broken in fragments. Her hands shook. She sniffed, dabbed her face with a tissue. She looked in the glass. Uppermost in her mind was failure; but failure at what? Having not known what she had wanted, the collapse of hope was unlimited. Tears of self-pity erased her image from the glass, washing away her view of herself as rain washes away the view through a wet window.

Her crying need now was to make contact with someone who knew who she was, so, fumbling a gettone into the call-box outside the cloakroom, she dialled Kim. He knew. He knew she wasn't a nobody in a tart's dress, her Christian name hung around her neck like a price-tag in a toyshop. He saw through her disguise.

'Who is it?' his voice quacked in Italian.

'Oh Kim——!' She leaned forward urgently and spoke English without thinking: 'Oh Kim this awful thing happens, I have such a terrible time—Kim?'

For the line had gone dead. The receiver purred in her ear.

Worse was to come. Upstairs in the palazzo where Kim had his apartment her key would not open his door. He had dropped the latch. The time bulb which lit the stairway went out. In the dark she leaned her head against the cold iron of the lift-cage and cried. She felt as empty as a mirror in a deserted room. She crept downstairs and away through the streets to Marietta's flat, stealing from pool to pool of lamplight, her fitful figure now lit, now extinguished, whilst the ancient permanence of Rome brooded against the stars.

NEXT MORNING, IN the upright gilt chair which she had chosen in preference to the more comfortable sofas disposed around the foyer of her hotel, which was altogether a less raffish place than the scene of Ettie's rout the previous night, Mrs Vannick sat waiting for Kim. She smiled: lighting her face, lighting anyone who passed near, her smile made her look still happier. She was recalling Kim's determination to impose upon her, whether she needed it or not, his solicitude. It was a present of great value to her. 'You'll want to rest' he had said, driving her from the airport, 'so shall we dine about nine?'

'I am ready for anything darling. Shall I find my way to your flat?'

'No no I'll collect you. Or is nine too late?'

'I will be ready whenever you come.'

And the hotel was so carefully chosen, just what suited her. This morning she sat contentedly, tranquil as at Larkford, unaltered, an upright stroke of assurance in the pillared entrance hall through which she watched for her son's coming from the sunlight and heat framed by the door. Dressed in cool clothes for walking, her needs contained in her handbag, she was the picture of an Englishwoman ready to enjoy, as she said herself, anything.

That Kim was late did not signify: his father too had usually been late. Waiting with her own reflections was no hardship to her. She had not been in Rome since before the war and in her quiet way she was excited, invigorated by flying from London and dining late outdoors with Kim. 'You must be exhausted' he had said to her after dinner 'so I won't come before eleven tomorrow.' She had agreed as she had agreed a thousand times to be ready at whatever hour Reggie had specified, travelling or at home, with his air of bringing order into her life for her. Ready, waiting, she had always been, looking as though she had just come downstairs, although probably she had been down hours earlier to dispose of tasks which Reggie did not even know she undertook. Patience contained her energy. Today she had already been out shopping and had bought Kim a tie, wanting to have at hand a token which made tangible the love she bore him. Ever since he had gone away to school only presents had enabled him to say the words she knew he wanted to say: Thank you. So, although she herself had never found it difficult to express love in words, she had always taken him presents. She could see him running across the bleak Gothic hall at Blewston, his preparatory school, and herself stooping to greet him through his school-induced awkwardness, or manliness; and then, when she had given him some small token present, the warmth and love in his kiss of thanks, and the excited muddle of boasts and fears, trout flies and conkers, which he had poured out to show her. Then, in those days, there had been nothing he needed that she could not give. Later, at Eton, it had become a matter of tact and intuition to find out what he needed, for the integument of secrecy, which he thought was independence, had begun to armour his heart. Even so, through chinks in that awkward armour of tail-coat and hard collar, she had glimpsed his true feeling in the preparations he had made for her visit. Once when she and Reggie had gone to his room for tea, an apparently off-hand invitation, he had produced from a drawer in his desk three bowls of jelly made especially the day before. She saw into his unchanging heart through little windows such as that. She understood him. Reggie did not. Reggie, worried and reassured by turns, was constantly tapping masters' opinions as though they were barometers, fearing or hoping that each movement of the mercury was a permanent indication of his son's character. Because of the war Reggie had scarcely seen Kim until he was five. In those five years which had seemed so long, and still were so vivid, Kim's true identity and direction had been fixed on their course, so she believed, and she did not allow that he could change. It was necessary to her to believe this: her children's lives, Kim's especially, were recompense for the splintering of her own life by war and uncertainty. So she believed in Kim, she had faith. Tom and Clara might try to agitate her about Kim's erraticism, but they troubled the source of her serenity no more than school reports had done. Kim was just the same, she was sure. She had come to find out what he needed. She didn't doubt that she could supply it. She looked up confidently to face the future.

And Kim stood in front of her. 'The traffic's appalling' he said, stooping to kiss her, 'utter chaos.'

She took his hand. 'Some coffee darling?'

'We can't Mother no, there are policemen all round the car. You ready are you?'

'Quite ready' she said rising.

'Or if you want coffee I can move the car.'

Indecisiveness? Or solicitude? 'We will have some coffee at the Borghese shall we?' she suggested, leading the way into the heavy sunlight outside.

The night before she had said that she would like to see the pictures in Villa Borghese first of all. She didn't very much care where she and Kim went together, any more than she had cared on visits to his prep school whether they visited Kenilworth castle or watched cricket, but a plan there had to be, the wheel of the day had to be set turning so that the cogs of minutes ran sweetly in companionship, and neither Reggie nor Kim ever set their shoulder to that wheel. So she always decided in advance, and when the time came to go she gave the appearance of being taken.

As his car drove along the brow of the Pincian Hill Kim made a gesture, a proprietary wave of the hand, at the roofs and cupolas tremulous with heat below them. 'You get rather a nice view from up here' he said.

She looked out. Traffic and parked cars. He did not know how tranquil it had been to walk under the stone pines up here before the war. But she tried to see what he saw. 'It is the most beautiful of cities' she said. 'How you must love to be here.'

'Yes I do.' Then, drawing blinds on his feelings he added 'Some of the time I do.'

'I think you are so wise to have stayed long enough to feel you really know Italy' she said. 'To feel that you have lived here.'

'I do live here.'

She said nothing. He was too young to know how this Roman 'life' would contract in retrospect, how he would forget the names of streets and the language, and friends' faces too, in the long real afteryears to come. But she never tried to teach anyone a lesson which time would teach them.

At Villa Borghese he bought their tickets. The first entrance ticket he had ever bought her, she remembered, had been for a cinema in Cambridge. The first invitation he had ever issued had been to tea in the dog-kennels at Larkford where he and Clara had pretended to live. The past, the foundations of the present, were as much in her mind as anything she now saw, following him across the chequered floor. In the dimness of the first room, amid fair marble forms like whispers, she suggested gently 'Shall we do as usual?'

'What?' He strained to catch her meaning. She said nothing. Then he recollected: 'Oh yes let's.'

So they separated to walk through the rooms alone, to meet later and look again together at each other's favourite paintings. As a small boy, when they had gone to the National Gallery together, he had taken her again and again to see 'Ulysses deriding Polyphemus'; and time and again she had stood in front of it, watching him, saying nothing derogatory of the fiery chaos on the canvas but waiting for his taste to change and always showing him briefly, on the way out, her own favourite picture, which was Piero della Francesca's 'Baptism of Christ'. Its stillness would one day, she believed, impress itself upon him in place of that swirling mythic instant seized upon by Turner. She was prepared to wait. However opaque the façade he showed her she had

70

patience and faith to wait until events opened a window into his heart.

Opaque his façade certainly was. At dinner last night the questions he had asked ('How's Clara? Tom all right?') had been so superficial that a stranger might have asked them. She didn't know what questions he should have asked, only that he should have revealed that a part of his mind at least constantly inhabited his home: he should have re-animated the ghost of himself which, for her, haunted Lark-ford. 'Did the white owl nest in the elm this year?' or 'Apps catching any fish this summer?' Her trust would have fed upon such questions. As you might look for the bubbles sliding under ice by which a frozen brook reveals its flow, so she looked for indications that Kim's direction was constant.

Dutifully she tried to attend to the statuary. For a time Kim was ahead of her, she kept him in view, then he was gone. He was in none of the rooms she walked quickly through. She heard his voice in the entrance hall and looked in: his back flat against the wall, he talked into the tele-phone.

'Look I'm sorry I locked you out' she heard him say, 'I was—anyway I'm sorry.'

He was speaking French.

Mrs Vannick collared her spying eyes and ears and dragged them away. French! She carried her faculties upstairs and set them down amongst the paintings she was determined to enjoy. But reflections interposed themselves between her mind and the painted scenes. Her eyes did not pass through the glass, they saw instead, superimposed on the paintings, her own uneasy reflection. French! To hear his familiar voice speak a foreign language so fluently shocked her. She knew of course that he spoke French, yet something about his fluency in the foreign language offended her. He had learned sums without becoming a mathematician, Greek without becoming a professor—why not French without becoming so foreign?

But he had not learned French without changing. That

was what made her reflection uneasy.

When he had come back from that year in France, partly spent with madame Deffin and partly in Paris, there had been an unexplained alteration in his character. Reggie had called it 'developing' and had welcomed it. To her it was as though inside his mind he had built one room more than the windows on his façade accounted for. She had held his new friend Evelyn Sele responsible for this secret addition. She had said nothing against the older boy at the time, as she had said nothing against 'Ulysses deriding Polyphemus' (or, earlier still, against Kim's obsession with *Sir Gawain and The Green Knight*, although the story had let loose in his child's mind a kind of panic fear which stalked him by day in the woods at Larkford, and by night haunted his dreams with the whetting of the axe). She had waited, and Evelyn Sele had gone away.

Or had he? Was his influence still at work in the window-less room in her son's mind? Unease fluttered its wings in her own mind, the same unease she felt when glances flitted quick and dark as bats between Tom and Clara, or when she heard the gravel works agitating the garden at Larkford. Change. The threat of change she could only meet by faith in the immutability of what in the end really counted; by transferring her thoughts from the oscillation of the pendulum to the stillness of the pivot. By an act of will she ordered her eyes to focus not upon the glass of the picture in front of her, but to pass through that reflecting surface into the painted heaven beyond.

Half an hour later she came down into the entrance hall. Seeing Kim at the bar with a glass to his lips, and because she wanted whatever was wrong with him to have a recognizable cause, it occurred to her that he might have taken to drink. She approached the bar.

'That was lovely' she said simply 'I did enjoy it.'

In rising Kim caught his foot in the bar stool and sent it clattering. 'Have some coffee' he suggested, setting the stool on its legs for her.

Reggie's clumsiness had always irritated her, but she liked to see the inherited trait in his son. 'I should like something cool' she said, 'is that Coca-Cola you are drinking?'

'Another Coke' Kim told the barman.

So he hadn't taken to drink. She must look deeper for his trouble. Though they talked about the paintings their hearts did not meet. Listening to the academic interpretation of a Titian upstairs which he repeated, she thought of the day he had sat on the nursery floor explaining to her the workings of his clockwork train. She did not like a didactic tone in children, and had said ironically 'Wonderful are the works of a wheelbarrow'. Now she interrupted him, fishing in her bag:

'A present for you darling.' She gave him the tie she had bought.

'Oh it's beautiful.' Pleased, his face lighted.

'The gift is small, but love is all.'

'The sampler in your bedroom' he responded, placing the quotation. His mind might have entered her bedroom that moment and seen it on the wall. He pulled off his tie and knotted the new one round his neck. 'How does it look?'

'I knew it would suit you.'

'Thank you Mother. Thank you.' He kissed her cheek, held her shoulder for a moment with a pressure of his hand.

'I intend giving you a proper present' she said, 'we must see what you need in your flat to make you comfortable. Can you cook there? Is there a good kitchen? Or do you have to go out to meals?'

He put up a defensive hand on the tie as though her gift was a Trojan horse from which invading questions poured. 'Yes' he said 'I mean no, breakfast and things, but I don't have people to dinner or anything. Shall we go if you're ready?'

Thinking that he meant to take her to his flat she rose. 'I don't suppose it is worth your having silver and so on out here' she said as they descended the villa's steps in the heat of the sun. 'I thought it would be rather nice by the by, rather nice to let Clara have the Victorian table silver. What do you think? You will never need more than the Georgian set we have always used, there is two dozen of everything in that you know, quite enough these days. And poor Tom seems not to have any family silver.'

'Whatever they want' Kim replied vaguely, walking apart, out of touch, until they reached the car. 'Now I don't know what you'd like to do next. We can't have lunch for a bit.' He stole a look at his watch.

She would not ask to see his flat. When he too was in the car she enquired 'Have you anything you should attend to? I can very easily amuse myself.'

'We could—or ...'

His attention had departed. He wasn't wondering what they should do, she realized, he was worrying. She watched him, waited.

'We could—go to the Forum?' he suggested at last. 'It's rather nice there always.'

'I should love that.'

On their way across Rome an incident occurred which seemed to relieve Kim's preoccupation. In Via Veneto he suddenly stopped the car, jumped out and crossed the pavement to a café table. He spoke to a man hidden from Mrs Vannick by a panama hat and a newspaper. She could see from its headline that the newspaper was in Arabic. She was surprised, rather shocked, at how quickly her son in his pale suit merged with the foreign crowd on the foreign street. It reminded her of the fluency of his French. But when he came back to the car his brow had cleared. He smiled, 'Sorry, a man I had to see'. They drove on.

Presently, waiting for some lights to change, he pointed at a long blank wall fronting a wide avenue. 'That's the wall Mussolini built to hide the slums before Hitler came' he said.

'What is behind it now?' she asked.

'I never looked. Slums still I suppose.'

'What a dreadful creature Mussolini was.'

In the Forum, descending to the Via Sacra, Mussolini and the war were still in her mind. 'I don't know how we have forgiven the Italians' she said, thinking of how the foreign crowd had swallowed Kim on the foreign street. She had not forgiven them.

'We've forgiven the ancient Romans' he said 'and they won. Veni vidi vici—we've forgiven that.'

'Caesar is part of our history though.'

'So's Mussolini.'

'No Kim no, not in the same way. What affects one's own life isn't history yet.'

'It's all history to me' he said.

'Remember the bombed church I told you about? The whole sky burning above it?' She saw the spark light his eye. 'That isn't history to you Kim. Your own memory is not history.'

'But my memory is impartial' he said, 'if you'd told me about Dresden burning I'd have had the same nightmare. The flames of Dresden burned the same sky. The whole thing together, all the burning and killing on whatever side, the whole war and its causes—that's what's all history to me. What isn't history is what I'm left with. Wreckage and hate, and the sky burned out.' He sombrely surveyed the broken arches and tumbled stones of the caesars. 'Who won and who lost doesn't matter very much.'

'Believe me Kim, had the Italians won the war——'

'But they didn't, that's the point. That's what's history. Rights and wrongs and what might have happened—that isn't history it's speculation. And propaganda and self-justification. And hatred.'

'It's all very well now to say it doesn't signify, who won' she said. 'To disparage what Father and his friends did, going to the war. But it is ungrateful. It is most ungrateful.'

'It was their war, they caused it.'

'Kim!'

'Well, they did, their generation. Other people's fathers. I'm not grateful to them for causing it, no I'm not. Or for

75

the wreckage they've left. It would be a poor sort of gratitude that kept the hate alive and caused another war. Anyway look' he said, putting out a hand which did not quite touch her arm, his attempt at apology, 'look at the first war if you want to know how I feel. I bet the first war didn't mean much to you.'

'That was different.'

'Why? You must have been about the age I was in the second war.'

'I was brought up entirely in the nursery. We hardly knew my mother.'

'I don't see what difference that makes.'

'Don't you' she said sadly. 'Ah well if you don't.' She moved beyond reach of his hand. She was alone.

From the rutted stones, through the fallen grandeur, they had approached the Palatine Hill, and now they entered the tunnel in its flank. Sun and heat were extinguished. The damp of this subterranean place took Mrs Vannick's mind back to that vault where she had buried Reggie. Poor Reggie buried, and buried with him her own physical life, all she had shared with him. It was a hard thought to bear, that he had taken with him what they had shared. Now Kim renounced what she had shared with him. He didn't see what difference it made, to be brought up in the nursery like a dog in a kennel. And Clara had gone. The tunnel smelt of beaten earth and she walked uphill wearily, her shoulders bowed.

At a turn in the passage came the sound of falling water, and she felt the gloomy air on her face ruffled by its draught. She caught up with Kim at an iron portcullis let into the tufa.

'I love this place' he said.

She looked through the grille into a cavern hollowed from the rock. Water spattered on a hoary river-god, his huge cramped presence in the grotto like a giant asleep behind the bars of his watery cage, an ancient and minatory creature. Falling water and ferns made it cold. She shivered. Such

76

figures belonged in the follies and sham ruins of Romantic landscape, which she didn't care for, but she tried to share what Kim said he loved. She tried; and in the same way that notes of music heard by chance, perhaps through an open window, can seem to arrange themselves into a melody familiar to the passer by, so the ferns and falling water produced on her inward eye another scene. It was a moment before she could place it: she saw a stream, a ferny stone cascade, colours of rhododendrons, the scent of yellow azaleas—'The Paradise Wood!' she exclaimed aloud.

'Yes' he said. 'Come on it's cold. You'll like the garden at the top better.'

When they broke out of shadow into sunlight they were on a plateau ruled square by gravel walks. The geometry of gravel and rose beds was trimmed with orange trees and backed by a formal pavilion. They might have emerged from the Dark Ages into Enlightenment. Here even the shadows were neat as cut-outs. 'This indeed is lovely' she said.

In the echo of her own rose garden she found harmony. As she stooped reading labels the familiar lingua franca of botany was as heartening as the feel of the soil between her fingers. Ah the kind earth! In its friendliness her fingers quickened like cuttings which take root. She pictured Kim coming to walk here, but walking in spirit between the old walls at home.

'I am so glad you brought me here' she said. No response. She looked up.

Ten yards away Kim stood at the parapet with his back to her. She joined him and looked down, as he did, into the Forum. A wilderness of rank, tough greenery flourished amongst the ruins, fig, olive and vine, acanthus spreading green fingers over marble, all sea-green as water welling up from below, splashing a spray of creeper against walls, a green sea reclaiming fallen arches and broken columns as the flowing tide reclaims castles of sand. Creeping and spreading upwards the appalling vigour of growth assailed the Capitol.

'I love it' he said.

On the plateau behind them stood purpose and order. Pruned roses under clipped trees, weeded beds neat as graves. He kept his back to it. She looked at his face. Though he said he loved the view his eyes were troubled, mirrors of the disorder below. Was it impossible to will to him the only fruit of her own life, her serenity? If the fruits of experience cannot be bequeathed then malgré lui each person's life is purely selfish. She looked at her watch.

'Lunch do you think?' she suggested.

'Yes. Lunch. Let's.' He stayed at the parapet. 'I don't know why I love it' he said 'but I do. It's the perfect view.'

She was looking over the wall when she saw a quick grey shiver in the grass, a mangy tail. Her fingers gripped Kim's arm. 'A rat!'

'A rat? Well it's got its living to make I suppose. Come on, lunch.'

Mrs Vannick tried to enjoy her lunch despite the dismal restaurant Kim chose, and the dead flies on the tablecloth and the way everything tinkled as each tram shook the street in passing. When they had finished their meal the choice of restaurant was explained: a sly, yellowish, bald man appeared with a suitcase from which he took, and secreted under Kim's napkin, a carton of French cigarettes. Mrs Vannick's instincts were offended.

'What a curious way to buy cigarettes Kim.'

'They're much cheaper.'

'You mean they are stolen.'

'I don't know where he gets them. He leads his life and I lead mine.'

'Surely you have the money to buy cigarettes in shops' she said.

'I don't smoke Mother' he replied, opening his hands wide, 'I promised to get them for someone. I'm told the ones you get in shops aren't made in France and taste disgusting. Shall

78

we go if you're ready?' His knuckles whitened with tension as he waited half-risen from his chair.

The restaurant had been chosen not to please her but to serve the purpose of buying cigarettes from a thief for whoever he had talked to in French on the telephone. This hurt her extremely. The candour of her eyes showed her hurt. 'Yes I am ready' she said, and they went out into the street.

'If you'd like to have a rest this afternoon I could drop you at the hotel' Kim suggested.

'Very well' she agreed. Now she saw through his solicitude. 'What will you do darling?'

'Oh—muddle about.'

Of course he had his life to lead. Like the thief and the rat, he had his life to lead. She could only wait. 'Then tonight darling' she said 'if you can dine with me I'd like to take you somewhere really nice. My treat.'

'That would be lovely.'

She got into the car. 'And maybe——'

When he was in the car himself he said 'Maybe what?'

'I thought just, maybe is there someone you would like to bring?'

He had stuck his head through the window to reverse the car, and he didn't answer. She folded her hands in her lap. For the first time she began to fear that patience was not enough.

4.

ETTIE HAD NO patience, but her resilience served the same purpose; as a sapling bent double under a fall of snow appears patient, and will spring erect when the snow melts, so she recovered. She had awoken on a sofa in Marietta's flat and lo! the burden was gone, melted in the morning sun. To avoid explanations—she regretted that she had told Marietta so much in the middle of the night—she had gone out to a café from which she could watch Kim's door whilst sipping coffee. When Kim emerged and drove off she let herself into his apartment and ran a bath. Yesterday washed off her like the dust of a journey.

She was painting her toe-nails when the telephone rang. Usually—she didn't know why because the question didn't interest her—Kim unplugged the telephone from its socket before he went out, but today he had not. She picked up the receiver and listened.

'Ettie?' It was Kim's voice. 'Are you there? Ettie answer.'

'Yes I'm here' she admitted cautiously.

'Look I'm sorry I locked you out. I was—anyway I'm sorry.'

'Did you lock me out?'

'You know I did' he said uncertainly. Her confidence fattened on his uncertainty. 'What are you doing now?' he asked.

'Just resting. I got so late last night.' With one hand she resumed painting her toe-nails.

'Look I'm at the Borghese gallery. Ettie I wish you'd come.'

She laughed. 'You've got your mother you don't need me.'

'It's just what I do need' he said intently. 'Listen, will you be in this afternoon? I'll dump my mother. Please be there Ettie.'

'Oh Kim' she said 'if you have lunch at that place where the smuggler comes you might get me some cigarettes.'

'Certainly. Ettie I wish——'

'Wish what?'

'Tell you this afternoon. Be there will you?'

'Gauloises don't forget.' She hung up.

Let him sweat. She painted her nails assiduously, with a careful hand, smiling. Why Kim was upset she didn't care, she cared for facts not their cause. For the moment—the only point in time where her footsteps alit—Kim was upset, and the effect of that fact was that she had the advantage over him. If you people the world with opponents, and have no aim beyond momentary advantage, you profit by another's weakness. You only win what someone else loses.

80

But the stilling of last night's uncertainty about Kim left a silence in her mind which soon filled with disquiet about Jack Peel. There she had lost. Faced with the consequences of her own actions she had run away. She had thought that she was big enough to play with anyone in the playground; but evidently she wasn't, she needed ground-rules, her own setting, an acceptance that she was more substantial than she appeared. She required her family name as well as her pet-name to be known. If people didn't know who she was, nor did she. From Jack Peel's game she had run home, or tried to. It was a defeat.

Ettie resented defeat with fierce irrationality. Incapable as yet of self-analysis, and unable therefore to distinguish what was important to her from what was not—unable indeed to know when she was serious—she could not trivialize defeat of her play-acting rôles. Her involvement in each moment, each rôle, was total: consequently each defeat was absolute, and rankled in every part of her being. Revenge she must have. She painted and prepared her woman's body whilst her unformed mind busied itself with schemes for getting even with Jack Peel. Her woman's body, in a child's pose cross-legged on the bed and with a child's expression of intentness in the tongue poking between the lips, was an adult weapon which a schoolgirl furbishes for the return fight with a playground bully. Another time she would be ready.

When she had finished preparing her body she had nothing else to do, and so she fell asleep.

The instant before waking there came a weight on her mind like a hand on the lark's nest pinning its wings. She fluttered. She woke. The weight became Kim. He was making love to her. She could not rid her mind of the dream-weight. Her leaps upward were broken-winged, she failed to take flight. All she felt was her nose bumped and her hair dragged, and weight and roughness, and dry hurt. In making love Kim left no mind hovering above the bed like a cold mirror to mock the bodies' antics, and this she loved, she loved the sense that she contained the whole of him, as she never could at other times. Usually she watched fondly for the return of his neutrality, as savagery withdrew into the deeps of his eyes; it reassured her that caged in the mind she didn't understand was the animal she did. Today she only felt trampled flat. She moved away from him.

'You get my cigarettes?' she asked.

'On the table.'

She rose. She wanted light and air all round her. His need, what he had taken, had only to do with himself; that was what had damaged her. The selfish resent selfish usage most fiercely: it involves them in what they want least to consider, the private causes of other people's distress. She went next door and lit a Gauloise. The thick blue smoke wreathed her in an explosion of her separate French identity. She felt better, straightened herself like a flower trampled in his footsteps. Then she went back and sat smoking on the bed.

'I needed you last night' Kim said. He did not notice that her silence was antagonistic. Often she left the room when they had made love; she did it so as to bridge the moment of tenderness when she felt tempted to tell the body next to her that she loved only him, and then, for some reason, to start crying. He lay looking up at the ceiling. 'I needed you and you weren't there' he repeated.

'Why lock me out then. You said you locked me out.'

'Because you weren't there.'

'You should have told me it mattered.'

He sighed. 'It's no good if you have to tell people.'

Silence.

Then he said 'The point of having your own life and people you choose in it is that they should know what matters without you telling them.'

Picking a shred of tobacco from her tongue she considered this. But why should she have to try to understand? To interpret his silence, to see through his opacity, to suffer his hurts which she didn't want to matter to her? 'I don't know what you mean by people from your own life' she said, 'it's all your own life you lead.'

82

'No it's not!' he told her fiercely, 'what's forced on me isn't mine. Only what I choose—this!' A sweep of his hand enclosed the flat and her in it.

Again she felt oppression pinning her lark's wings. She got up and went to the window to be sure that the street was there, and people and cars passing in the world outside.

His voice pursued her: 'What's over, this past people keep forcing on me isn't mine, isn't me any more. It isn't. My life is a place I choose, people I choose. What I choose.'

At the window her thoughts had separated from his words and returned to herself. No one in the street knows who I am, she thought, only Kim knows. Her existence seemed to depend upon him. Was that oppression? Suddenly she was frightened by the very independence of him which she had sought at the window. Independence was annihilation. She turned and looked at him. Something gipsyish was revealed in his nature when he was naked, or when he was by the sea or in the country with his hair blown wild, and this appealed most deeply to something hidden in herself ... struck a chord expressed in a refrain running in her mind 'An old brown dog a big front porch and rabbits in the pen, I'm going to be a country girl again'. What they appeared or pretended to be, their clothes, his hair brushed flat, disguised them from each other. She went to him naked and kissed him.

'You choose me don't you' she said in his ear.

He put his arm round her. She nestled against him: the unwavering column of her cigarette smoke rose above them. Into the room, remotely, penetrated the noise of Rome passing. Life passing.

Life passing her by. The moment she was secure Ettie saw, as if from the window of a moated grange, the lighted travelling coaches streaming by. But she tried to resign herself to peace, if Kim needed it. If Kim needed her.

'You see' he said presently 'it's nothing but confusion her coming here.'

Ettie stiffened. Even his hand absently stroking her arm

83

wasn't thinking of her. 'Your mother you mean?'

'Yes. Yes, she keeps making out all the time she knows what I'm really like. And how can she possibly.'

'She is your mother.' Ettie got up. The hand which had stroked her body now indifferently stroked the pillow.

'She was' Kim said. 'You can only mother children. I'm not that any more.' Realizing that Ettie had gone, he looked across the room at her. 'You don't care what I was.'

'Not a bit.' She was fetching out of the cupboard the raincoat she used as a dressing gown in her determination to travel light.

'And I don't care who you were' he told her.

That was rather different. Steadying the cupboard door she steadied her naked image in the long glass. Behind her reflection was Kim's on the bed. It was enough: two reflections, a bed, the Roman sun. Enough for the moment.

'Trouble is with a family' he went on 'they won't accept you can alter. You know? Christ, you can go bald and they won't believe it, they think it's some phase you're going through. It's the indulgence drives you mad.'

Settling her hair outside her raincoat collar Ettie watched him. Even to her he looked very young. 'So is that why you came to Rome' she suggested, 'to get away from ...'

'From what?'

'From everything before?' She wouldn't name his mother.

'Is it why you came?' he countered. 'Is Rome nothing but ruins and refugees?'

She went into the bathroom. One of the reasons she wouldn't name his mother was that behind Kim's mother stalked her own. Admit one prying mother and you admit into your mind them all, and with them their associated concepts: guilt, deceit, lies. The words exploded like flashbulbs shocking light into the dark places of her life. They made her feel squalid, as a child feels when the sheet is pulled back and light reveals the night's dirty sins. She ran another of her innumerable baths.

Cleansed and dressed once more, making up her face, Ettie

told Kim, who had dressed too and was wandering restlessly about the flat, that she had an appointment with the sarta who was making her some clothes.

'I'll drive you there' he said immediately.

'You'll only have to hang about' she objected.

'What do you mean hang about? It's at San Giovanni isn't it, I'll look in the church. Come on if we're going.'

'Museums in the morning, churches in the afternoon— quite the little tourist suddenly' she mocked on her way out.

'In the end there are plenty of things in Rome besides silly people' he said, slamming the door shut behind them.

On the landing where she had wept in the dark last night Ettie remembered the terrible gloomy permanence of Rome, and herself slipping from pool to pool of lamplight through the streets. On impulse she jumped onto the broad mahogany bannister and slid down it to the next landing. 'Don't you like silly people any more?' she called to him.

When he caught up with her he was laughing. He took her arm and together they descended, the clack of their heels echoing in the stone stairwell of the palazzo.

His cheerfulness soon evaporated in traffic jams. Ettie knew that the sawing horns showered sparks on the powder-keg of his temper, and she shrank from the explosion. They were jammed at the bottom of Via Nazionale when the flash-point came. An urchin ran along the line of cars hitting their roofs with a stick. Kim yelled at him. For that the child cracked their roof twice, and Kim sprang out of the car. The two of them dashed across the pavement and disappeared into the slum streets hidden behind Mussolini's wall. Ettie was too surprised to move until horns screaming behind her goaded her into the driving seat to put the car up the kerb. When Kim didn't reappear she abandoned the car, and the embarrassment of being in it, to follow him.

Immediately she left Via Nazionale the world changed. Dusk, cobbles and the vile rookeries of the poor surrounded her. She had walked only 50 yards of alleyway when she

85

heard issuing from a tenement the caterwauling of women's voices screeching abuse. A door stood open into a hellish interior. In its flaring light three furies screamed at Kim. The oldest of the three croaked over a table where she was flattening a shirt with an incongruously new electric iron; another waved a bottle from which wine splashed; the third, her face swollen with shouting, kept her hands over her ears. Kim, so slim, so disdainful, looked the unhorsed knight in the hands of a rabble. It was war: Ettie hesitated to side with the object of such violent hatred. She did not enter the tenement. A very old man rose with great difficulty from his chair and struck a feeble punch at Kim, who pushed him in the chest. He collapsed like an overcoat slipping off its hanger. At this the brawniest of the furies snatched up a meat knife. Kim grabbed her wrist and fought with her at arm's length. Then, flung by the crone, flashing in the light, there flew through the air the electric iron trailing its flex. Struck on the knee by this missile Kim kept hold of the knife-arm attacking him and was backing towards the door when the third fury belted his arm with her bottle. It was a tremendous blow—Kim doubled forward over his arm. The scene froze. In the silence Ettie could hear wine leaking from the upturned bottle onto the stone floor. When Kim backed out of the room none of them came after him.

Ettie could not bring herself to touch the object of such hatred, who limped beside her over the cobbles nursing his arm, in case its fury was not yet spent. Keeping clear of him she measured the distance to the safety of Via Nazionale as she had measured, last night, the distance from Jack Peel's hotel to the world she knew. Kim had started to laugh painfully.

'You know I think they broke my arm?' he said.

His gasps of laughter shook the scene into a new pattern. What had been frightening became absurd. Ettie fixed thankfully on what was ridiculous and laughed too. 'You see the old man fall over?' she gasped.

'You see the old woman?' he wheezed. 'You see she had to

unplug the iron before she threw it at me? Unplug it!'

So, gasping with hilarity and pain, they reeled through puddles of lamplight until they regained the sane world they knew, of traffic jams and floodlit ruins.

When Ettie had helped him into the car she asked 'Do you know the way to the hospital?'

That made them laugh so much she could hardly start the car.

However, by the time they reached the Salvator Mundi laughter was exhausted. From the solitary confinement of his pain Kim said nothing. Beside him Ettie could not help feeling wonderfully free from pain. She was not involved. Their arrival at the hospital was to her like seeing Kim off on a journey; when porters had taken him away she would have left, gladly as you leave a station, had the nuns not assumed that she would wait until his arm had been set. So she sat in the waiting room turning over picture papers. The brawl in the slums faded from her mind. She regretted her missed fitting with her dressmaker. She was bored.

At long last a nun came to take her to Kim.

For Ettie, who had been educated at a convent school, the hospital's nun-haunted passages led her not onward, not nearer to Kim, but back into herself and away from him; the linoleum between blank walls was joylessly familiar to her, and reimposed the guilt-ridden context of school upon her mind. She remembered the frisson of secrets—a lipstick, a letter from a boy—shared in corners of passages just like these, and the large black shoes of nuns slapping the lino as they approached to discover the secret and to grieve over it. Their holy grief inflated secrets into sins. Their sorrowing piety loaded her with guilt, and with remorse. In moments of exaltation in the chapel she could have crawled to their altar to beg shriving for peccadillos which she had been conditioned into regarding as sins. But her sense of guilt was too general to be dispelled by penitence; it was impossible to avoid sinning in a religious establishment which made all rule-breaking sinful. Because the nuns were constantly in a state

87

of anguish about their pupils, and the nuns were presumably in a state of Grace, she came to think of anguish and Grace as being much the same, and to think of guilt as her lot in this world and the next. She had absorbed the precepts of the convent more thoroughly than she knew.

She had learned the lessons of guilt and self-denial so effectively that guilt still corroded, and self-denial still negated, any view she might take of her own identity. She believed in her inmost heart, where the stern duenna still presided over her soul, that she was nothing.

Even now, in the hospital corridor, she imagined grief and anguish for her short skirt and painted face to fill the mind of the nun who led the way. She felt guilty, ashamed of her appearance, ashamed of being bored by Kim's injury. Adding to her burden of guilt, the nun referred to Kim as her fidanzato; here as at school it wasn't proper even to share an accident with a man you weren't engaged to marry. Smarting with guilt she turned upon its cause outside herself, Kim. She entered his room full of bitterness against him.

But he looked so absurdly neat in bed, the sheet drawn up to his chin, like a child she had come to say goodnight to, that at his bedside she smiled down at him—could only kneel and shake her head tearfully and cover his slack hand with hers. His mild, wondering gaze followed the tears down her cheeks one by one. 'Oh Kim' she said, 'poor poor boy.'

Presently he murmured in English very quietly 'I think my mother is waiting for me at her hotel. Will you ring her up?'

She withdrew her hand from his. As if she had reached out to rescue from the tide a child whose feet were already on a rock she felt foolish, and nothing dams the springs of pity quicker than that. The tears dried on her cheeks, crusty as barnacles. She only stayed because it was awkward to go.

Once again, with faint petulance, he asked 'Will you ring her up now?'

'Yes all right.' From the door she asked roughly in French

'Do you want anything else?'

'My mother will bring what I need' he replied.

Downstairs she told a nun to telephone Kim's mother and escaped to the car. Escape, which had been impossible at school, was possible now. Escape from guilt. She would make amends, she would stay quietly in Kim's flat all evening. She drove away rejoicing in her youth and freedom.

5.

WHEN, AFTER LUNCH, Kim had dropped her at her hotel, Mrs Vannick had gone straight upstairs to her room. She felt old and tired as she unlocked the door. But a few moments alone with herself refreshed her.

Arranged about the room, points of focus catching the eye in the negative ground of hotel décor, were scintillas of her personality in the form of small but quintessential possessions: photographs of the family, silver hairbrushes, her dressing gown over a chair, a bronze figurine of the Buddha on the bedside table where most people would have kept a clock; books, flowers—so assertively superimposed on the room was her own context that even the receptacle in which flowers were arranged did not look like a vase you would find in an hotel, but like a vase brought from Larkford. As the Cross makes a Christian church out of a hut by the Zambesi, so Mrs Vannick's heterodox talismans furnished her room by the Tiber. The quintessentials of her context travelled with her, like a missionary's, to combat facts with faith.

She sat in her dressing gown brushing her dark, silvered hair to loosen the knot of headache behind her eyes. All would be well. All must be well, she insisted, letting the rhythmic brush-strokes whisper peacefully. She had faith.

Both present and future, she firmly believed, depended upon roots set fast in the past. That nothing came about in isolation, that every event was explicable in terms of its antecedents, was the continuum in which she had faith. No event—not war, not the death of her husband—broke the rhythm if you interpreted it aright. *Was, is* and *will be* are all affirmations of *to be*. You looked back, and found reason for going on. Her past was clear print on clean pages, not a word blotted or a line smudged, nothing she was ashamed of: a text from which to draw comfort, a source upon which to base prophecy. In the light of faith, all must be well. If she waited patiently something would happen.

She did not mean that 'something would happen' in the sense that Reggie or Mr Micawber had meant it, that something unlooked for and self-evidently delightful would turn up; no, it was something retrospectively predictable that would happen. What, she did not know; but that it would be of a piece with the existing pattern she firmly believed. Fulfil now oh Lord the desires and petitions of thy servants, as may be most expedient for them.

She left the dressing table and sat down in a chair with a book in her lap, the hours until eight o'clock, when Kim would pick her up, ahead of her.

Instead of reading Lord Chesterfield's letters she massaged the nape of her neck with her fingertips, her eyes closed, thinking of Reggie. Had he been there she would not have talked to him about Kim, she would only have replied peaceably to his speculations, trying to imbue him with her tranquillity as he paced to and fro upsetting ornaments and moving chairs ... She remembered him entering her room one night ten or more years ago when she was reading in bed. 'Pretty rotten report that of Kim's don't you think?' he had asked. It lay on her table. She had not read it. 'I know you think these beaks make a great caboodle about nothing' he had continued 'but you can't turn a blind eye to what the outside world thinks. It's the world the boy's got to live in after all.' Then had burst out the real irritant of the report: 'You see this wretched chemist beak has the gall to say he's "a bit of a misfit"? Misfit!' In delving for a clock-key that he had dropped in the fender he had managed to upset a brass trivet. Uproar in his part of the room threatened the peace in her own. 'I don't know what to think' he confessed when he had restored order and was staring moodily at a chalk drawing which hung over the fireplace. He was not inactive for long; he reached up and began to straighten the picture.

'Please don't Reggie' she begged him.

'Oh, sorry, you trying to sleep?'

But he wouldn't go, he found no distraction from his worries alone in his own room. 'Awfully clever likeness that' he said, for the drawing was a portrait of his father, 'old whatsisname got him to a T. That to-hell-with-you look in his eye.'

'I often think Kim is like Father' she suggested.

'To look at you mean?'

'And in character.'

'I hope not' Reggie concluded from his study of the drawing. 'I hope not. I mean to say, all very well being an odd bird then, if you had ten thousand a-year. It's a very different story nowadays.' He looked up into his father's heavy-lidded, contemptuous eyes. 'God knows what would become of Father nowadays.'

'He might have been more adaptable than you think, if things had been different. If he had had to adapt.'

'Might have been. Never gave any sign of it.' His gloomy reflections encroached upon her lamplight.

'Darling if you are worried about Kim why don't you have a talk with him' she proposed. She had often watched their 'talks' from the window, the two of them yoked to the garden roller, plodding up and down the tennis lawn side by side whilst the rain pattered on their hats and the wet dim park fell away beyond them; and she had watched Reggie emerge from the 'talk' with relief, like a boy from punishment, whilst Kim wandered away unperturbed. In a sense Kim was older than his father, and it was Reggie's plight she wished to ease. 'I am sure a talk with him would set your mind at rest' she urged.

Reggie rubbed his chin anxiously. 'I would but he's so ...
Unapproachable. Guarded.'

'He's at a difficult stage.'

Reggie seized on that. 'You find him difficult?'

'At a difficult stage, I said. Underneath he is just the same.'
Even to comfort her husband she would not share his unease
about her son. But clearly she would have to send them
further than the tennis lawn. 'Why don't you take him off
for a day or two, just the two of you, away from here? You
could go and fish Tinker's river in Wales, he is always asking
you.' She reopened her book. 'We could do with a salmon
for this race-week party of yours' she added.

What she did not add was the line which ran in her mind:
When life fails, what's the good of going to Wales? Reggie
placed too much reliance upon circumstances and other
people, on salmon fishing or schoolmasters or going away,
to achieve what could only be won by his own effort, to
achieve the trust and understanding which he longed for
with his son. He wished situations mended without effort on
his own part. He shrank from conflict. He could not bear
hostility. If it was possible he conciliated, and then escaped
as rapidly as he was able, leaving behind him, like the ghost's
melodious twang, an impression of his charm. And she
couldn't be angry with him because he always made her
laugh. It was all a joke, an improvised play in the theatres
of country houses ... she remembered a verse he had written
for a country house game years and years before, which
expressed both their dilemma and his attitude towards dilem-
mas:

> When Adam joked and Eve laughed
> Who paid off their overdraft?

In the same scrawling elegant hand had come his letters
home from the war. That too had been a joke, a game invented just when he was sick of being grown up. That he had
been glad to escape to the war was the worst damage that

the war had done her: her self-reliance and her fortitude dated from that realization. She could not count on Reggie. Because he enjoyed himself so infectiously it was not generally noticed, except by her, that he took detours around all situations that he would not enjoy. Along he swung, sanguine and high-spirited, as if the earth was flat and made expressly to bear his weight, and it seemed captious to point out that he was zig-zagging downhill. 'Don't for God's sake let's worry about money yet' he had continued to say whilst unopened bank statements had filled the drawers of the library, 'something is bound to turn up.'

What had turned up was a heart-attack, which had killed him instantly. He had escaped again.

Because of the damage the war had done her, because of Kim's dereliction and now because of Reggie's death, Mrs Vannick's idea of what was permanent had been driven back from one outpost to another as she had discerned that stability was founded not upon this, not upon that, until only Larkford and herself remained, the Capitoline rock above the ruins, the formal garden upon whose order encroached the vigour of the wilderness rattling its tin money-boxes in her ears. Although (of herself and Reggie) it had always been she who had faced up to their responsibilities, she soon found that facing these responsibilities alone was a different matter: whereas before she had been looking after Reggie's interests since he wouldn't do it himself, she was now—ostensibly— looking after her own interests. By his death her altruism became selfishness. To stay on at Larkford was selfish—she read the accusation in Tom's face, heard it in the rattle of the gravel works. To refute the accusation she must discover Kim's best interest and pursue that. More clearly than he knew himself she must know what Kim wanted.

Such determination to know is not impartial: in combating facts, faith bends them. She tended to find under stones sermons she had already hidden there. Like a writer whose slipshod use of tenses confuses his reader's sense of time, Mrs Vannick's memory confused her view of actuality by presenting past and present with equal vividness. Rather than having to recall the past she had it constantly in mind, its focus quite as sharp as the 'now' around her. Such a very clear memory is itself a form of distortion, since it does not allow what is distant to grow small.

Although she took no particular note of time passing from minute to minute, eight o'clock found her awaiting Kim in the foyer of the hotel: her mind, ranging widely over past and future, was like an astronomical clock which tells also the time of day. Ready and waiting, she was by no means subservient to the person she awaited. She sat in the hallway trim as a tulip, but there was nothing meek about her.

When she made out that the porter standing at a respectful distance in front of her chair wished to speak to her she smiled. 'Yes?'

'There is a telephone call for you signora.'

She rose and followed him to a cubicle into which she allowed herself to be shut. Through the glass he pointed at the telephone. She picked up the receiver. 'Hallo, Kim?' she enquired.

A female voice poured Italian into her ear.

'I do not understand.' She halted the voice firmly. 'Attendez s'il vous plaît.'

She set down the instrument and, after a little difficulty in extricating herself from the cubicle, found the same elderly porter and brought him to interpret the call. They were so squeezed together in the box that his decorum suffered, and Mrs Vannick's mind occupied itself with this damage to the man's professional dignity until he replaced the receiver. Something had happened, as she had known it would.

'Is your son signora' said the porter when they were outside the cubicle. 'They telephone from the hospital.'

Still the light fell calmly upon her face. 'My son is ill?'

'Not sick, is hurt. Is not bad,' he hastened to say when he saw the blow take effect, 'but I think you go to see? Wait now and I call you a taxi.'

He touched her arm before he went into the street, the light firm reassurance of his hand reminding her of Apps's when he helped her into a car. She always awoke kindliness in a uniformed breast. When she went out into the violet dusk he said, leaning into the taxi before he closed its door, 'Is good you are here signora, is lucky for your son.'

She did not know where the taxi took her. Interminably unreeled the streets, sometimes leafy, sometimes glaring with shops. Something had happened, an irreversible event: unlike Reggie she did not expect events to do her work for her, but she expected them to show her what work must be done. She would soon know; urgency sharpened her sense of purpose. Across the river the taxi burrowed into the biscuit-coloured mass of trasteverine Rome, by ancient lanes, lamps splashing light onto her clasped hands, lamplight silhouetting her taut figure. The driver turned in at a gateway, ascended a drive, stopped. She asked him to take from her purse what she owed, and entered the grave building.

Ceiling lights burned down on silent green corridors receding from the empty hall. She could see no reception desk, only a panel of opaque glass in the wall. Uncertain, she hesitated. Abruptly the frosted glass panel shot upwards: in the opening a nun's face confronted her. Mounted on its wimple the face was a steel-engraving which the hatch framed, a face no less opaque than frosted glass. Nuns were impenetrable creatures to Mrs Vannick's eye. She asked for news of her son. The female incapable of motherhood disappeared. There was a telephone conversation in Italian. Mrs Vannick waited. Like mist isolating a traveller the foreign language and the foreign faith descended between herself and her son.

Soon, rustling along the passages, came another habited creature to act as her guide. The corridor she was led along seemed to lead inward, away from the light, as a forest track leading inward leaves the wide sky behind. Believing what she was told, that Kim had broken his arm in a car accident, she was less concerned about how he was than about where he was. In her Protestant mind the suspicion of enchantment, of imprisoned souls, arose from the rustling hieratic figures passing to and fro in greenwood depths. Kim had to be rescued.

It was a surprise to find that his bed, when at last they entered his room, stood by an open window. After so many interior passages she had not expected to see the sky at this end of the tunnel. Two or three quick steps, the first hurried movement she had made, brought her to his bedside. But Kim, looking up at her, seemed still to be at some infinite distance beyond.

Her guide whispered that he was drugged. Mrs Vannick waited until the door closed. Then, kneeling by the bed, she asked 'How do you feel darling?'

Kim sighed. 'Strange. Stupid. Someone attacked me, a woman attacked me.'

'No darling' she soothed 'these are nuns, I am sure they mean to be kind. You were in a car smash, no one has attacked you.'

'Didn't a woman hit my arm?' His eyes appealed to her for a ruling, ready with belief even before she spoke.

'I am sure if one of them knocked your arm it was by accident' she told him, 'but don't worry about them darling, we will get you out of here directly and into a proper hospital. I daresay there is an English nursing home' she supposed.

He smiled faintly. 'If you live in Italy you have to go to an Italian hospital mother.'

It went against all her instincts, to be ill abroad; she even travelled with a spare tube of English toothpaste. But she only contradicted him in her mind, saying aloud 'We will see, darling'.

'Anyway I'll be able to go home in a couple of days they said.'

Home! Her eyes lighted. This was the event that had turned up to reward her patience. She foresaw the care she would take of him, the summer days strolling at Larkford. 'I will book our tickets' she said.

'Oh not to England, home to my apartment I mean.'

He didn't know what he meant, she decided. He was confused. 'We must wait and see' she said. 'Darling I think you should sleep if you can. I will stay by you if you like.'

'Please ...' His voice petered out.

Please yourself, did he mean? Or Please stay? There he lay, injured, vulnerable—rescuable. She stayed. She remembered promising him, when he had suffered nightmares as a child, that she would always be near. 'Where will you be?' he had implored; and she had realized that even then such a promise, if taken literally, was dishonest. Even when she had held him in the hollow of her hand she could not always be there. Nor had she ever wanted her children to be dependent on her in that literal sense. In the war, in an isolated house, proximity had conditioned both the children and herself to physical interdependence; but what she had meant them to learn was not dependence but security. Comity. She had wanted them to recognize their relationship to a context wider and more stable than the individual self, and to find, as she did, in the seasons and in the setting of the stars that immutability which the ticking of the clock denies. This is what she had intended to teach; but a dominant will accomplishes more than it intends, to everyone's cost, and dependent upon her the children had become. It made her slightly contemptuous of them.

Quiet as her own thoughts came words from Kim's lips: 'Mother, you remember breakfast once in the war?'

'Indeed I do.' She could feel the iron frying-pan in her hand, hear the children's voices echoing in the kitchen. Various Boards had taken away her servants and she had looked after the children alone.

'Remember the poisoned berry I ate?'

The projector casting pictures on her mind shuddered and stopped.

'What berry?' No answer. 'No darling, you never ate a

97

poisonous berry, I would remember that' she insisted. Mended, the projector's serene images flowed on in her mind. Breakfast, Miss Hay the governess arriving in her little Austin . . .

'And the lamb that died in the wood?'

Another detonation shook the landscape she remembered. 'Which wood Kim?'

Silence; as if he didn't know or wouldn't pronounce the wood's name. When he spoke it was a suggestion: 'Where I saw the Green Knight?'

Ah, now she grasped which way his mind was wandering: into nightmare. She saw her chance to discover more. She drew a chair close to his bedside. Through the ice of his opacity, which anaesthetic had shattered, came his frightened true cry from deep water. She drew near the starred hole in the ice and let down her hook to fish. 'Kim, what is wrong?' she asked.

'What is wrong?'

She waited, aware that she must eavesdrop rather than interrogate.

'I don't know about right and wrong' he continued wearily 'or East and West. I don't know if it's wrong to work for a whole system you don't care about. Just for money. Just for money so you can go on . . . can go on living inside the system you don't care about. Because I don't care about East and West. If the Firm knew me they'd know I don't . . . it's all ruins. But I suppose they think I've chosen. Chosen!' His eyes opened, glinted with self-mockery or despair. 'They think people choose but I never chose anything. Nothing! It's just that I try and stay where I know . . . which keeps on shifting. You know—do you know what they asked me now? For a list of friends so they could tell me which ones could be useful to them. Then I realized. Just to try and stay where you are you have to sell everything. You have to sell out.'

His eyes closed. Silence. Some altogether loathsome shape nudged her hook below the ice. 'Kim, what do you do in

Rome?' she asked, hands already over her ears, so to speak, to blot out his reply.

'Don't you see?' Again he revealed the troubled depths of his eyes. 'Ah if you don't' he murmured, and closed his eyes once more.

She straightened her back from his bedside. She didn't want to know. She wound up her hook and line away from the jaws of that Leviathan. 'Well if you don't like it Kim' she said 'I should come home.'

Very carefully he withdrew his plaster arm under the sheet. In the white, silent room the light burned very still.

She went to the window. Against the indigo night brooded the crowns of palm trees. Below lay a courtyard darkened by their baleful and metallic moonshade. His window gave not onto freedom but onto a jungle clearing: the corridors had not led through the forest but into its ultramontane depths. He was lost. She turned back.

'I should sleep if you can' she said, repeating childhood's charm against the terrors of the night, 'you will feel better in the morning I am sure. The main thing is to get your strength.'

She kissed his brow cold as stone. It was all she could do. No use promising she would be near, because she could not be. He was lost quite alone, and must find his own way. If the compass with which she had furnished him at the beginning of his journey no longer distinguished East from West or right from wrong, she could do no more. She left him.

6.

NEXT MORNING Mrs Vannick visited the hospital again. After the heat of the streets Kim's room was cool and airy, white curtains puffing in and out, Kim sitting up cheerfully in bed in the pyjamas which he said his cleaning woman had brought him earlier from his flat. To all appearances a night's sleep had quite restored him. Mrs Vannick was not entirely reassured. But she struck a balance between the chimeras of the night and the pretence which sunlight made possible, that there was nothing wrong with him but a broken arm. She knew the value of optimism.

She divided her day between the hospital and the Vatican museum, regaining her own balance in the presence of paintings, in the sun's warmth, in dining at her hotel with a book for company. She would be, whatever happened, the person Kim trusted her to be in the place where he looked for her. She would be herself.

On the following morning—Kim was to be allowed to leave hospital later in the day—Mrs Vannick walked to his flat with an armful of flowers to make it pleasant for his return. Not having told Kim what she planned she relied on the porter for a key. She found the address without difficulty, the ponderous door of the palazzo standing ajar off the street. She stepped in; shadowy stone, the singing of stone silence in her ears, eclipsed sunlight and the noise of traffic; again she had the sensation of stepping into ultramontane depths of foreignness. Only her flowers glowed in the gloom. No porter answered her knocking on the closed mahogany doors. Finding Kim's name on a numbered mailbox she took the lift upward, its iron gate clashing, the iron cage creaking up through several floors until she saw Kim's number beside a door. She pressed the bell in hope that his charwoman would answer it.

The door was opened to her by a girl. Fragrance like the scent of a child asleep came from the lovely face drowsing in clouded hair. She stood clutching together the lapels of her macintosh, on bare brown legs, and smiled. Her cheek was creased where she had slept on it. 'Yes?' she said in Italian.

What a beautiful neighbour Kim had! 'I mistook this for my son's flat' she said, smiling too, 'Kim Vannick. I am sorry to have wakened you.'

Ettie bit her lip with a pearly tooth. There was amusement

in her eyes. 'Oh' she said on a light breath indrawn 'oh, come in I—I stay here you see. Come in.'

Mrs Vannick followed the rippling raincoat through the hallway into a room warmed and gilded by bars of sunlight through slatted shutters. Here the girl turned, welcoming her in. 'I am asleep when you come' she said 'I am so sorry.'

'I had only waited a moment' Mrs Vannick assured her, as if accepting that the only explanation she need be offered was that the girl in her son's flat had overslept.

'Roses!' Ettie came forward, would have touched the flowers, but seemed to think better of approaching Mrs Vannick too close.

'Will you put them in water for me?'

'Thank you.' She accepted the flowers as a gift to herself; and indeed the buds of yellow roses complemented her. 'Shall I cook some coffee?'

'That would be nice.'

For the moment Mrs Vannick was content to play the guest. Grace and pertness such as this French girl showed was ownership, incontestable. The flat, the flowers, the sunlight itself seemed hers in the sense that to youth and beauty the visible world belongs. There was no contesting her right. So Mrs Vannick stayed put where she had been invited, and waited. Their true relationship would emerge.

When Ettie returned carrying two coffee cups she had pulled on a sketchy T-shirt and tied back her smoky hair with a purple velvet bow. She had emerged from the mac a trimmer, tougher proposition. Offering a cup she asked 'Do you speak French?'

'Alas no.' Guest or not, Mrs Vannick would choose the language.

'I thought as Kim speaks it so well ... but of course you sent him to France quite young.' She hit a cushion with her hand so that dust filled a bar of sunlight. 'You sit down? I never speak in English with Kim' she went on, taking a pack of Gauloises from a bureau, 'I don't even think of him as an English man not hardly.'

'You think of him as a Frenchman? Surely not.'

'Not anything, just étranger' the girl replied through blue smoke wreaths. 'Stranger you say it?'

'Foreigner.'

'Forestiero. Kim and me too, oh so many in Rome, all of us strangers, foreigners ... siamo tutti forestieri.'

'You have lived here long?'

'Here?' She was taken aback, looked round the room.

'Here in Rome' said Mrs Vannick smoothly. That the girl's cigarettes were established in the bureau gave her presence in Kim's flat a history, but for the moment she preferred not to learn that much history. Ettie told her that she had come to Rome a year ago and had a job translating film scripts for an agency run by a friend, and Mrs Vannick appeared to listen; whilst all the time she was adjusting herself to the facts which had been presented to her on the doorstep of the flat. If she had been a woman who regretted her actions she might have regretted coming to Kim's apartment so early in the morning, for had she come later it would have been possible to maintain, if only as a polite fiction, that the girl was a visitor, and this she would have preferred; not so as to deceive herself but in order to get off to a happier start with Kim's friend, whose hostility she felt, and was sorry for. The girl's antagonism did Mrs Vannick very little harm, but it soured the natural happiness with which Ettie had awoken and answered the bell. Of the charming creature who had opened the door to her Mrs Vannick could have made a friend. Now that she had put on a mask, a disguise, it would be harder. However, things were as they were and she must begin. 'Now tell me' she said 'what is your name?'

'Yvette Arvers' the girl said, lifting her chin to pronounce her name clearly. 'But' she added 'one calls me always Ettie.'

Although Mrs Vannick disliked the forwardness of calling a stranger by a pet-name she dived in at once: 'Well Ettie, you know that Kim will be here by midday?'

'Yes, I go to fetch him.'

'Is there food in the house? And his room ready? He won't be able to look after himself you know. My intention in coming was to prepare a welcome' she said, adding rather grandly, 'In case he hadn't a servant, do you see.'

'Well no, we had a woman—Kim had I mean' she said, her pertness somewhat rattled, 'but she came always so so early and now, yes, I was just going to begin cleaning when you come. Now I begin' she asserted, retreating through the door with their coffee cups.

This time Mrs Vannick followed her into the kitchen.

'Please, you mustn't see the mess, I am going to clean' said Ettie, pushing up her sleeves and running taps in the sink.

'Bachelor kitchens are always like this are they not?' Mrs Vannick observed the lovely rounded arms in the sink and the slim body tautening the T-shirt. 'Does he have sauce-pans or anything of that kind?'

'We never eat at home.'

'We shall have to now. We shall have to get what is needed for cooking and so on' said Mrs Vannick as she looked into the bare cupboards.

'I am sure Kim is going to want to eat out still.'

'He will have to do what is best for him' said Mrs Vannick firmly. 'Now what I propose is this, that I should go out and buy what is needed whilst you do what you can here before fetching Kim—his car I suppose was damaged in the accident was it?'

'The accident?'

'When his arm was broken.'

'Oh that accident. No it wasn't. I have had her mended in fact.'

'I see.' For the moment Mrs Vannick leapt the crevasse of deceit. 'Very well Ettie, I will go out to the shops now.'

'But how will you buy shopping if you don't speak Italian? Or do you speak Italian?' wondered the girl, doubtful now at what capabilities Mrs Vannick might next display.

'Oh I shall manage.' She smiled. 'Then shall I make some

lunch for all three of us here?' she suggested as she left the kitchen.

'Yes please stay to lunch' Ettie called after her; but it was evident to both of them that their relative positions, of host and guest in Kim's flat, were already reversed.

Mrs Vannick would not have prevailed over Ettie so easily had not a large part of the girl's character—and that part the fundament of her early life—been conditioned to accept authority. Out of Mrs Vannick's eyes looked the nuns of her convent school. By their light she saw herself as a slut amid squalor. The image she saw, like each latest reflection of herself, convinced her of its truth. The apartment, now that she looked, was filthy. There were no utensils to clean it with. She tried, but the dirty underclothes she used as rags only smeared grime from the flat onto herself. Disgusted, fishing hairs out of the basin plug, on the edge of tears, more and more thoughts to cry over slopped into her mind. She was a failure—the incurable failure which keeps in mind no steady idea of what would constitute success. Crying, she packed her belongings into her suitcase. When she saw how little difference their removal made to the appearance of the flat, she cried the more.

She left her case at Marietta's apartment, which served also as the office of the translation agency, and drove to the hospital to collect Kim. In the car she told him resentfully 'Your mother burst in at dawn'.

'You were in bed you mean? God what chaos.'

'You needn't worry, I've moved out.'

'You can come back at night. She won't be there at night.'

Ettie didn't answer, driving fast, her face set. She hated the tenderness with which he treated his arm. The thought of bone-ends grating inside the plaster filled her with revulsion for him. Also it made her own bones feel fragile.

'Where will you go?' he continued. 'You can sleep in the spare room if you want.'

'Oh shut up Kim.'

Neither spoke again.

When Ettie opened the apartment door Mrs Vannick came forward, drying her hands on a new tea cloth. Kim's painfully white face, his lips and eyelids red as weals, his sling and his limp—for the electric iron had damaged his knee—hurt his mother like injuries to herself.

'Welcome home darling.' She touched his hand.

She only touched his hand, but the impression Ettie received was of mother and son falling upon one another's necks. She pushed past them into the sitting-room carrying the holdall of things she had taken Kim in hospital. Shutters and windows had been opened wide; heat and brilliance flooded the room in place of the usual glimmer of shadowy parquet, and on the rosewood table plates and cutlery had been laid around the vase of roses. Ignoring superficial dirt Mrs Vannick had cleansed the very atmosphere of the apartment.

'Now' said Mrs Vannick 'lunch is almost ready. I thought you would find an omelette easy to manage, Kim.'

'Anything'll suit me.' He limped across the room to try the drop-leaf of the bureau, seemed satisfied to find it locked.

His mother watched him. 'You hurt your leg too did you, in the—car accident?'

'Only my knee a bit. It's perfectly okay.'

'Did the doctor look at it?'

'Please don't go on about my injuries Mother.'

'You can't expect us to ignore them.'

'No you can't' put in Ettie.

'I'm perfectly okay.'

'You are not, Kim, and trying as I know it is for you there is no call to be peevish with Ettie and me.'

'No there's not' Ettie echoed.

'Come Ettie, could you help me with our lunch?'

Ettie followed Mrs Vannick towards the kitchen. So determined was she not to be on Kim's side that she did not fully realize her only alternative, which was to be on Mrs

Vannick's side. Her selfishness was not positive enough to amount to independence.

Left alone, Kim opened his bureau with a key taken from his pocket. He seemed anxious to make sure that its contents had not been disturbed; anxious, not eager. He looked extremely careworn. Then he relocked the desk and limped to the kitchen.

Whilst Mrs Vannick whisked eggs Ettie showed Kim new utensils on the shelves and provisions in the cupboards. 'Look' she said in English, 'look how your mother has bought all things you need. See, all you want.'

'Do I want them?' he asked in whispered French.

She disassociated herself from his whisper: 'Look, even a tea pot. You can get jam and stuff and have tea now.'

'I don't want tea' he said irritably, walking out.

At lunch the burden of conversation fell upon Mrs Vannick, who questioned Ettie on conventional topics: asked her where she was brought up, what brothers and sisters she had, whether they had children, and so on. Ettie's answers were evidently news to Kim. By his mother's way of judging friendship he knew nothing about her. Nor did Ettie know anything about Kim—was surprised, and interested, to hear about Tom and Clara and their twin sons. Mrs Vannick asked her at last how long she had known Kim.

'Since six months—is that how you say it?' she appealed to Kim, who had only joined the conversation to correct her English several times.

'For six months is what you say.'

'I know I am stupid in English' she muttered.

'You speak it very well' Mrs Vannick told her.

'I don't express myself—je suis pas moi-même je veux dire.'

'No one can be quite themselves in a foreign language' Mrs Vannick pointed out.

'Kim is, in French. It's true Kim, no? You speak from your mind.'

'Of course I think in French if that's what you mean, yes.'

'Ah but you see' explained his mother 'that is only to say that the pretence is in your mind rather than on your tongue.'

'What pretence?' Kim asked, piqued.

'The pretence that you are what you are not, a foreigner. Tell me Ettie' she went on 'speaking of appearances, where would you advise someone of my age to look for clothes in Rome? I thought it would be rather fun to buy one or two things.'

On this subject Ettie was full of ideas. To be consulted by someone as elegant as Mrs Vannick seemed a commendation of her own appearance, and she was flattered. Clearing away lunch she suggested rather shyly that she should show Mrs Vannick a shop she had described.

'I should love that if you are not too busy. I should be most grateful' Mrs Vannick replied. 'And you Kim darling, I would rest if I were you: why don't you get right into bed and perhaps you could sleep?'

Kim was sullen. The plaster cast seemed to have caught him, he was like an animal dragging a trap. He watched them clearing the table together, listened to their voices in unison in the kitchen, limped into his bedroom. The pillows were heaped against the headboard for one occupant. Ettie came in, shook his hospital things out of her holdall and was going out when he caught her arm and whispered in French 'Come back tonight'.

'I can't Kim.'

'Don't let her interfere.'

'She hasn't interfered. I like your mother.'

'Don't you see? Can't you see she's only trying to charm you?'

'Charm works Kim. You should try it.'

He let go of her arm. 'I'm sick to death of charming' he said, and sat down on the bed.

She hesitated for an instant, and then went out to the hallway. In explanation of the holdall she said to Mrs Vannick 'I bring Kim's things from the hospital'.

As if innocently Mrs Vannick said 'But I thought that you were staying here?'

'Oh no!' In the candour of those eyes, steady as altar candles, Ettie was shocked by the suggestion. 'I only stay while Kim is away. Now we go?'

'Goodbye Kim' called their two voices.

The bedroom door slammed.

'You have somewhere to go tonight?' asked Mrs Vannick as they waited for the lift rumbling up towards them.

'Yes. Yes I have.'

Ettie looked away to conceal the leap of excitement in her blood. Jack Peel had been in touch with her again, and she had agreed to dine with him this coming night. Although the lift descended slowly, excitement thumped her in the gut like a free fall.

She enjoyed shopping with Mrs Vannick. She enjoyed the deference which Mrs Vannick commanded in the spacious, deep-carpeted, gilt-chaired couturier's. It reminded her of shopping in Paris with her own mother, without the irritation of being a dependant, a daughter; for from Mrs Vannick, whose good opinion she was by no means sure of, she enjoyed as a treat what would have irritated her as a chore with her own mother, whose love could be taken for granted. She was not interested in the affection of those who were bound to love her. They sat together on a gilt sofa. 'I wish I had dressed up more smartly' Ettie said.

'I think young people's clothes are delightful nowadays' Mrs Vannick replied. 'All these colours and odd fashions; it seems to me you are free to be whatever you choose. To be an individual, at any rate in appearance. Of course it makes it harder to decide I suppose. But in my day one simply had no choice. As one has no choice much at my age now' she added, though not sadly.

The sales girl showed them clothes. Mrs Vannick made Ettie try a dress or two, and in the intervals talked in the most natural way about her own life in England. Ettie was soon learning about Tom's plan to extract gravel at Larkford. 'Can't you stop him though?' she asked, quite angry at the threat to this idyllic house she pictured, 'can't Kim?'

'Has he ever spoken to you about it?'

'Me? I didn't know even you lived in the country.'

'Didn't you? Ah didn't you' Mrs Vannick mused. Presently she said 'He should really come home and consider it all. He will I am sure.' Ettie tried to assess whether it mattered to her, if Kim went home. Then Mrs Vannick said 'Perhaps would he bring you one day?'

The suggestion captivated Ettie. What enamoured her was not the idea of going to Larkford but the idea of being liked sufficiently to be invited. She sat alone thinking of it, for Mrs Vannick had gone to try a coat and skirt. The suggestion wasn't thrilling, indeed it offered the opposite of excitement, peace. A country house, such as her grandfather's in Burgundy where she had been born ... she pictured the landscape she had seen in English paintings, the wide washed sky and watercolour light, and in that landscape, in that context, she placed Kim amongst antecedents and possessions, amid a family and responsibilities. She saw him for the first time as a figure related to its ground, substantial in a way he wasn't in Rome. And his mother liked her well enough to invite her into that picture.

Later the two of them walked along Via Sistina together. 'You must be such a help to your mother, with your taste' Mrs Vannick said. 'I am afraid my daughter Clara is always trying to persuade me into widowish garments of one description or another, black very often, and it does lower one's spirits. You have cheered me up.'

Ettie laughed. 'I don't think my mother is interested in me telling my advice.'

'You go on being interested in her all the same' Mrs Vannick advised, 'you will find your interest returned.' They had reached the top of the Spanish Steps, where their ways parted. 'I won't ask you to come and have tea with us' she said 'you must be weary of talking English to me. But come and have lunch or supper in the next day or so will you? Please do.'

Ettie said she would. Impulsively, as if conferring a blessing or an absolution, Mrs Vannick kissed her. Then she stood a moment longer at the balustrade, looking down on Rome. The splendour of evening light made a golden lake in which domes floated, tolling dark bells; below the gilded surface scurried traffic and people, cars gliding like fish, life scuttling through streets tenebrous as a lake's depths.

'Yes, it is the most enchanting of cities' Mrs Vannick mused. And then, laying her hand on the girl's arm before she left her she added three words: 'For a time'.

For a time. The words tolled like one of the bells whose tongues rolled gloomy thoughts across the city to Ettie's feet, iron tongues reverberant of the past, warning of the future. But Mrs Vannick had gone, taking with her that larger scale, that broader context of past and future which she had suggested to Ettie's mind. She had gone: Ettie no longer needed to please her. The present was enough. She descended the wide steps into the clamour of Rome, and excitement at the coming night once more emptied her gut with the thrill of falling.

7.

ON THE NIGHT of Kim's accident, coming back from the hospital to his apartment, Ettie had spent the evening on her own thinking that she would wash her hair, play records, even perhaps read a magazine. But time was a remorseless enemy to Ettie. Sly at slipping through the hourglass when she wished to catch hold of the minute's tail, the hours fought her inch by inch when they had her alone. That evening not a moment had died meekly. In the pauses between one record and another there yawned abysses of silence. Soli-

tude she did not know, only loneliness; and loneliness was
one more facet of failure.

> If loneliness meant world acclaim
> Everyone would know my name,
> I'd be a legend in my time.

Most of Ettie's emotions were expressed for her by the lyric
of one pop song or another: indeed the inside of her head
resembled a transistor radio, the crackle of bad reception
occasionally pierced by gobbets of schmalz. In the emptiness
of Kim's apartment her own hollowness resounded. When she
remembered that Kim unplugged the telephone she blamed
him for severing her from the world, hurried to plug it into
the wall, and rang up Marietta.

'I wondered where you were' her friend said, 'there are
some flowers come for you from that film man. He rang up.'

'Did you give him my number?'

'After what you told me he did?'

A pause. 'What sort of flowers?'

'Orchids.'

'Orchids! He's really trying.'

When she could get Marietta off the line she rang Jack
Peel's hotel. The switchboard wouldn't put her through but
took her number. Then she waited. Waiting for a telephone
call gave point to her existence, which had had no point
before. It transformed her from a beggar standing aimlessly
at the roadside into a rich woman waiting for a taxi. In a
few minutes the telephone rang.

'Ettie? They tell me you called.' His voice bounced the
ball into her court.

'Oh——' She hadn't thought what to say. 'Oh—just thank
you for the orchids. So lovely, they are by me now.' She
expected him to apologize.

He didn't. 'That's okay. Sorry you got sick and ran off the
other night.'

'I am sorry too. It was silly' she apologized.

'Forget it. Listen, you busy later in the week?'

'Why?' Be cagey, she thought.

'We could maybe meet up Friday.'

'Yes fine' she agreed, 'Friday is fine.'

'Only it'll have to be a raincheck in case we started shooting nights, okay? I'll let you know, right?'

'Right.'

Ettie recognized that she had started from the stronger position and had yet lost the round. Never mind: she had something to look forward to. She was in motion again.

She was in motion again, like the pendulum swinging. When she had left Mrs Vannick at the top of the Spanish Steps she walked to Marietta's flat and dressed herself up for the evening. She picked clothes for the kind of girl who wouldn't have lost her head in Jack's hotel. Then she took a taxi to Palazzo Roccaleone, for Jack had left a message telling her to meet him there. The palace housed a club and an embassy as well as Marco Roccaleone so that, since she didn't know what was Jack's social context in Rome, she didn't know from which façade of the courtyard to expect him. He came out of nowhere: before she could get out of the taxi he hopped in and directed the driver to a trattoria in Trastevere.

Lamplit glimpses of Jack's blue jacket and polo shirt hinted that she had dressed for the wrong occasion. The smoky yellow light of the trattoria confirmed it. Families filled the tables, uxoriousness prevailed. She had prepared herself to win the wrong war, the one she had lost last time. Jack lounged back and lit a cigarette from his crocodile case. She dimmed the wattage of her bosom as best she could by folding her arms across it.

'Were you with Marco at his house?' she asked. 'He is a wonderful musician did you know?'

'Wonderful?' The cigarette bobbing in his mouth was very white against his tan. 'He'll never get anyplace.'

'You think he needs to?'

'I know everyone needs to. Look, all he does is sit in that

palace like he was another piano stool, writing stuff no one's going to hear. You know what he does when he finishes some masterpiece? Sticks it in a drawer and starts another. Christ!' A grissini snapped between his fingers. 'He's like me when I was in art school, these kids farting around painting stuff so wild no one would buy it and telling each other they were geniuses. Scared to put it on the line.'

'But Marco is one of the most rich people in Rome. He hasn't need to sell his work.'

'Everyone needs to sell what they do sweetheart. Especially the rich. How else you get to find out what you're worth?'

'Maybe Marco knows what he is worth.'

'You think Marco wouldn't love to get paid?'

'I think he wouldn't mind much.'

'Then I'll put you straight.' He let the waiter set plates in front of them. 'I just been talking to him about scoring a movie and I tell you, no beggar couldn't have jumped on a loaf no quicker.'

'So he is getting somewhere' she said 'if he is writing film music for you I mean.'

'Shit, he won't score the picture. Go ahead and eat.' Whilst she obeyed he watched. 'He might come up with couple of ideas we'll use is all.'

'But he'll be paid.'

'Not the going rate he won't.'

'Why not?'

'Because he's a schlmiel sweetheart. You know what he said when I made him an offer? "Don't worry about the money, the money's the easy part." He could paint that up, it's the schlmiel's motto.' He watched her eating her Parma ham hungrily. 'Marco'll never get airborne, too much inert weight to get off the ground. That palace, that's some shell to hump around.'

'Most people would think he was lucky' Ettie said.

'Listen' he said, 'getting in a palace is easy if that's what you want. Getting out is another thing—getting out of that shell if you were born inside, that's something else. And why? Because there's no need. You don't have to move. Fatal. You look at tortoises, they don't do too well.'

'Better than hares.'

'Only if you believe in fairy tales. Believe me instead, these guys who have it made only look like the lucky ones. You finished?'

Hungry, but aware of the coarseness of stuffing herself whilst he watched without eating, she had laid down her knife and fork. The next course came rapidly, even the waiters hustled by his energy. He crushed out his cigarette and ate. Meat he took seriously, shovelling it into his mouth, washing down the shovelfuls with gulps of wine so that bits of food floated in his glass and smeared its rim. He was too busy eating to talk.

'You said you went to art school?' Ettie enquired. She wondered what he had been like before he had been taught, or had taught himself, to order hors d'oeuvres he didn't eat as a preliminary to wolfing meat.

He looked up. 'You want to know where I come from? That what you mean?' His eyes fingered her thoughts inside her head. 'You want to hear how the other half lives?'

'If you want to tell.'

'About how I used to bike home from school and slip up in my father's puke so I busted my ass on the doorstep? That the kind of thing?'

'If it's true.'

He hit a brick wall, stopped: stopped eating, sat back in his chair. He pushed away his plate and lit a cigarette. He looked weary. 'Stuff like that happened to people like me' he said, 'it's true like history. Like it happened to someone else my whole childhood. True but irrelevant, like having ancestors in woad and skins is irrelevant.'

He had picked himself up but he was different. He was a meccano figure knocked out of shape. Ettie, not usually interested in people's background or context, was intrigued. 'Tell me what was it really like' she said.

When he spoke he had shed his Americanized voice: 'Well, there was art school and hanging about. Hanging about in this caff you could go in and sit if you had a couple of bob. Rain one side of the window, steam the other—the steam come off the hot-plate where they heated up the meat-pies. And by the till where you go up and get change for the juke-box if it's your turn to pay you find they got a big box packed full of indigestion pills. You live off meat pies and Vimto you learn to love them pills. That do?' he asked her. 'That sound real?'

'Real yes. Really you?' she wondered. She thought of him faking Venezuela in the Roman piazzetta. Faking backgrounds was his business.

He smiled. 'Reckon about the same time' he said, 'about that time some chauffeur was collecting Marco Roccaleone out of school and driving him home to the palace. You believe that don't you? You believe the kid in the limousine was Marco right enough?'

'Yes' she admitted 'I know it was.' That was why Marco's past didn't interest her: she already knew it. 'He hasn't changed you see.'

'He hasn't even got out the fucking car and sniffed the air yet you mean.' Jack had picked up his momentum again. 'He stopped in his shell all his life.'

She couldn't divest her mind of the idea that privilege is enviable. 'It is unfair isn't it?' she said.

'That life's unfair sweetheart' he replied 'is the one chance we got. Just so long as life's unfair then the kid in the caff I told you about has a chance. You get a fair society, like in Russia or someplace, you got no snakes and no ladders. No dice. I tell you, the day some two-bit huckster can't make it from used-car lot to White House, that's the day I vote Communist. The way things are in the West right now you just have to find out how to be unfair and you got the whole crooked system working for you. How to load the dice is all you need work on. So long as there's dice in the game you got a chance they'll turn up box-cars.'

She wondered 'How do you find out how to be unfair? How did you, first?'

He opened his cigarette case. 'Fixing smokes in art school' he said. 'Want one?'

The crocodile case he had given her, but had kept, was extended towards her. Should she claim it? Did he remember? His eyes were blank as a gambler's offering her a card. Her courage—her nicety—failed her, and she took only a cigarette from the case. 'So how did you fix smokes in art school?' she asked. Her magpie wits picked up slang like tinsel.

'Having the teacher send me out to buy his. He'd always give me a couple out the pack.'

'How could you make him send you?'

'By acting humble enough to run errands. More in that for me than having him swoon over my brushwork like the other kids wanted.'

She objected 'How is that unfair though?'

He replied 'You make what they want serve what you want. I learned how you do that.'

'How?'

'You define your ambition. Sounds easy but people don't do it. Precisely define to yourself exactly what you want next. Not dreaming about the top of the ladder, that's Johnny-head-in-the-air stuff, no—focusing on the next rung of whatever ladder you find your feet on, that's how. You schlepp around art school complaining it's unfair they don't let you paint the Sistine Chapel and you get nothing: you focus on climbing on teacher's back, you find he'll carry you to the cigar store. You see' he said 'the process of thinking about what you want eliminates what's impossible already. Then you're left with what's possible, and you go for it. It's the people with vague ambitions or no wants who get to be trodden in the shit in the end. Like that Marco Roccaleone.' He looked in her eyes. 'Like you maybe? You a schlmiel?'

What did she want precisely? The cigarette case was all

she could focus on. She didn't like to ask for it. 'Like me' she admitted.

With coffee and sambuca in front of them he asked 'You have any trips planned in the fall?'

'Only to the sea maybe. I don't know.'

'No place you want to go?'

'Oh many! Everywhere, but ... they are so far. I thought in Paris if I got to Rome everywhere would be near but ... they are still far.'

'Nowhere is near everywhere' he said.

'You, where do you want to go?' she asked.

'Where I'm sent. I still run errands. When we wrap up the studio stuff here we're all of us going to Spain on the new picture.'

Her eyes went out of focus, dreaming of Spain. 'You are lucky.'

'That's the way the dice roll. You want to come?'

'Me?' Spain, the idea, wouldn't focus. Was it what she wanted? Or what he wanted? A ladder, or a snake? Did she want to be there, or did she only want to be well enough liked to be invited? She didn't know herself clearly enough to know the difference. For a moment the invitation lay open like a trap which might shut on her fingers if she took the bait. Then he snapped shut his cigarette case and pushed back his chair. It was too late.

'Listen Ettie' he said, looking at the watch on the underside of his wrist, 'I have to check with Sol in case he wants to shoot tonight. He needs a moon and he's the only person allowed to say if it's shining or not. You want to stop by the hotel with me?'

What did *he* want?—for she couldn't choose. 'Can't Sol make any of the film without you?'

'I'd be a schlmiel if I let him find that out. Come on and I'll drop you home.'

As she followed him up the step into the street the stain of failure widened and widened till it permeated all her mind. Only when the choice had been made for her did she know what she had wanted. Not this, not this. But it was too late.

When he dropped her she couldn't immediately face Marietta or her flat. For her friend was a girl whom another ten years of time passing had turned into a caricature of Ettie herself: in Marietta and her flat she faced her own future. So she walked on the off chance to Kim's palazzo. But the heavy door was closed and his high windows dark. There too it was too late. Walking back through the streets she thought, Now is over. The bells which had tolled were silent. *For a time* had come and gone.

As she waited for sleep on Marietta's sofa, her clothes on picture hooks or strewn amongst empty glasses she thought of the two stools she had fallen between: the peace of Kim's apartment, the luxury of Jack's hotel. On her own all she could achieve was a sofa. She put her thumb between her lips and sucked it. Like a genie conjured by this action came rescue: there was always the past, she could still go back to Paris.

8.

ALTHOUGH MRS VANNICK continued to sleep at her hotel, and took herself off alone to look at pictures, or a church, for an hour or two each day, she spent most of her time with Kim. She cooked, she cleaned the flat, she made him more comfortable with small purchases, and she talked: if nothing particularly intimate was discussed they yet fell, by propinquity and interdependence, into living upon intimate terms with each other.

It might have seemed that her work and the things she bought would tend towards establishing Kim more immovably in the rented flat. But she did not think so. She was furnishing his mind with the idea of home. She was anglicizing the Roman apartment. She was extending her influence by creating around him her own context. She could not help extending her influence, as a lamp cannot help dispelling darkness. After a couple of days she could enter the gloomy vestibule off the Roman street without that first dire sense she had had of slipping and falling into foreignness, for upstairs were floors she had swept, the stove she had cooked on, the flowers she had arranged; the context she had created by her own work. Purchase is one way of acquiring possessions, but work is another; she had come to own Kim's flat in the sense that a gardener comes to own his employer's garden.

Whenever Kim let her in—he said he had only one key—he had apparently been sitting unoccupied in a chair. There were neither books nor papers spread about, and his bureau was always locked. The telephone never rang. He was secretive. The flat she made her own, the flat she lighted; but not his mind, which was full of shadow. Kim was a tall dark tower she had seen trembling, shaking bats out of narrow windows to shriek and wheel like black holes in the Roman sunlight. But the tower had not fallen, and the bats had floated back into its crevices. She trusted in the tower's foundations.

When she found that the telephone had been unplugged from the wall socket behind his bed she did not reconnect him with the foreign city beyond the windows but called to him 'I wonder that Ettie hasn't telephoned'.

'What?' He was sitting next door with the paper she had brought him unread on his lap. Quiet and thoughtful, he took a moment or two to comprehend her questions when she spoke. 'Oh Ettie. I suppose she's . . . I don't know.'

'I asked her to come to supper' said she entering the room 'and she said she would love to.'

'Something else probably happened.'

'Yes, one is so afraid of missing things by being in the wrong place at that age. Especially anyone as pretty as Ettie' Mrs Vannick said. 'Indeed I have often noticed that the more attractive you are the more you think life owes you, and the less hard you feel obliged to try. I remember Clara so well at that age. Most discontented, nothing suited her.' So she talked, making things comfortable around her injured son.

The day was approaching when she would have to leave Rome if she kept to her original plan of staying for a week. She would not extend her visit unless Kim suggested it, for she had arranged to stop the night of her return with Tom and Clara in London and it was not easy, she well knew, to rearrange Tom's plans. Tom was always so busy. Tom—his name tolled rather threateningly in her mind as she went to bed on Sunday night, for on Tuesday she would have to face him. In Tom she recognized, if not an adversary, certainly a person of determination whose intentions were not easy to oppose. He would expect results from her journey as if it had been a business trip on behalf of a company; the results of a mother's journey to see her son would not impress him. Knowing Kim only since adolescence Tom thought that he needed to be forcibly shaken into changing his nature before he would face responsibilities, whereas she believed that Kim had only to be restored to his true self—not changed but un-changed—for all to be well. This un-changing needed caution and restraint, like the touch required to awaken a sleepwalker, if he was not to be permanently alienated. Kim was very testy. He disputed any implication that his life in Rome was impermanent. When she said that Lord Chesterfield convinced her of the value of the Grand Tour as part of an Englishman's education he retorted:

'That was 200 years ago. Anyway touring isn't living however grand the tour.'

'Three or four years they often stopped abroad. How long is living?'

'It isn't the time Mother it's the attitude. They were always on their way home, a tour is a circle where you're facing home the minute you start out.' He added rather bitterly 'And they knew what they'd done would be some use to them in the society they were going home to live in.'

'All steps in development have value Kim, if you take them with a purpose in mind. Because each stage doesn't last doesn't mean that its value won't endure.'

In the bitter, self-absorbed tone with which he now spoke of himself he said 'My life seems to have been a series of self-sealing compartments. Nothing leads to anything, nothing's been any use. It's been all stops and starts.'

'You might say a river is all stops and starts if you look at each pool separately' she pointed out. 'But it is all one river. And you can't stop the water flowing' she added.

'I know you can't' he groaned. He got up and paced about as though that truth was unendurable to sit down under. 'You know' he said 'when I was leaving school the headmaster told me this story—it was about the only time he ever spoke to me—he told this story about a child praying for a bike for Christmas and his parents couldn't afford one so when Christmas came and no bike from Heaven his father said "Sorry God didn't answer your prayer"; and the child said "Oh He did, He said No".' Silence. 'I mean I don't know if you see the connection' he added lamely.

'Yes I see the connection. "Fulfil the desires of thy servants as is most expedient for them",' she quoted.

'But how can anyone be that meek and still be a human being?' he demanded.

She didn't answer that question, she repeated what she had said before: 'Instead of regretting what is taken away by time passing you should think of what is left. For example' she said 'I am sure you thought of yourself as living in France the time you stayed with madame Deffin, but now looking back you can see that you were not, it came to an end. Yet learning French has been of lasting value to you.'

He thought about that. 'Wouldn't be much use if I lived in the back of beyond in England' he concluded.

'Value I said, not necessarily useful: there is the whole of French literature, wherever you live.' She paused. 'And you know that any friends you have of any nationality will always be welcome at Larkford.' He said nothing. 'Besides' she went on 'the broader the mind the less trammelled it is by living in the country. Look at Grandfather planting the Paradise Wood with the fruits of his travels. Look at the way those people coming home from the Grand Tour rebuilt their houses and laid out their gardens with ideas they had learned abroad.'

He was still silent. Then he said impatiently 'Ah but in those days if you learned the morals of a whore and the manners of a dancing master you had all the qualifications you needed to succeed in the world. It's a bit different nowadays. You ask Tom.'

She knew that he thought of himself as having travelled too far along the road to Rome to turn back. He did not know how short a way he had really gone. But his feet dragged, he looked back; she was sure that he would navigate himself out of the wood and onto the true line in time. Tom however would not be satisfied. Tom would want to know exactly what he was doing in Rome: 'What is the mystery?' she could imagine him asking. And she knew what the mystery was.

Before she went to sleep on Sunday night Mrs Vannick remembered watching a garden pond at Larkford electrocuted to stun any predators prior to restocking it with ornamental fish. Hitherto, goldfish had unaccountably vanished; though if you looked into the pool you saw nothing more threatening than a newt or two, and the chimneys of the house reflected amongst lily-pads. The electric current, however, had conjured out of the dark depths such evil presences that she had instinctively stepped back from the margin of that once pleasant pool. Tom was like a dynamo himself, determined to electrocute everyone's mind and restock it according to his own taste. He hustled one so, and to what purpose? To balance the books and show a profit. It was not her idea of balance, or of profit, the way he and Clara lived. Mrs Vannick reached out of bed and switched off the light.

But Tom continued to tramp about in her head. Whilst

Reggie lived it would have been gross impertinence for Tom to have questioned their staying on at Larkford, but now that Reggie was dead he, and the world too, looked on his interference as 'taking care of Clara's mother'. Well—she thought of Sydney Smith's recipe for happiness: 'Take short views, hope for the best and trust in God'. Faith, hope and charity. Then she thought of a verse which Reggie had composed at their wedding in reply to her godfather (an admiral) who had wished them 'plain sailing':

> Life's sea is rough
> My barque is frail
> Faith scans the trough
> For Charity's sail:
> Yet do I scorn to fear my fate,
> I have appointed Hope my mate.

Smiling she fell asleep.

'I am going to stay with Clara tomorrow night' she said to Kim as they finished supper next evening.

'Tomorrow?' He sounded alarmed at the proximity of tomorrow.

'I suppose I could alter it. My plan was to stay a week in Rome.'

'Tom would go mad if you altered it now.'

'Oh, Tom! I sometimes think it would do Tom a world of good if his plans were upset once in a while' she said.

'Nothing ever goes wrong for Tom.'

'He doesn't set his sights so very high.'

'What do you mean?' Kim asked.

'I mean that he has—well, safe ambitions. Within his reach.'

'True he's no high-wire artist.'

'Still, no one could be kinder to Clara' she said, determined to be just.

Kim said 'I think their life is hideously dull. It kills me the way they live.'

She knew that he foresaw such a life for himself if he came home. And so it might turn out. 'Anyway darling' she said 'the main thing is, will you manage on your own if I do go tomorrow?'

'I'll be all right I think.'

'What will you do about food and so on?'

'Oh, drift around.'

'You must see that you eat properly Kim. Maybe Ettie would come in and cook a meal?'

'I don't think Ettie is a brilliant cook' he said. Then he added 'But some girl might come in I suppose'.

This upset the picture. His mother preferred to imagine him only with the girl she had met. What he said next was worse.

'I've got to go away next week anyway.'

'Away? Where Kim?'

'The Middle East' he said, and stood up.

'The Middle East? Well Kim' she went on 'we will have to see how your arm is when the plaster comes off.'

' "We" won't be here' he said, stacking their plates with his left hand. 'Anyway, plaster or not I've got to go.'

She kept hold of her coffee cup so that he could not guillotine the conversation by removing it. She looked into the past for a parallel to reassure her. 'I was trying to think' she said, 'your wrist is the only other bone you have broken isn't it? That time at Blewston.'

Impatient for her cup he said 'It wasn't at Blewston Mother it was in Scotland I broke my wrist. You keep saying it was at Blewston but it wasn't.'

'I came to visit you Kim, I wouldn't mistake it.'

'Mother it was my wrist not yours.'

She tightened her lips and the skin wrinkled sadly. Her age showed. 'I won't argue' she said, stitching up the hole in her memory he had pushed his fist through, 'but I came to see you when you had hurt yourself at Blewston and you insisted that there was a cricket match you had to play in, remember?'

'No. And this isn't a cricket match I can tell you.'

'The principle is the same Kim. If you really want to play —really want to go I mean, then you——'

'My God, if it was a question of what I want!' he said roughly, and took her cup away with him to the kitchen.

She sat on alone, massaging the grain of the table with her finger tips. By polishing the rosewood she had made it so familiar that she had annexed it as a possession; and now strangeness arose everywhere to reclaim it, and to reclaim her son.

'Then why do what you don't want?' she asked when he entered the room again. 'Why do you go on Kim, if the road is so hard?' her voice appealed to him.

'Because it seemed the answer when I was approached. It seemed the easiest way. The easiest way of staying the same ... I don't know, I didn't think. Didn't think the Firm would be so—pernicious!' he spat out.

It could not be discussed. She knew what 'the Firm' meant, a cousin of Reggie's had worked for them and had no doubt had Kim recruited. So much for nepotism: Kim suborned, alienated, broken-armed, limping. She would not discuss it because, although she knew of the Firm's existence—as she knew that predators existed in the bottom mud of every pond—she balked at admitting the knowledge in so direct a relation to herself. Certainly there are rats in all old houses; but not at Larkford surely? Besides, she could not imagine what possible use her child could be to the Firm.

About ten o'clock she left him and walked back to her hotel. An hour later Ettie rang at Kim's street door.

When she spoke her name into the intercom there was a pause, as if the palazzo deliberated. Then the portone clicked ajar, a trap baited with the idea of peace, the peacefulness of Kim's apartment which had tempted her to try the door. She went in and rode up in the creaking iron cage of the lift. Kim opened the door in a silk dressing gown his mother had bought him, a sherry bottle under his arm.

'Goodness!' Ettie exclaimed in English. 'What a smart clothes!'

'Like it?' he replied in French. 'I'll give you one.'

She sat down. He would: he offered a present, not a trick like Jack's cigarette case. But when he spoke as though they had a future she remembered that she was leaving Rome. The shining table, the flowers, the peace. 'Kim' she said, agreeing to speak French if he chose to, 'Kim why do you unplug your telephone? I tried to call you.'

'To ... to keep things separate.'

'To keep me away from your mother you mean?'

'Yes that too I suppose. Keeping everything apart. It's easier.'

She shrugged. 'If you think always trying to make things easy is any solution.'

'I'm not looking for a solution' he told her irritably, 'I'm not a philosopher I'm just trying to get by that's all. From one bloody day to the next.'

Silence. Then she said 'Your mother told me so much you should have told me Kim, if I was going to understand.'

He got up. He seemed to bounce angrily about the room. 'How could she have told you, she doesn't know. I told you she'd just confuse everything telling you things.'

'Everything is confused Kim. You can only pretend it isn't, by keeping things apart. You can pretend for a bit, for a time, to each person a different lie you tell but ... The confusion, that's the truth. No one's a good enough liar not to have to face the truth in the end.'

'Oh God' he said, uncorking his sherry bottle, 'why don't you try and unravel yourself if you want to practise psychology?'

'I have I think.'

'Good.'

But he didn't look pleased. Instead he looked abandoned, as if she had booked her onward passage without him, abandoning him on the island they had shared. He stood weighing the bottle in his hand, wondering (she knew) what it was that she had understood about herself. He couldn't ask: to ask questions went against the principle he professed, that other people are opaque and must remain so, in their loneliness. He decided to take another swig of sherry.

'Anyway' he said 'there's no point bothering about my mother because she's off to England tomorrow. A nip of sherry? She bought this and I didn't like to send her back for whisky. Want some?'

'No. But Kim . . .'

'Yes?'

'Kim—can I sleep here?' Instantly she regretted it. Why had she asked, except that the flowers and the quiet high room was a refuge from Marietta's flat? 'I mean sleep in the spare room, I'll go early before you mother comes.'

Now he looked pleased, as if she had given up her onward ticket. 'No need to go early' he said. 'Tell you what, we'll take her to the airport if you'll drive. Then when she's gone . . .'

'Then what?'

'She's gone. It'll be just like before she came.'

'Yes.'

Silence.

'Kim' she said 'I'll go to bed I think.'

'The bed's not made up in the little room.'

It was the thought of his broken arm which decided her. 'I only need a place to rest' she said. 'Goodnight Kim.'

In the bare white room, as if all the sand had at last run through the hourglass and made a heap for her bed, she was soon at rest. Her mind was clear. On the pivot between past and future, poised upon that infinitesimal pinpoint, she had a clear picture of her own identity, immaculate and lonely as an angel balanced upon the point of a pin.

In the morning they drove to the hotel to collect Mrs Vannick, whom they found taking leave of the head porter. Ettie heard her say 'If your son does decide to try his luck in England be sure to give him that telephone number, won't you.'

The old man seemed charmed, and Ettie too found Mrs Vannick's kindliness convincing, but Kim, as if irritated, called out 'Come on we must go'.

Because of his arm he sat in front beside Ettie, but he talked to his mother in the back seat. Crossing the flat tract towards the sea, a landscape of umber farms and ilexes, and sheep grazing amongst ruins, he said 'I always think this is about the only bit of Italy Mr Stroud would recognize from *The Georgics*.'

'Mr Stroud' his mother responded. 'I haven't thought of him for years. Do you suppose he is still teaching at Blewston?'

'I know he is. Swindells told me. He's immortal' Kim said, speaking with horror as though of the undead. 'Think of him still teaching!'

'He is not so very old.'

'Not old? You know he got that wobbly neck in the first war? You might as well have a caveman teaching.'

'Principles don't change, Kim.'

'Well they ought to. Principles like his ought to, they've done enough damage I should think. Made enough people useless. Caused enough wars.'

Instead of disputing Mrs Vannick said to Ettie 'Mr Stroud was a master at Kim's first school. Very—what shall I say?'

'Obstinate?' Kim supplied. 'Prejudiced? Stupid?'

'Inflexible' his mother decided. 'But kind: do you remember Kim how he used to help you with your garden?'

'Help me? He made me dig it up and burn it, if you call that helping.'

'Oh ... I knew he took an interest. Your garden was mostly weeds as far as I remember.'

'Weeds to you. They were flowers to me' Kim said.

They reached the airport.

Whilst Ettie was parking the car Kim and his mother were alone in the entrance hall. The bustle and hurry of people,

128

and flight-calls raining down on the crowd, quickened and agitated Mrs Vannick. As though the thousand miles between Rome and England already separated her from Kim communication took on the urgency of a long-distance telephone call. She returned to what she had said to him before. 'If you so dislike what you do Kim darling, if you are not happy why do you not simply come home?'

For a moment, perhaps because the airport seemed as near to London as to Rome, he appeared to see it by the pellucid light she cast. Then his eyes grew troubled again. Maybe he reacted to the way she looked anxiously past him for her porter. He too returned to an earlier conversation they had had. 'I'll tell you the difference between living and Grand Touring' he said, 'living you get involved whether you like it or not. It's only tourists can leave if they don't like it.'

And she was leaving: half her mind was projected towards home already. All she could say was 'Kim take care of yourself. You are out of your depth.'

'No one knows what anyone else's depth is. Not from safe on shore they don't. Anyhow it isn't dangerous, don't worry.' He smiled.

'But your arm Kim?'

'My arm? Oh breaking my arm was nothing to do with it.' He laughed.

'It was not a car accident' she stated.

'No I lost my temper, somebody hit me. Nothing.'

She looked at him gravely. 'Kim you have lost your bearings' she said. 'Come home. Come to England at least, there are plenty of things you can do in England surely, with your education.'

'Mother education is useless: I haven't any qualifications, who on earth is going to hire me? The manners of a dancing master aren't any use any more. And anyway' he added disconsolately 'everyone's such miles ahead. People I despise are. Look at that oaf Swindells.'

Indifferent when she had told him of Swindells' visit to Larkford and its purpose, he sounded rancorous now. If only he could be goaded into competing. 'Of course' she said 'if you are going to despise people who succeed without half your ability ...'

'Ability's no use without qualifications.'

'Kim nothing is of any value without determination, and that is never to be despised.'

'Whatever its object?'

'Whatever its object. Little Mr Swindells is where he is because he knows what he wants. I have seen determination beat ability too often not to respect it believe me. Beat it in the short run that is' she added. 'Ability extends the horizon so, there are so many wrong directions tempting the able.'

'Talking about wrong directions' Kim said, 'did Swindells tell about me carting him off to Florence by mistake? That was a laugh.'

Mrs Vannick only half-attended; her ear was alert to catch her call to London through the multiplicity of flight-calls on the Tannoy. 'He did say something about having taken you to Florence' she said. 'Do you suppose Ettie will find us here?'

'Taking me! It was me took him to Florence' Kim insisted, as if responsibility for the mistake was a distinction. 'He rang me and I said I'd got to go and get my car from Anzio where I'd left it when I went on that yacht trip, would he like to come? Then——'

'What yacht trip Kim?'

'Didn't I tell you? Anyway I told Swindells to come on the train to Anzio and get the car if he wanted to see me. Then at the station we got on the wrong train and believe it or not went non-stop to Florence.' Kim laughed. 'He wasn't so much angry as frightened, frightened at things going wrong. I never saw anything so pathetic, him grovelling to the ticket collector and the railway police and everyone he saw in a peaked hat. Pathetic.'

'Well he had changed the story when he came to Larkford.'

'He lied you mean.'

'He said nothing about a mistake. It is a kind of determination' she said 'retrospective determination you might call it, to alter what did happen into what should have happened to fit in with his idea of himself.'

'And you admire that? I know you don't.'

'I don't underestimate determination' she said carefully. 'Ah here comes Ettie at last.'

Ettie had stood outside for a moment, watching them through the glass doors. The relationship of their two figures was simplified to her because she could not hear what they said: she saw Mrs Vannick tending away, looking round, giving the impression that she was trying to escape from an importunate dependant. That was the structure Ettie suddenly saw underlying their relationship. The impasto of what Kim said, even believed, about his relationship with his mother confused this more basic structure. Her insight made Ettie pause. Then she pushed through the swing doors and herself became a figure in the picture, for Mrs Vannick laid a hand on her arm as soon as she had sent Kim to buy her a paper.

'Take care of him my dear' she said, 'try to see that he doesn't rush off to the Middle East unless his arm is thoroughly well.'

The old firm hand seemed to Ettie to weigh her down, to transfer a burden. She knew nothing of Kim going to the Middle East, yet a promise was compelled out of her.

'And perhaps a little later on you will suggest coming over to see us in England' Mrs Vannick continued. 'I am always at Larkford and you would be most welcome.'

Again Ettie was compelled into murmuring a response. She wondered how welcome she would be at Larkford. Because she had so recently seen Mrs Vannick press her kindness upon the hotel porter her invitation—her charm—lost its impact. She understood that Mrs Vannick was a woman who was reluctant to sever acquaintanceships. It was part of her attraction, that by meeting her one seemed to form a connection with stability which would last. But did Ettie want it to last? She felt again the weight of that old hand on her arm. What did she want, in this future which had already begun—had begun by her choosing to sleep in Kim's spare room last night? Her head, so clear then, was refilling with the crackle and static of conflicting messages.

Now Kim came back with the newspaper and the three of them adopted the formal brightness of departure. They conveyed Mrs Vannick to the gate, where she kissed them both and was gone. They turned back.

Flight-calls listing cities matched the confusion in Ettie's head. What did she want? Madrid, Rio, London, Karachi. So many cities, a confusion of tongues. Then a flight to Paris called in French. Reality clear as crystal. It was as if clouds had parted and she had been called by name. She stood illuminated in that shaft of light. Her departure had been announced.

She stayed at Kim's apartment that evening, not caring very much where she stayed now that she had in spirit left Rome. She made supper with Mrs Vannick's bequest of food and utensils. There was a distance between herself and Kim which she made no effort to bridge. She had left, her mind was full of Paris. Between them on the table stood Mrs Vannick's flowers which hid Kim from her. She was thinking of telling him that she was leaving Rome when he spoke:

'I'm going to England I've decided.'

It was a blow, to be pre-empted. Now she craned round the flowers to try and see into the mind which had taken her by surprise.

'But—but your mother said you were going to the Middle East.'

'I keep telling you she doesn't know what I'm going to do.'

Ettie claimed 'I had already decided to go back to Paris. I mean before today I had decided.'

132

'Yes you should' he said. 'When?'

She regained the initiative: 'Tomorrow'.

She carried their dirty plates to the kitchen, not knowing why tears leaked out of her eyes. It was Kim not she who would be left behind. Yet the clarity in her head had become emptiness, lonely. She had nearly finished washing up when he appeared at the door. Leaning against it he said:

'Come to England with me from Paris. I'll collect you on my way. I'll start as soon as I can drive.'

She didn't reply, and in a moment or two she heard him walk away. Her head filled with warm confusion. Why had her tears stopped? She put away every plate and dried each pan, folded the cloth neatly and sprinkled bleach in the sink; but however long she waited her tears would not flow again.

When she went into the sitting-room he was waiting. Whether he now regretted his invitation she could not tell from his enquiring, half fearful eyes. She knew that he usually regretted the few decisions he took.

'Yes I'll come to England if you want' she said. She busied her hands tidying the table and added 'But you have to come to stay with my parents in Paris on the way'.

He sat without moving. He looked as though he had exploded a grenade and was now wondering how extensive his own injuries were. Then he said 'Okay fair's fair. But listen' he added, qualifying his committal, 'I won't stay I'll come to dinner, okay?'

'Okay.'

No sooner was the word out of her mouth than she knew that she had not decided, she had accepted. Again she had failed to decide, and her fate had moved quicker. Instantly, though she didn't know what she wanted, she knew what she didn't want. Not this. Alas, instantly was too late. Fate moved quicker. From the pivot, the pinpoint where the idea of herself had balanced in equilibrium, she slipped down the pendulum and clung to its swinging tip. The hammer blows of the ticking clock riveted her into the chain of instants, and the chain-gang shuffled onward. Not back, where she wanted to go, but onward.

'I'll go to Marietta's tonight I think' she said 'because of my clothes and everything.'

'Right.'

'But I don't see why you won't stay with me in Paris' she complained, 'I'll have to stay at your home I suppose.'

'That's different' he said.

'Why different?'

'It's miles from anywhere. You've no choice.'

9.

UPSTAIRS IN HER bedroom at Clara's London house Mrs Vannick sneaked about unpacking her needs for one night. 'We'll have dinner at eight if Tom's home' Clara had said, or shouted, soon after her mother's arrival from Rome. Busy as usual in the kitchen she had had to shout through the racket of the washing-up machine and the electric mixer, which had begun to give Mrs Vannick a headache in the confined underground space. 'Sorry about the noise, I like to get everything done before Tom gets back. You pop up and rest I should, you must be exhausted.'

It was an order. Suggestions, like requests pinned up in hotel bedrooms, were mandatory in this house where minutes were allocated and the schedule tight. Mrs Vannick crept about the house because she did not like to betray by the creak of a floorboard that she was not obediently resting. Here it was not a question of complacently allowing Kim to think that he ordered her life for her; here she obeyed Clara out of a sense of superannuation. Here she was Granny.

Though there was plenty of evidence in the form of furniture and ornaments she had given Clara that this house was connected with Larkford—far more tangible evidence of the connection than in Kim's flat—this house was in atmosphere utterly at odds with Larkford. In atmosphere it was Tom's setting, regulated to the busy tick of the metronome which oscillates without advancing. On holiday at Larkford Clara might reassume her childhood self, but assumed was all it was, the paper hat an adult wears for Christmas dinner. This busy little house was her setting now. Clara had grown up; she compelled her mother to be a granny. Of course it affected Mrs Vannick's feelings, that in relation to Kim she was still 'Mother' whilst here in London she was 'Granny'.

When she had taken her night clothes out of her case she lay on her bed. No point in unpacking her own context, the talismans she travelled with. She complied with the household's insistence that she was elderly and tired. She dozed.

In the street below her window a taxi stopped. Its door slammed. Steps crossed the pavement. The front door opened. It too slammed, and a tremor ran through the building, the tremor of Tom's return which spread unease upward like a draught to seep under her door. His footsteps ran upstairs. She sat up; shouldn't she be ready, wasn't she late? Her watch was still set by Roman time. In succession from the floor below she heard taps gush, drawers pulled open, shoes dropped, hangers squeak on coat-rails. A wireless began to publish news loudly through the house. She got up and began to dress for dinner, and in time made her way downstairs, feeling with her foot in grandmotherly fashion for each step, to her son-in-law's solicitous welcome.

At dinner—and Tom suggested that they carried their martinis into the dining-room directly he had poured them— he had a list of subjects to discuss with Clara. Out of politeness he did his best to disguise the agenda as conversation, canvassing Mrs Vannick's opinion on each item, but time was short and wandering from the point was checked. In this style the weekend to visit their twin sons at prep school was decided upon: guests for a dinner party in a month's time were chosen: a company cricket match was fitted into their schedule. As she listened Mrs Vannick thought of Kim saying, of a life such as theirs, It kills me how they live. And something was certainly missing from their agenda: was it life itself they hadn't time for? The engagements were stepping-stones by which they hurried across the river without wetting their feet. In due order would come the turn of Kim's name to be discussed. Mrs Vannick waited for it whilst the smooth machinery of the household fed Tom his dinner as a battery-hen is fed, from a trolley set with pre-prepared courses. With fruit salad in front of him Tom turned his attention to his mother-in-law.

'Now Granny tell us about your adventures in Italy.'

'Could I have a little sugar Clara dear? The oranges are rather sharp. Ragus esaelp' she tried, 'did you ever tell Tom about the Proper Language?' No, here in London Clara would not be diverted back to childhood. Mrs Vannick sprinkled sugar in silence. 'Yes I was glad I went' she said, 'poor old Kim. It was a stroke of luck my being there to look after him.'

'How did he seem?' Tom asked.

'Pretty shaky still. We were hoping to have the plaster off by Tuesday——'

'Yes but apart from his arm' Clara interrupted.

'Oh, just the same.'

Silence. This was no comfort to them.

'I think he finds what he does rather too much for him sometimes' she was compelled to amplify.

Interest from Tom. 'What does he do?'

Disbelief from Clara. 'I thought he didn't do anything.'

'Well' began Mrs Vannick 'it isn't the kind of work he would want talked about ...' She let the adumbration hang, she hoped darkly, in the air.

'Some scheme he's got you mean? What line of country?' Tom asked.

'Not a scheme quite, more ... secret work. I really don't think we should discuss it you know.'

It seemed that she might block their questions. She attended cautiously to her fruit salad.

Then Clara said 'Oh Mother really! Did Kim try and make you believe he's a spy or something?'

Mrs Vannick had not confronted her mind with the naked word. Now the bats fluttered out of their crevices, now the rat shivered through the grass. 'Spy, no; I am sure Kim would do nothing dishonourable' she maintained.

'Kim would be absolutely useless as a spy' Clara said flatly.

'Oh I don't know, all sorts of odd bods get caught up in intelligence' Tom said. 'Attached to the embassy is he?'

'I don't believe he is' Mrs Vannick replied.

'That's the trouble, out of a job at five minutes notice could be. At least if he was established on the embassy staff' Tom continued 'at least he'd have a measure of security as a civil servant. Security yes, recognition no; I'm told they never promote their cloak-and-dagger boys above minister rank. Did he tell you what they pay him?'

'No.' Mrs Vannick had thought that she need only hold up Kim's occupation like a Gorgon's head to petrify them: and here was Tom speaking of security and the civil service. Kim struggled in tumultuous currents, but Tom assumed that he had chosen a set of stepping stones. 'I may have given you quite the wrong idea' she said 'I am awfully stupid at understanding these things.'

'But he is definitely in intelligence?' Tom wanted to establish.

'Isn't it possible that he just helps occasionally? Just finds things out?' she appealed.

'But Mother that is being a spy.'

The stunned idea floated up from bottom mud into the light. The notion coagulated into ugliness by being named. Her son was a spy. Beyond the candlelight the shadows deepened and pressed in upon her.

In the silence Tom looked from one of them to the other before raising the next point. 'So what did you finally settle about Larkford?'

Her shoulders bowed over finger tips pressing on the table's edge. Clara took pity on her. 'Shall we have our coffee upstairs?' she suggested.

Alone in the drawing-room with Tom whilst Clara fetched

the coffee Mrs Vannick hastened to admire a new addition to their overcleaned and overlit pictures. Pleased, Tom told her that it had set him back a large sum but showed her a sale list in which a smaller painting by the same artist had fetched an even bigger price. She could think of no comment to make on this. It always surprised her that Tom had any money; at his marriage he had had none (the solicitors had been most careful to tie up Clara's settlement out of his reach) and she was used to people growing poorer rather than richer, belonging as she did to an eroded class. Reggie had grown steadily poorer throughout his life. Of the class which tends upwards and appears from nowhere, throwing up mole-heaps of dirt on noble lawns, she had as little experience as she had of the class above her own, whose wealth and possessions are so enormous that they cannot help growing richer.

'Did you meet any of Kim's friends?' asked Clara carrying in the coffee.

'Oh rather! Such a charming French girl—who drove us to the airport as I told you. Kim seems quite taken with her.'

'You didn't tell me she was French.'

'Did I not? I suppose I hardly thought of her as being a foreigner. After all Clara' she said, taking her coffee cup from Tom, 'you cannot expect Kim to have many English friends in Rome.'

'No I can see English friends aren't much use to a spy.'

'He has a life apart from what he does Clara.' But had he? *I didn't know it was so pernicious.* She remembered that he had been ordered to make a list of his friends.

'Now you were telling us Kim's views on Larkford' said Tom. 'If he's settled in this undercover job of his out there what does he want done?'

Clara too looked expectantly at her.

'Well Tom' Mrs Vannick began 'I don't think he wants the whole place dug up for money—for gravel that is to say. I don't think that is his idea.'

'He'd rather raise the necessary by an outright sale? Probably best.'

'For the time being he would rather that things were left as they are. That is what I understood' she asserted. Kim made poor cover from Tom's fire.

'But Mother—I thought we agreed the only point of you trailing out there was to get him to understand that things can't go muddling on. Can't he get that through his head?'

'Clara I went to Rome to see Kim, nothing more nor less' she said.

'And you got no forrader, is that right?' Tom supposed.

'Not what you would call forward Tom, no.'

Silence.

'You see Tom' she tried to explain 'money has never been very important to Kim.'

'He's managed to spend a fair amount' Clara said.

'Because it has been there Clara, because he has always had some money. He has never run into debt and he has never made money: that is what I mean by money not being very important to him. Perhaps I should have said that he has never been concerned to make more money than he needed. He was telling me just this time' she said, endeavouring to build a platform for Kim to stand on, 'he was saying that the whole business of capitalism isn't what he cares for, that it doesn't appeal to him. We had such good long talks' she added.

'Capitalism may not appeal to him but he lives like a rentier' Tom said.

'And I'd have thought a spy was doing his level best to support capitalism' Clara said.

There was no answer. It was impossible to reconcile Kim's contradictions into a settled purpose. *I don't ever seem to have chosen.* Darkness, darkness. And here in this house so much unwelcome light. The lustrous veneers, the very rays of the lamps, seemed polished to their full value. Light bounced about the room but penetrated nowhere. Nothing was revealed but polished surfaces. She watched Clara clean a speck of cream off a shiny table: Clara was not even thinking of her brother, but of her furniture.

'I propose' Tom announced to end the silence, 'I propose—with your approval—to push ahead with some exploratory work at any rate into the potential capacity of the Larkford gravel bed. This cement chap Swindells is our man. We needn't commit ourselves, he'll do the work in return for an option. That agreed?'

Husband and wife looked at Mrs Vannick.

Defenceless, out of her context, superannuated. Where sentiment was like something spilled on the furniture which Clara would mop up Mrs Vannick did not like to speak of her home. Here the money boxes of the gravel works rattled louder than a human cry, a broken voice. She nodded, not trusting her voice.

And Tom passed onto the next item: 'By the by darling, I've got a working breakfast with our publicity people tomorrow so I'll have to make an early start.'

Clara replied 'I must be in Bond Street when the shops open or I'll never get done so I'll start with you.'

'Eight sharp then. But what about Granny?'

Mrs Vannick focused through a mist (was it tiredness? The tiredness they all kept wishing on her?): 'Please don't worry about me. I will catch the old morning train and go home. And now my dears' she went on, rising she hoped erect as ever, 'I think I will go to bed. I am tired, after all.'

Tom said goodbye: Clara, with the mixture of efficiency and agitation which made the house so uncomfortable to stay in, fussed her mother with arrangements about tea and toast in the morning. From the door, summoning her clear silver tone, Mrs Vannick said:

'I will see you in September when you bring the children down.'

In these utilitarian lives of theirs, structured around the ferro-concrete of 'must' and 'have to', Larkford had its use too, for holidays.

*

Clara, who believed that she had no time for reading during the day, sometimes read in bed after Tom had turned out his light. Tonight she laid down the magazine she had been staring at and asked,

'Do you really think Kim's working for the secret service?'

She could call her brother a spy to her mother but not to her husband.

'There are all sorts of twopenny-hapenny jobs in intelligence' muttered the snuffed-out shape beside her. 'You may be sure Kim's only playing around.'

Clara said 'I suppose he could run this gravel thing if he came home. Mother thinks he will—will come home I mean.'

That woke Tom up. 'And play around at that? It's a serious business Clara. Potentially there's a lot of money involved.'

'Oh, money!' She slapped the magazine onto the floor. 'Sometimes I wonder.'

'Look, with a mortgage on this house and a mortgage on the house in Hampshire if we get it I can tell you we need the money from Larkford gravel' he told her. Already Larkford sounded more like a company than a home. 'Even if we didn't' he added 'there's the twins to think of. Kim's children too for that matter. The right deal now, get rid of that house, and we're all set up.'

'Kim may never marry. He may not want the money.'

Tom closed his eyes and resettled himself. 'Course he will' he murmured 'he'll be just like everyone else in the end. I'll get him a job when he comes back don't you worry.'

'What sort of job could Kim do?'

'I got a lot of pull with our advertising people, he can be a copywriter. All you need for that is this famous education he's been so busy acquiring.'

Clara said no more. If Tom was to regenerate the whole family then to maintain him in working order was her first care. He had taken his pill and he must sleep.

Yet there nagged at her mind something left undone that she ought to have done. She had loaded the washing-up machine and cleared the dining-room; she had put the candlesticks in the safe, locked the windows and switched on the burglar alarm; she had laid a tray for Mother's breakfast —Mother, that was it! She had been too busy all evening to talk to her mother. Talked of what? Told her about the house in Hampshire? Told her that even for holidays they no longer needed Larkford? Told her about the two rooms over the stables in the Hampshire house in which she and Tom had agreed that 'Granny would be perfectly happy'?

It was as well that there had been no time to talk to Mother. Clara put out her light and lay down with her arms around her husband.

10.

THE REALITY OF homecoming was not the illusion Ettie had remembered from afar. Even at the airport, when she heard her flight to Paris called, her flight did not seem to sparkle like other flights. She envied travellers hurrying to other cities. In Paris her home opened to receive her, and closed around her, as if she had never been away. For a day or so she talked, told her parents a version of her travels; then she was silent. For want of air the fire went out.

At the same unalterable hour her father's doorkey rattled in the lock as he came home from the office. Her mother had not finished the tapestry she had started before Ettie went away. Both parents were deliberately incurious. They maintained their inward-facing stance, backs to the world, warming their hands at the thin flame between them.

'You're back' people said to her on the telephone. She was. And yet she wasn't: with Kim coming there was no point in attempting to be back. The thought of his approach blotted out the light as if England itself, sombre rainy land, rumbled towards her on tumbril wheels. Her fate.

At the end of a week she rang the hotel where Kim had said he would stay. They had no booking. Why did he not come? She did not want him to come, yet she did not want him to stay away because he was enjoying himself elsewhere. What did she want? Nothing. Whatever was not this. She didn't tell her parents about Kim or about going to England, as if the future might not happen if she didn't speak of it. So long as she remained uncommitted there was a chance of something happening.

Something happened. Tapped on the shoulder in Avenue Kléber she turned to find Jack Peel breathless from running after her. A rainbow leaped across the sky. 'Saw you from a taxi' he said, 'you want to come to lunch?'

Dazzled she let him steer her arm to the taxi. She was in, the held-up traffic flowed again, they were off. She had a second chance. At once she went back to the point where she had failed to choose before. 'Jack you know that cigarette case you gave me? I want it' she said.

He clapped the pockets of his speckly tweed jacket. His clothes contrived to look as French in Paris as they had looked Italian in Rome. 'Must be at the hotel' he said, 'right after lunch you get it.'

She got it right after lunch, got laid quick as a touch-welding job done on the roadside to keep a machine in the race, in his hotel room whose window gave onto a courtyard. In this courtyard an old man gardened, tending the window-boxes, singing softly to himself, and throughout Jack's assault Ettie never lost awareness of the gardener's proximity; it was his shadow on the net curtain which was as much part of the experience as Jack's body. Neither touched her core. Afterwards she watched the shadow splash water from a hose and listened to Jack whistling in the shower. She was inviolate, her mind unruffled. She had kept her head. That was Jack's failure, and must therefore be her victory: all you can win is what someone else loses, if the world seems full of enemies. Jack had lost. When he came out of the shower slapping his flat stomach she smiled. She had met and beaten that thrusting male vigour his body promised. She smiled.

'Come back in bed.'

'Can't sweetheart I have to get on.' He pulled on a fresh shirt, crisp trousers. He was sexier in his clothes than out. He looked a big catch but she had beaten him. That he hadn't smashed her apart in bed as Kim did was what built her up in her own mind. She didn't feel like crying or like telling him that she loved him. She loved herself, and luxuriated in the bed.

Jack's energy was already directed elsewhere, driving him on towards what he had not got. Sex was trivial to him. 'I have a meeting with Sol' he said, giving his watch a couple of quick winds as if to synchronize himself with the sun in heaven, 'you hang on if you want. We'll be all through in a couple hours, take in a movie maybe, what you want. Talk about you coming along to Spain you think?' He kissed her in passing and was gone, the machine back in the race again.

Left alone, Ettie's idea of herself sparkled in her own mind like a solitaire on black velvet. Unsmashed, unmelted, she dazzled herself. She could play with anyone, and win. Her head was clear. She could stay or go, just as she chose. She dressed and left.

But next day Kim rang up. It was a wet dark afternoon and Ettie's mother, stitching at her tapestry under the lamp, answered the telephone. She handed it to her daughter, her plucked eyebrows lifted. 'Someone called Kim? English.'

Tumbril wheels. Ettie took the receiver. 'Yes?'

'Ettie could you come and meet me, I'm in the bar down the street.'

'All right. I'll come now.'

'Ettie wait—the thing is I've got no money. Could you bring some? Much as you can.'

When he rang off Ettie looked in her bag. She had only a few francs and had to borrow from her mother, who showed no surprise in case it was mistaken for inquisitiveness. Because of the rain it didn't seem worth tidying her hair before she went out, so she pulled on her mac and went as she was. In the downpour the last bastion of her sandcastle identity slipped and subsided.

Kim's car was double-parked outside the bar, two black half-orbs which the wipers had cleared peering through the filth of the journey. The Rome number plate, the car itself, unloosed so many feelings in her that she ran the last few yards to see Kim himself again. There he was at a table, wolfing a sandwich, a bird of passage dropped from the clouds. Now she longed to fly with him, if only for the splendour of flight. She sat down and put her mother's banknotes on the table.

'Thanks' he said 'I had to carry on eating till you got here. Couldn't pay. I've had a terrible drive.'

'I expected you before. Why didn't you come before?'

'Before what?'

Before yesterday, she meant. Before it was too late. She said nothing.

He said 'I meant to get here sooner but you know how impossible it is leaving places.'

'I left.'

'I know you did. People asked why.'

'You told them?'

'I didn't know myself' he said.

It irritated her that he did not pick up the money she had brought: that he set no store by French banknotes which looked to her so much more valuable than other currencies. 'You do know' she said. 'Rome was over.'

He shrugged. 'Rome maybe. Life is continuous dammit. Nothing is ever over. I wish it was so easy.'

She couldn't bear to watch him eating his sandwich. Its size made him look avid, bread and bits of meat falling from his mouth. She looked away. 'Did you go to the Middle East after all?' she asked. 'Is that why you're late?'

'People kept asking me to things. Parties and things.'

'You never go to parties.'

'Don't I? I met you at one.'

She said nothing. But she wondered if he had met someone

else. Jealousy hooked her back into his life as no other emotion could have done.

'In the end I drove up without stopping' he said. 'I only left last night.'

It brought Rome nearer again, the continuous road covered so fast. Coming by road he had re-welded the link which her air-flight had severed. Nothing is ever over. 'You must be exhausted' she said 'you won't want to come to dinner with my parents.'

'Yes I will. I'll go and sleep now and I'll be all right.'

So casual, she thought. And he looked so gypsyish, a wanderer, a wild free bird migrating north. The cry of the widgeon travelling swiftly above the clouds alone. What she loved in him still attracted her. 'How about your arm?' she asked, remembering it for the first time.

He looked at his arm as if he had forgotten too. 'It's all right I think. I seem to be whole again.'

Yes, he was whole again. 'Kim why don't we just go out and have dinner when you wake?' she appealed. 'Like before—wouldn't it be simpler? Simpler than coming home?'

'If you think trying to make everything simple is the solution.'

They were the words she had used to him. 'But Kim your mother understands, my parents don't. You don't know my parents.'

'You don't know my mother if you think she's simple. Only strangers look simple. But people won't stay strangers whatever you do. You can't help getting to know people and then it's confusion deeper and deeper. Interconnection—you can't stop it. You can't stop the water flowing' he said with the hopelessness of someone who has tried. 'So I'll come to dinner.'

'I'd better go and tell them then.' She stood up.

'I'll be there at eight.' He took a paper-clip out of his pocket and pushed the banknotes into it. The clip already held some Arabic currency.

'So you have been in the Middle East' she said.

'Yes.'

'Kim you say there's this connection but your secrecy—it's like holes in the bridge I keep falling through.'

'I never said there was a bridge. If you want to cross the river you have to wade.'

She left the café. There in the street waited the car which had come for her. Not a tiger which hunts you down, but a cat you've tried to lose which reappears ineluctably at your door. Her fate. The rain fell as it would fall in England.

However, by the time she went to bed that night it seemed to Ettie that her fate had been avoided, for Kim did not come to dinner. The solution after all was very simple: he failed to turn up. After dinner she rang Jack Peel, and on her way to bed she told her parents that she might get a job on a film and go to Spain.

'Oh.' Her father shook out his newspaper. 'For long?'

'I don't know. For a time.'

Her mother worked away silently at her tapestry, stitch by patient stitch.

In the middle of the night her father wakened her. 'This English friend of yours is on the telephone' he grumbled through the door, 'he says that he overslept.'

'Tell him—will you tell him——'

'I won't tell him anything. You're supposed to be grown up you can deal with him yourself.'

Ettie heard him stump away down the passage. She half rose, wondering what to say to Kim. Then she realized that she need say nothing, need do nothing, for the dark water between herself and Kim to widen. She had only to leave the receiver off the hook until morning. She would repay her mother the money Kim had borrowed; if money was all it cost her to buy back her freedom from fate, then freedom was cheap. She lay down and went back to sleep.

PART THREE

MORE THAN A year later, on an October morning in London, Ettie walked with a basket on her arm along a street of neo-Georgian houses, or maisonettes, in one of which, so she had been told by his office, lived Kim. The misty air made wraiths of the young trees from which leaves dropped singly, sadly, like notes drifting from a clock as the hour strikes.

Vaguened by mist at either end this street existed unattached to the rest of the world. Ettie did not think it likely that Kim, or anyone she had ever known, lived here. The little houses were without depth, so many stage-flats painted neatly on the mist. Inside them she could imagine nothing; neither her eyes nor her imagination could penetrate the façade. Speculation like a handful of gravel rattled off their windows. Only her feet on the pavement, and her keyed-up awareness of being in this street for a purpose, were substantial. She was making a stage-entry and she needed a response. If Kim would pull aside a net curtain and see her, or open a door and greet her, the action could proceed. She believed he was there because his office had told her that he was at home with a cold, and she had brought him a picnic lunch in her basket. But he did not appear. It was hard to believe in the existence of anyone behind those stage-flats painted on nothingness. Determined to act she approached his house. But her feet carried her past his door, and on towards the mist she had come from.

Two days earlier she had met Kim by chance in Shepherd Market, close to the hotel where she and Jack Peel were staying, and they had gone together into a café to snatch at what seemed to her a chance to think about the past instead of the future. She had no future. Though she had come from Spain with the film company, and was part of its entourage at the hotel, when the party broke up and took apartments she knew that she and Jack would part; they only awaited the small event which would separate them. Then what? Nothing, she didn't know, was walking through Shepherd Market worrying; and here was Kim, hurrying along ghost-pale, walking swiftly out of the past, part of the crowd yet looking up at the sky in a way that no one looks who is happy living in cities.

In the café the first thing he did was to pay her back the money he had borrowed from her in Paris. She didn't want to let him buy back his freedom.

'It doesn't matter Kim, I don't need money. I thought you'd forget.'

'I don't forget anything.'

'I didn't mean forget in that way: I meant you didn't use to notice whose money we spent.'

'Money's different when you earn it.' He held out the notes to her. She noticed that he kept them in a wallet now, not on a paper-clip shoved in his pocket. 'Take it' he insisted.

She crumpled the notes into her coat pocket rather sadly. He talked, his voice rapid and agitated. She hardly listened, he told her nothing she wanted to know, his voice screening instead of expressing what she listened for, and they drank coffee she couldn't taste. With his black shoes and his worried air of haste he had joined what Jack and his friends called 'the subway crowd'. At the tables round them nobody stayed long, couples met and parted. In a minute they too would part. And all he told her was that London wasn't too bad, he got away at weekends if he could—'I really live in the west country' he told her.

'I know that Kim' she broke in. I know you, she longed to shout. 'After all, you have forgotten' she reproached him, 'you have forgotten what I know.'

He looked at her. 'I'm so used to strangers' he said.

'In your own England?'

'Strangers to all I've been. Telling them takes so long.'

'I know. Why bother?'

'Why bother' he agreed. He finished his coffee. 'People don't get the picture anyway.'

Silence. He would go in a moment.

'You said once it's no good if you have to tell people' she said. 'If you have to explain there's no point explaining you said.'

'I thought then there was an alternative. I thought you could choose people who knew.'

'You can. Can't you?'

He sighed. 'Not if you work you can't choose anyone. There's a man shares my office' he said 'I see more of him than I see of any human being. Today I said to him it was killing me having to drive someone home at dawn every morning because she hasn't got a car and he said "Tell her you'll get so tired you'll lose your job and then you'll have to go back to Bristol". The point is I don't care if I get sacked, I want to go back to Bristol, which I suppose is where he thinks I come from. I mean there we sit he and I, day after day doing the same thing in the same office, you'd think we'd know each other. Not a bit. His idea of calamity is what I want to happen. He doesn't know, and I couldn't explain to him. We look opposite ways.'

Out of this all she considered, jealously, was the girl who stayed till dawn. It was too late. She stubbed out her Gauloise, buttoned her coat. 'Why not go back then' she said.

Through the clatter of cups and the ringing of the till he made a strange answer: 'Because an angel guards that gate whose sword turns every way'.

The words weighed heavy and cold as stones. 'I must go' she said.

'So must I.'

Her coat, even her body, were burdens she shouldered to lug onward. Like other couples they parted at the door; and, as happens at partings, one takes with him the sense of reality whilst the other is left, as Ettie was left, to readjust herself to an emptied world. She was a mere reflection again in a hall of mirrors, as she had been for a year, seeing in other people neither her real self nor theirs, but seeing in the surface of each, distorted by each, the reflection of her own appearance. In Kim's company, in place of the mirror there was glass; she looked through it and saw him, and knew that he looked back and saw her. It was to reclaim her identity which existed in Kim's mind as a savage reclaims his photograph from the camera that she had materialized out of mist in Kim's street. She had passed his door, now she went back. In reknitting that continuity which she had broken she saw her one chance of existence. She rang the bell.

When he opened the door she slipped in quickly like a seep of the mist. It was dark in the hall. Kim closed the door and followed her into the sitting-room. She didn't put down her basket. Mist drops pearled her hair.

'Take off your mac, sit down' Kim suggested, his voice thickened by his cold.

She did neither. 'Is it yours this house?' she asked. Is it you, she wondered.

'Borrowed. I borrowed it from some business friend of my brother-in-law' Kim explained.

'Tom' she said, to show him how much she knew.

'Yes Tom. Tom fixed me a job a house the lot. The whole treatment.'

'A job in a bank I suppose.'

'What makes you think I work in a bank?'

'I just thought you might. Look I brought a picnic Kim, isn't there a better room?'

'Better in what way?'

'More like somewhere people live.'

He looked round the room. Prints were stamped round the walls. Armchairs sat about like fat women in satin stuffed with dinner. Bleakly the grey London light stared in. 'You're right I never come in here' he said. 'I suppose I'll get used to it in the end.'

'Why get used to it if it isn't yours?'

'Because I'll end up with one of my own just like it. You order them on the telephone from Harrods I believe.' He smiled. 'Come on up, I camp upstairs. How thoughtful to bring a picnic.'

At the turn of the stairway he stopped. 'How did you know I'd be here?' he asked. 'And how did you know where I live?'

'I rang up your work. You told me where you worked.'

'So you know I don't work in a bank.'

'I know what you do Kim.'

'Then why say a bank? A bank would be even worse.'

'It's just an expression Jack and people use. People I know use.'

He resumed his stair-climbing. 'An expression of contempt no doubt.'

'In a way. The way they describe people not like them. Yes, I suppose contemptuous.'

'You share his contempt? Jack whoever he is.'

'It's just the point of view film people have on anyone with safe jobs, like they talk about the subway crowd. I picked up their slang. You do pick up people's views.'

'If you don't make them pick up yours you do.'

'Make them pick up yours?' She caught at the idea. But its brilliance faded: she had no views that she knew of.

'This any better for a picnic?' He had opened his bedroom door.

She went in. So that was the bed where the girl stayed till dawn. Clothes and papers ploughed into the room's blandness gave Kim's personality a roothold here. She put down her basket, took off her mac. She wondered if she would ever take off all her clothes in this room, wake in that bed. 'How long have you been living here?' she asked.

'Six months? I don't know, seems forever.'

'It doesn't look very permanent.'

'Nowhere I've lived ever did. From Cambridge on I only ever camped. Looking back you can see. I never seem to have arrived anywhere.'

'This is better than hotels at least' she said, 'at least you can make a mess and it stays messy. In hotels you get so sick of people in uniform tidying up so it looks like you just got there. And restaurants every meal.'

There was a trace of American in her voice now. 'Hence the picnic?' he asked. 'A change?'

'Have you got any plates? Any glasses?'

Whilst he was gone she took out of her basket the ingredients she had chosen with such care. She spread out the picnic like so many tubes of colour and painted on Kim's floor the landscape she wanted them to live in. Simple food you can't get in hotels, and a bottle of white Burgundy to wash the picture in its sharp French light. An old brown dog, a big front porch and rabbits in the pen, I want to be a country girl again.

Singing to herself she went to the window intending to open it, for there lingered in the room another scent than her own, but the metal frames were locked. She looked out of the back of the house. Mist confined her view to the back of the houses opposite, a mirror image of the terrace she was in herself. Back and front the houses were painted on the mist. Even inside this house it was difficult to believe in the substantiality of their interiors. Below, there was a tract of concrete squared into concrete gardens dividing the two terraces: above, the mist was a dome enclosing the mutter of London. Planes scraped continually across its slate. On the windowsill a sparrow sat looking in at her.

'You've got wings little bird' said Kim's voice over her shoulder, 'why don't you go and live in the country?'

He tapped the glass but the bird did not fly away. She remembered how he had looked at the sky when they had met in the street, as men who love cities never look.

'You want to talk English do you?' he asked.

'Yes. I let you be yourself now. Not the French translation.'

'And you, what are you? The film version?'

She smiled, treasuring the spark of jealousy. 'Does the window open a bit?' she asked, tugging at the catch.

'No don't touch it! It's got burglar alarms' he explained, 'getting out's as hard as getting in.'

156

'Not much to steal is there?'

'There ought to be. There's supposed to be if you live here' he said. 'There are safes built in and burglar alarms and wires all over the bloody place—I think they start with the burglar alarm and build the house round it' he said. 'It's the machinery is in charge in these houses. You listen, all you hear in this house is switches clicking on and off to run the house while you're supposed to be out. Out a-making more like the folks with plenty of plenty. You upset the house it starts screaming for the police. We're prisoners living here' he said. He had put his hand on hers to stop her opening the window-catch. Awkward to hold, her hand seemed more awkward to drop. Now he dropped it. 'Prisoners. I watched a woman over there' he went on, nodding at the terrace opposite, 'I watched her fighting her way out of the french window to do her gardening this morning—gardening poor soul, do you know what she did her gardening with? A brush and pan and a duster. All she can do is brush the soot off the aucubas. Think of all the concrete between her feet and the real earth. And her little tubs of soil from Harrods on top.'

'You shouldn't mock.'

'Not mockery, pity.'

'I expect in her mind she was hearing birds and the wind in the trees.'

'Like us picnicking?'

'Do you pity us?' she asked.

Just then a plane over the rooftops bombed her mind senseless with noise. When speech emerged from the shaking rumble which tramped away into the mist he was saying 'I thought you'd have flown away in one of those by now. I've heard them go and I thought you'd be in one. Up in the blue leaving all this.'

Was it he who thought he had been left behind when they had parted at the café? She said 'There's no point going anywhere. I've tried that.' She turned away from the window. 'Let's have our picnic.'

They shared the picnic food between them on the floor. With the companionship of eating came companionable talk. Ettie did not attend closely, ever, to people's views; she absorbed from their tone, from their mood, from being close to them, whatever impulse gave them life. She twined through their branches as the ivy climbs the oak. Her view of the world was the same as her host's. This compliancy fostered a sense of rapport with widely differing individuals, as the ivy climbs whatever is erect.

'It's a treat not to have to get back to the office' Kim said when an hour had passed. His cold seemed better, his voice clearer.

'Kim you must miss being free now you work.'

He leaned back from the demolished picnic. 'Freedom is only a background' he said. 'In the end you have to try and put something in the foreground. You get sick of the space being empty.'

'You have to work you mean.'

'Work is better than nothing. Even the treadmill is. Even the house of correction is a substantial building compared to the ruins of what might have been. You see' he went on 'it's all ruins behind. It's a landscape with ruins, looking back at Rome. It fills me with despair. I had the chance—or I had the time, if that's a chance. But I got nowhere. Honestly the treadmill's a relief, if you don't know what else you want to do.'

'You can still choose what you work at though. I mean if you hate your advertising you can change.'

He shook his head. 'It doesn't matter. You work for work's sake if you come to it my way. Come down to it. The opportunity to choose is the very thing I'm sick of you see. One of the troubles with education' he said, 'with over-educating people from the point of view of giving them what's of use, is that discrimination outruns ability. I mean you get too choosy. Not that not that, you say to yourself— that or that wouldn't fulfil what I could be. So what's left? Nothing. Almost everyone educated is underemployed in the

158

jobs they do' he said, 'you have to accept that. Look I'll show you what I mean.'

He took from his table a storyboard, six little drawings for a television commercial, and spread it on the floor for her. She wanted to be shown, did not care whether she understood or not.

'You see we're selling a fixative that sticks people's false teeth in' he explained. 'This little character goes and stays in the boss's weekend cottage, here boss offers him an apple in orchard, here little man's dentures get stuck in apple, here they fall out because he doesn't use our glue—see? Now look what the account executive wrote in the corner.'

Ettie read ' "I like the apple theme, we get subliminal spin-off from the Eden/sex-temptation syndrome" '.

Kim said 'All it is is a half-minute spot selling tooth-glue, but they try and tell themselves it's the Fall of Man.'

Silence. He sat back against the bed and clasped his knees.

'You see they will try and make use of what's better than useful' he went on 'they try and use stuff that's too wonderful for dentures. To justify his education and what he might have become this man I work for won't deal in any coin smaller than Original Sin. But you can't draw up Leviathan with a hook. You can't, but he won't listen to that. And maybe I won't either—I helped write the thing.' He stared contemptuously at the storyboard, then said 'We've cheapened Eden into a weekend cottage. We've confused Sin with embarrassment. God we made the boss of some company and Man—look what we made of him. The skeleton in his own cupboard. The sum of the fears we can exploit.' He looked gloomily at the six frames in which the characters were drawn as skeletal matchstick-figures with empty O's for heads. 'You know there's a legal fiction, the man on the Clapham omnibus? Well there's an advertising fiction, it's the skeleton in the cupboard of the man on the Clapham omnibus. Like consumer profiles is another fiction we deal in. I tell you' he finished 'I look out of the window, all I see is the profiles of skeletons dusting soot off tubs of laurels.'

Silence. She wanted to protest at the bitterness of his tone rather than at what he said, which she hadn't followed too closely: she didn't like self-contempt in anyone to whom she attached herself. For the ivy to climb, the oak must stand. 'But Kim' she protested 'you aren't really one of them.'

'No one's a cypher in the consumer profile to himself' he said. 'Everyone who's given up—everyone in what your film friend calls the subway crowd—they're all secret misfits you know. We all treasure up what we might have been ... but we end up growing a little moustache maybe, and carry on catching the Clapham omnibus. *"We all dwell together to make money from each other. This is a community."* Do you know that poem?'

He took Eliot's poems from his table and read her the chorus from 'The Rock' in which the quotation was contained. Her mind remained busy with its own concern. She wouldn't let him sink his individuality in the crowd Jack despised: she couldn't bear the thought of Jack's contempt if he knew. 'You don't belong catching the bus' she insisted, 'you've always been the opposite—what about the man in your office who said about going back to Bristol? You're the opposite of him you said.'

'Going opposite ways I said. Same bus stop. You see' he said 'the point is I've been where Melvyn's going. What's his ambition? A sports car like the one I had at Cambridge. A house in Chelsea like this one. Knowing girls in films like you—look, if Melvyn saw me this minute you know what he'd say?'

'Lucky Kim?'

'Right.'

'You don't think you're lucky?'

'Is it lucky in the long run if the stork drops you higher up the mountain than Melvyn'll ever climb to?'

'It looks lucky' she said, remembering how Jack had once described Marco Roccaleone: He only looks like the lucky one.

'The worst of privilege is looking lucky' he said. 'What people don't know is that if you haven't got used to climbing early on you're no good at it. There's no need and you've no momentum. Melvyn's got momentum, he climbed into the office we share and he'll carry on climbing. All that's opposite about us is the direction we're going in, him up, me down.'

It was evident that there was no momentum left in Kim. She felt his inertia. The room was full of despondency. *What is the meaning of this city? What will you answer?* At the window mist and the grey rumbling town, roofed by planes lumbering to and fro from similar cities. She had been there. They were not her destination. Not Rome, not Madrid, not Paris even—not even Paris, to which she had forced Jack to take her for Christmas, and from which she had persuaded him to take her away again before Christmas had come. Not that, not that. This then? No.

'Kim this isn't the way you ought to live' she said.

'I know that. But people think it is.'

'Who thinks?'

'Tom and people. Even my sister Clara. Even my own flesh and blood.'

'I don't.'

'You know too much. You're already in the picture as they say. No one else seems to be.'

She looked at the unmade double bed he was sitting against. 'No one?'

He stood up. 'Yes dammit my mother knows. When all's said and done' he sighed 'she does know a thing or two. She's like Cerridwen in the Welsh poem: whatever I try and turn myself into she knows it's only me. When I believed in what I was she infuriated me not believing; but now it's rather a comfort she knows I'm not this.'

Ettie remembered Mrs Vannick with great clarity; even her name spoken was like a sighting of the Pole Star. 'You are lucky' she said 'I mean truly it is a good fortune to have your mother.'

'Is it?' Kim questioned that too. 'I'm beginning to think

161

that the only really lucky people are the people who've had it made plain from the start that you are utterly alone in this world. Everything else is lies. It is. Privilege makes for illusions, protection saps independence. It does. It's a false climate being protected. You get to the point where even reality seems like treachery.' He paused, then said 'I mean no one would ever think my mother ever betrayed anyone, but I thought when I was a child she betrayed me.'

'How betrayed?'

'Well, going to school. I didn't think she'd let that sort of thing happen to me. I thought she caused what happened.' Another pause. 'And earlier than that. Almost the first thing I can remember isn't being protected it's being abandoned, because protection was just the norm I didn't notice.'

'Tell me.' She was sitting on the floor, he walking to and fro. She wanted to be told not because she wanted to know but because she wanted him to confess to her. 'Can you remember?'

'I can remember like yesterday.' He leaned against the window, shadowy. 'Clara and I were walking along the drive at home before breakfast, it must have been in the war, I remember the iron railings had gone to make guns we thought—Clara was ahead and I called, but she didn't take any notice. She had pigtails then. By mistake I'd swallowed a berry out of my peashooter, we used berries from a thorn tree I suppose it was we'd found in the middle of the garden. Dark and bitter to taste. I knew it was poisoned. I knew I'd die. But when I tried to tell Clara she put her hands over her ears and chanted "I can't hear I can't hear, if you don't talk Proper Language no one hears". You see she'd invented this language which was ordinary words pronounced backwards. I could say Ragus esaelp and the useful things I needed to say but I didn't know how to say this awful thing that had happened to me in her language. She had pigtails. When I found my mother to tell her she was making breakfast in the kitchen and the minute she saw me do you know what she said? "Go and wash your hands darling." I thought she'd

162

know even without me telling, the way she came in the night if I had nightmares and said she'd keep me safe. But in this crisis all she said was "Go and wash your hands darling".'

'And did you?'

'No. I went to say goodbye to my hen before I died.'

She thought about it. The story was extraordinarily vivid to her: in anecdotes, not in abstractions, people and ideas came alive to her. She imagined the two children under a rainy sky darkened by war, she saw the malignant tree in the midst of the garden and tasted its bitter fruit. 'You know how to tell things now' she said.

'Still not in the proper language' he said. 'All languages I've ever learned are still bent pins when it comes to fishing up what I want to say.'

'You say it to me so I hear.'

'You know already.'

The bed seemed to swell in her consciousness until it filled the space between them. That was one way. But she said 'Kim —will you take me to Larkford?'

He looked away, thought for a moment. 'Take you to Larkford.' He tried the idea out. Then he faced her. 'Yes. All right. I will. I'm going down on Friday night and I'll take you.'

Two days lay between her and Friday, two days' march to the walled city. She must get out before what she knew was right went astray. She gathered up the fragments of the picnic hoping that Kim would not keep her from leaving whilst the way was clear. He did not. He let her go without even asking where she would reappear from on Friday.

In the street, although yellow leaves had been floating off the trees all the time they had talked, and floated down now, singly and silently, there seemed as many leaves left still to fall. Winter had not yet come.

PART FOUR

I.

ALONG THE LANE rushed an open Rolls, now sun-splashed, now flickered with shadow, swift and dangerous and leopard-quiet. The racing scenery seemed all in movement, all flowing with running sunlight and the shadows of clouds, and the car kept pace with the grand fleet footsteps of sun and wind. So it seemed to the driver, his black hair tattered in the slip-stream, a coal-black moustache hooked over his mouth, music scattering to the four winds as he tore along. But the Rolls was not quite under control: the best endeavours of its engineers had succeeded, and the driver was insulated from the danger of such a car's weight and speed. Anyone but the driver could see that there was almost sure to be an accident.

Jack Peel in his new disguise was the driver. On his way back from Cornwall, where he had been looking for locations to fake some second-unit footage of Spain (and Spain had been tricked out in the movie to look like Italy), he had turned off the London road because he had recognized a village name on a signpost. Larkford was the name; and Larkford was the postmark on the parcel Ettie had sent him in April. All the parcel contained was his cigarette case full of Gauloises. The postmark was his only clue to her whereabouts since she had vanished from their London hotel one Friday last October. As if she had regretted shutting the door in his face she had sent him in the spring this one clue like a key pushed out to him through the letterbox. The knowledge that he still existed in her mind intrigued him. So when he saw the signpost he turned off the London road and came hunting her. The unstoppable weight of his car flashed along the lane like a fragment torn off another star and hurled through space. It had to hit something.

The mail van coming around the corner hadn't a chance, stove in the metal along the Rolls' flank, shrieked by; the momentum of the Rolls carried it into the hedge and smashed down a gate before it stopped. Jack thought the world had stopped, so profound was the stillness after shock. He looked back. The scarlet van crouched in the lane, its engine grumbling. Sunlight and cloud shadow still passed swiftly along the valley. He climbed over his buckled door and walked back. A ferrety face frightened into shouting abuse leaned out of the van. Jack strolled towards it. The arch of his eyebrows and the hook of his moustache lent his face an expression of sardonic imperturbability. The youth's shouting dried up.

'Okay' Jack said 'so I was in the middle of the road. This road only has a middle.'

'In a fucking Rolls-Royce it has.'

'You want to fetch the fuzz in?'

The youth's hands shook putting a cigarette in shaky lips.

'Better forget it okay?' Jack suggested. 'You were coming pretty fast.'

'What about your damage then? Cost a bit that.'

Jack looked back at the buckled metal of his car. A knife in his heart. But he had learned to pretend that possessions don't matter. 'It'll stand a little beating around' he said mildly.

The youth jammed his van into gear. Scattering stones as he dashed off he yelled 'Fucking Rolls-Royce! You want to look where you're fucking going!'

Jack smiled. It was because of the resentment that extravagant possessions aroused that their owners could afford to underplay them. Resentment was recognition, it satisfied him. And he liked the way he had played the scene. Print it, he said to himself.

When he turned to look at his damaged car it was like turning from a studio set to face reality. On camera the Rolls had been a stage prop, expendable, its function to bring out the best in the actors; off camera the car became his own again. Upon him fell all the trouble and expense of repairing the damage. He looked around him: he was in the middle of nowhere. Whereas before the accident the landscape had been fleeting impressions, speed and the sun flashing, now there was stillness and permanence. His dusty moccasins on a dirt road. Silence.

And then, by degrees, the silence filled. First he heard the wind, remote in high firs; then birdsong in the hollow of the wood. His mind, like the silence, filled with intimations of harmony. He looked about him again, not this time to discover how far he was from a telephone but to examine his surroundings. A wood bordered the lane on one side, on the other the valley dropped to a stream which ox-bowed through fields quilted with fat hedges. Bare-backed downs enclosed the valley. In the shade of the trees which sheltered the lane the air was very still.

Beside the wreckage of the field gate was a small gate into the wood. On impulse, like a child leaving a wrecked toy, Jack abandoned his car and pushed open that squeaky wicket gate.

At first he strolled under mighty firs, his path splashed now and then by sunspots whose restless pools coloured the wood's floor. These evergreens were the shelter trees for the heart of the wood. He strolled on scuffing cones with his moccasins; until there were no longer cones and pine needles underfoot but moss and leaves, for now, still unaware of what lay ahead, he was walking beneath oaks and beeches which formed this windowed chancel beyond the dark nave of firs.

He wondered what it would cost to repair the car. Keeping up the hire-purchase payments was trouble enough. He budgeted as if his enormous weekly wage was a secure annual income, treating himself as though he would never be out of work; canniness, in the film industry, is a suspect virtue. Thrift looks too much like poverty to be risked by anyone but a famous millionaire. Poverty—overnight collapse and secret burial—is to the film industry what the Black Death was to a medieval court, a contagion shunned and feared, mortality put out of mind by music and cloth of gold. The Rolls was Jack's certificate of health. If he could barely afford to keep it, he certainly couldn't afford to get rid of it. For he had his worries: after the war film he had designed for Sol Wenkel, which was almost in the can, he had nothing lined up. His career as Sol's designer had become static, and he needed to move on, make a picture of his own. If you aren't going up you have to be going down. Through the wood his worries tracked him. He walked with his head bent.

He walked with his eyes on the ground until like a gout of wax dropped from a candle a scarlet flower fell at his feet. He looked up. The wood was lit with flowers. Their profusion took away his breath. Here, there, everywhere flowers glowed and blazed, trees towering, leaning, immense candelabra flaming in sunlit glades, gloomy torchères refulgent in green vaults; banks and drifts and clouds of colour and scent were interspersed with the Gothic columns of English trees and were roofed with their tracery of leaves. A paradise. Yet not a garden; there was a wildness in the scene which made it seem fortuitous. Such rampancy overflowed the bounds of design, went beyond what man could use: the flowers bloomed for their own glory, and faded and fell unlooked upon: the whole splendour of the wood was overgrown, forgotten. Consider the lilies of the field. If he had looked through the windows of a deserted mansion, and seen an uneaten feast by the light of tapers burned low in their sconces, it would have given him the same sense of an unearthly owner.

Jack's response to this extravagance running to waste was to pull a miniature camera out of his combat jacket. He wouldn't look for long, except through a viewfinder. The evanescence of so many flowers made him aware of time passing, of the night at hand when no man shall work. How best to use the light? He held to his own eye the Gorgon's eye of his trade, to petrify the wood.

He soon let it drop. A viewfinder cropped the scene to nothing, didn't frame a shot worth printing. The glory of the wood lay not in its detail but in its entirety. Here was a narrow red-trunked tower of great leaves, wonderfully gloomy, patched with deep scarlet; but photographed alone it amounted to nothing. The grandeur of the wood lay just outside whatever shot he framed.

A camera was no use to him. It took his five senses and his

whole brain to comprehend such prodigality. Comprehend: but what use could he make of it? It was too wonderful for use. That it should run to waste seemed quintessential to the prodigality of paradise. Unseen, unsung, the flowers faded and fell. He who had planned the planting had framed a symmetry within which growth, decay and regeneration were contained by his design. Time only rooted his concept deeper in the earth. The years did his gardening. He had set in motion an organism which would run forever by its own momentum. Who had he been? There was no sign of human life.

And then in the middle of the wood he came upon a swing. On cords immeasurably long it hung like a pendulum from the rooftree of the creation, empty and still. Yet the swing furnished the wood with the idea of children: a child might come running through the trees to play. No one came. In the glade drowsed the unruffled flowers, and no one came. Only, high above, the wind inspired the firs, first one, then another, rocking them gravely. That immense whisper was far off in symbols faint, a forgotten language. But it tempted Jack, or the child in him, to swing. He seated himself on the split log suspended between the two ropes and pushed himself off.

No sooner were his feet off the ground than he felt himself fused with the harmony of the wood; as the moving deck and straining mast of a sailing ship connect you to the harmony of wind and sea. The ropes creaked, the bough far above began to undulate, the wind of his own momentum blew in his face and he was sailing body and soul. As the rushing scene flew by, its perspectives liquefied by dizzy motion, it was as though the pendulum was once more set swinging and the clock began to tick.

When he got off the swing he knew what he must attempt to do. He must try and make a film which would express— would catch on the wing—what he felt about the paradise he had found. Multifarious as its flowers and scents, ineffable as the whisper in its trees, his intimations must find expression and form in a story. It could be done. With the right story he could take the place in its entirety and annex it, make it his. He would show the splendour that went to waste but, because it was he who showed it, for him it would not go to waste; he would harness its power and make it serve his purpose. If he had a story. If he had an idea. What followed— development money, a package, leverage, distribution deals— all that wheeling and dealing was work he could do. What he needed to know was the story. The idea behind the wood.

Walking as he thought back to the car he was deceived by the trees and lost. He found himself on a high ridge, the wind scattering leaves from his footsteps. Far below he saw the stream and began to descend towards it. Nearer, looking down through alders at the current stealing by, he saw the figure of a man lying along a branch above the water, fishing. As Jack watched, a fish took the dapped fly. He saw the rod glint as it dipped towards the swirl. He heard the reel screech as the trout leapt in a necklet of splashes, then tick out line as the fish tugged across the pool. A commotion shook the tree out of which the fisherman was trying to clamber, cursing all creation as he struggled.

'Can I help?' Jack called.

'Yes can you land the fish if I bring it in?'

'I'll try.'

'Damn this tree!'

Jack slithered down till he stood on the bank. Nettles grew fiercely between him and the water. He smoothed his moustache, hesitated. Damn these nettles.

'Quick he's coming in!'

Jack ploughed through the mean-toothed nettles and jumped down the bank. Cold water leaking through his moccasins contended with the heat of the stings. Whatever you do in the country you get hurt, he thought, watching the line cut through the water towards him as the reel overhead wound in. The fish flurried, Jack grabbed, he caught the slippery dart of life in both hands and held tight. 'Got it!' he cried, delighted.

'Brilliant!' The fisherman was scrambling out of his tree.

'What shall I do with it?'

'Kill it.'

Jack hesitated. Then he struck the trout's head on a stone. What had been quick went limp. In his hands a dead fish.

In a shirt and torn breeches, his shanks bare between knee and gym shoe, Kim looked like a Romany. His long narrow eyes were alight with pleasure. 'It's a good fish, it's nearly a pound I should think' he said, peering over the bank.

Jack held up the fish for him to take. Already its translucence had faded. Its tacky scales came off on his hands. He said nothing, washing his hands in the stream. The water had the brilliant quickness of the trout, as if what he had caught had slipped back into the river, beyond catching. When he climbed the bank, Kim had dropped the fish inside his shirt and was pulling the line clear of the tree. 'What do you do if there's nobody by to land them?' Jack asked.

'I never think that far ahead. I just try and catch them' Kim said. 'And I don't really mind if they get off' he added, winding up line, 'in fact in ways I like it. They could be any size if you lose them.' He smiled.

'Sorry I spoiled the illusion.'

'Oh I've lost plenty. I been losing the big fish all my life' Kim assured him, 'one or two this size are useful to eat.'

He was busy reshaping the bedraggled fly with a corner of his shirt. Jack had the feeling that he would go in a moment, this stranger who was so much at home by the river, yet that if he could be delayed he would answer questions. But what questions? What did Jack want to know? The difficulty lay in framing the question. He asked tentatively,

'What's the idea behind this wood?'

No answer. Had the stranger not heard?

'What's this wood called?' he asked.

'Depends who you ask. Why?'

'I think' began Jack irresolutely, smoothing his moustache, 'I think it could be what I'm looking for. I have a feeling there's something hidden here. You know the swing?' he added, to fix upon something tangible.

'I know the swing' Kim admitted cautiously.

Jack took a step nearer. 'What's it doing there? Who put it there? Who swings in it?' He wanted to polarize the wood around people and action.

'I could tell you the facts' Kim said, but didn't.

Silence. Then Kim said 'You asked what's the idea behind the wood. If you mean purpose I don't think there is one. But ideas ... there are as many of those as there are names.'

The tip of his rod was broken, which was why he had been dapping from a tree. Anything broken irritated Jack. 'You live around here?' he asked.

Kim stuck the fly in the rod's cork handle. Then, as if he had decided to tell the whole truth at once and be done with questions, he said 'Yes I live in the wood. We live in a caravan in the middle of the wood.'

Two of them. With two people you already have a story. Jack's interest increased. 'Who does the wood belong to?' he asked.

Kim seemed to resent that question. 'I don't see it matters who owns it.'

'It's yours' Jack guessed.

'I inherited it if you call that owning.'

'I call that owning.'

'What I mean is I didn't buy it and I didn't work for it I was just born here.' Kim seemed anxious to disclaim responsibility. He sighed, looked round at the wild disorder of his inheritance. He pulled at the long hair on the nape of his neck and his eyes gazed past Jack at peeps of blue infinity between the leaves. He looked sad. 'Owning the way I do is nothing' he said. 'If I could hang a swing for my son in an oak tree I'd planted myself, then I'd feel I owned this place.'

The extravagance of the idea expressed what Jack felt too. He said nothing. The stranger knew.

'What I mean is it doesn't matter me owning it' Kim said, 'you can go where you like. In fact I think it's supposed to be open to the public. But they never come' he added, as if saddened by this aspect of public behaviour.

'I work in films, I make movies' Jack said, to assert his independence of the public. 'I was just driving by in the lane back there when the postman hit me.'

'Hit you?' exclaimed Kim with interest.

'Hit my car.'

'Oh.' Disappointed. 'I hoped maybe you'd hit him back.'

'You have a war with the postman?'

Kim waved his hands. 'People writing' he explained. The world seemed to catch up with him. 'I must go and catch another fish' he said.

'So it's all right if I look around your woods?'

'Look where you like' said Kim. His frankness implied that Jack would find nothing.

'And you live in the middle someplace?'

'Here and there. The caravan's got wheels.'

Jack watched him go, a ramshackle figure stumbling on long stalky legs through the lacy sunlight of the wood. The rod springing in his hand gleamed now and then like a sceptre as a sunshaft caught the cane.

2.

THE TWO TROUT bumping inside Kim's shirt as he walked up towards the caravan gave him the sense of being a bread-winner which earning money never gave him. From Monday to Friday he worked for money in an office in the market town. Saturday and Sunday he and Ettie lived in the wood as though they were gypsies. Now he heard Ettie singing in the caravan as he approached through the glade. When she saw him through the window she called,

'Catch something?'

He held up the two trout. 'Enough?'

'Plenty. See' she said, showing him the frying-pan smoking in her hand, 'I trust you, I had the butter hot already.'

He went up the steps, gave her the fish and stood at the door of the little kitchen watching her dextrous hands slit and clean the trout. It still surprised him that those hands knew such skills; had always known them, as if in readiness for this life whilst leading others. 'Where's Aiuto?' he asked.

'On our bed probably.'

'Why does he never come out with me instead of lounging about on the furniture?' Her dog irritated him.

'You forget you've got him and then I worry about the road.'

It was the dog's name he disliked most. Ettie thought it was a joke to call him Help in Italian; she seemed to think she scored off the English in some way, calling 'Aiuto!' across the English fields and talking to her dog in French. To Kim it was not cosmopolitan but insular, to think that a foreign language was some sort of secret code amongst superior people. His heart still jumped when he heard her call Help. However, it was a trifle. He didn't care.

'Talking of the lane, that maniac postman hit someone at last' he remembered to tell her.

'Oh? Who?'

'A man I met poking about. Bogus American.'

Cleaning the fish suddenly seemed to need extra concentration. She bent over the sink. 'Bogus-American you mean, or bogus and American?'

'Just a phony. He said he was——' Kim stopped. He wouldn't tell her the man was a film-maker. No point blowing on those embers in her life. The split trout writhed in the spitting butter and she didn't ask what the stranger had claimed to be.

He went out and lay on the grass waiting for lunch. The glade was still, the grass warm, the sun hot. In the climate that his grandfather had contrived, his creation basked. The wind passed high above. All that could not be excluded were the sudden dark footsteps of the clouds. What is the idea behind the wood?

He closed his eyes. He didn't know. He lived here as if it was the back of his own mind, a fastness secure even against introspection. *O my soul, be prepared for the coming of the*

Stranger, Be prepared for the coming of him who knows how to ask questions. He will go away, Kim thought. He'll look round, find nothing, go away and forget about it.

Ettie carried out their plates and they began to eat. He was aware of the silence between them, aware of having something to conceal. She might overhear his thoughts. It still shocked him, after six months of marriage, to have someone so indivisibly close to him, another inhabitant of his mind who might overhear his thoughts. He watched her picking flesh neatly off the trout's backbone. The stranger would go away. They were safe.

> Who is so safe as we, where none can do
> Treason to us, except one of us two?

Presently, looking for some screen of words to hide his thoughts, he said 'I must try and get this hay turned today so I can burn it before Monday'.

She looked up at the grass he had scythed into swathes in the glade. 'Remember we're going to tea.'

'It'll be a good excuse for leaving early.'

'You know we'll be expected to stay to dinner.'

He felt a bone in his mouth, picked it out. 'Well it's not much to ask. Supper occasionally.'

'I don't say it's much to ask. I just point out it'll be you accepts to stay on.'

'Well don't point out what I'm going to do before I do it' he said. 'Anyway you're wrong, it's you that's all smiles and Gosh how supers when the time comes and my mother asks.'

Avoiding the bones in her fish with surgical precision she said in a firm voice 'I don't say Gosh, Kim. It's the girls you might have married who say Gosh and Super.'

That was true. 'Well you smile anyway' he told her.

'I like your mother, you know I do. Or you say I am charmed by her' she added 'I don't care which.'

Kim said nothing. It was he who had taught her to pick her words so warily, to make distinctions that didn't matter to her. It saddened him. Feeling at fault he said roughly 'Yes, so charmed we have to move into a caravan.'

'You know I was quite willing to stay on at the house.'

He took her plate and stacked it on his so that the clatter expunged her thoughts from his mind.

'Save the skins for Aiuto' she said.

He said 'I rather wish we had a cat.'

'They're not company like Aiuto is.'

'I like the way cats come and go. I wouldn't have a cat for its company I'd have it for its independence' he said. 'And to eat fish heads.'

'You're not here on your own all weekdays.'

'People who depend on dogs for company' he told her 'aren't facing loneliness you know, they're just looking the other way.'

'You could say that about people who depend on people.'

'I probably will' he said 'when I'm through with people.'

She laughed. 'I wouldn't be without Aiuto now.'

'An old brown dog, a big front porch and rabbits in the pen' he sang.

'I'm going to be a country girl again' she chorused with him. Her singing voice had a far stronger foreign accent than her speaking voice, as though the country she sang of was far away, and she an exile in this wood.

In the afternoon Kim worked in the glade, turning the scythed grass. He didn't want a shaven lawn around the caravan, he wanted the balance between wilderness and garden which seemed to be maintained naturally in other parts of the wood. But not here: once he had started trying to perfect that balance the task was endless. Ettie helped, then wandered off with her dog. Later she passed through the clearing again towards the caravan.

'I am going to get ready' she called.

Kim ignored this. For a visit to his mother he was always ready, and never ready. It was the natural balance of his feelings. Ettie upset it, he thought, because she made an occasion of each visit; she questioned what was natural; even whilst complying she resisted. She 'got ready', and in consequence he too couldn't help preparing, which was an unnatural posture for going home. Before, he had just accepted: come back from Rome, come back from London—capitulated. There had been no one else living in his mind in those days, no one watching from within and describing his actions as surrender. How could it matter now, after all he had surrendered, whether or not they stayed to dinner? Could she not understand that tidying grass and going out to tea were equally futile if compared not with each other but with what might have been? He didn't tell her; assertions require defending once you have someone else living in your head. There was nothing left worth the effort of defending. He worked on until she emerged from the caravan in different clothes and called out 'Ready?'

'Ready.' He stuck his hay-twitch in the ground and joined her, tucking the tail of his shirt into his breeches.

'Aren't you going to put on some stockings?' she asked, fixing on his bare legs to criticize. 'In case we want to stay to dinner.'

'I've got clothes there if we stay. Come on.'

Most of his clothes were where they had always been, in his own room at Larkford from whose cupboards he had never moved them, to Rome or anywhere else. When he and Ettie had come back from their honeymoon to Larkford, after Christmas, they had expected to occupy the principal upstairs rooms of the house as had been agreed. But Mrs Vannick had not moved into the newly converted nursery wing. She had pointed out that Ettie would be far more comfortable in the new quarters, that she would find far more room for her clothes in modern cupboards than in her own inconvenient arrangement of presses and tallboys. Ettie had complied; they had moved in. But when at the beginning of the summer they had moved out to the caravan—for a holiday, on a chance impulse—Ettie had left behind her nothing. She had left those modern cupboards open and empty. What she had done with her clothes Kim had not asked. His clothes remained where they had always been, for he had never moved them from his own old bedroom. If they stayed for dinner or stayed for the rest of their lives he would find clothes enough; there was no need to plan in advance. At Larkford nothing he might do would catch him unawares, or be out of character.

'Isn't Aiuto coming?' he asked as they walked through the summer wood together.

'No he's better staying behind.'

It irritated Kim that she wouldn't take her dog to Larkford. It was like a mental reservation she made, leaving part of herself behind before she would enter his home. But he let it go. He had taught himself to accept that small things didn't matter; now the small things amounted to everything. Nothing mattered any more. When they came to the wicket gate Ettie pushed it open and crossed the lane. But Kim stopped and stared at the Rolls.

'Good God! Look at that. Take a look at that Ettie!'

'I know,' she said, climbing the style on the further side of the lane, 'I saw it earlier.' She walked away across the field.

'It's been hit. It must belong to the film man I met' he called. He vaulted the style, nearly fell, staggered after her. 'Why didn't you tell me you'd seen this marvel?'

'Why didn't you tell me he was a film man you met? Anyway it's only a car.'

'Only a car? It's a dream on wheels.'

Like a meteorite fallen in the lane behind them the car continued to disturb their magnetic field as they walked on.

'You don't want a car like that' she said.

'Yes I do' he claimed. 'Now I'm just old Moly, but once I was Mr Toad.'

Presently Ettie's shoe, one of the smart pair she had put on for tea, came off in a patch of marsh. 'Honestly Kim' she said, leaning on his shoulder whilst she put the shoe on again, 'I think now you pretend you haven't got a car at all, always walking this miles to the house.'

'It's a shame to get the family saloon soiled at weekends.' Then he said 'How could I pretend, I have to drive the damned thing to work every day.' Yet he did pretend.

As they traversed the steep fields with the stream below them the truth depressed him. He never stopped pretending. At weekends he pretended he was a gypsy: in the week he pretended to be a clerk, working all day in the local office of the gravel company, driving to and fro in a clerk's suit in a clerk's car. Thinking that it would bring peace and quiet he pretended to be this, he pretended to be that; and all the time he knew that he was neither. It was all pretence, as if he was still a spy, a sleeper bedding down in his cover. An agent awaiting further orders. *When the Stranger says: 'What is the meaning of this city? Do you huddle close together because you love each other?' What will you answer?* Linking his arm through Ettie's he tried to match his stride to hers and hide himself in that pretence of unity.

They separated to negotiate a hawthorn hedge which checked the rough little fields scrambling along the valley. Beyond it they walked apart on smoother turf under noble trees. In the placing of these groves the eye detected the influence of purpose like a magnetic force polarizing nature; one felt part of an arrangement; one looked instinctively for the house which had imposed its views upon the countryside. Upon Kim the majestic trees, and prospects between them to blue woods and bluer distances, always had the liberating uplift of homecoming. But the moment she came through the hawthorn hedge Ettie entered an enclosure. She never forgot that the lake in the valley below had been contrived by damming the stream.

Through a gate they entered a shrubbery which screened the kitchen garden. Above its wall the gables and twisted chimneys of the house rose like a keep within a barbican. The tunnel-dark of the shrubbery, smelling of rotted leaves, made their approach seem stealthy. What Kim resented was that tension mounted, he couldn't help it.

If tension had a voice it might have uttered precisely the

humming-top drone which came to them from the garden beyond the wall. His mother humming.

'You go on' Kim said, 'I've just got to see if. . .'

They parted. Kim loitered round the outside of the garden wall, kicking leaves, his hands in his breeches and his eyes on the ground. Had he looked up he would have been forced to consider the breach which frost had made that winter in the kitchen-garden wall. He didn't look up. Why had he never noticed this maddening humming of his mother's before, he wondered. Now, amplified into the foreground, it was everywhere; behind a wall when you were in the garden, outside the window when you were in the house. Maddening. From the first time that he had seen Ettie's lips tighten when she heard the sound it had begun to madden him.

By that time, too, in the early spring, other discordancies had begun to replace the euphony of wedding bells. Marriage had been a shock. By March, recovering from the shock, he had begun to feel the impatience which succeeds convalescence as buds break from the pruned wood. Impatience for what? 'That untravelled world whose margins fade forever and forever as I move.' Because it had seemed to solve without effort on his part the problem of where he and Ettie should live he had agreed to live at Larkford. 'After all it is your house' his mother had said. It was made to seem that he was entering upon his inheritance. Through Tom the arrangement had been made that he should work for the gravel company, a subsidiary of Swindells' cement group, which was biting its way towards the estate. The group had an option on the Larkford gravel bed; this was satisfactory to Tom, who thought they would take it up, and to Kim, who didn't think about it at all. What Kim worked at, once the collar was round his neck, didn't matter to him. Or he thought it didn't. Meanwhile Larkford was continuity, convalescence after the shock of being married, for which living with Ettie in Rome had in no way prepared him. The peace of the old house, winter light filtered through the leaves of magnolias and its colours the subfusc of Persian rugs on stone floors, was rest. Fires glowed on the heaped ash of winters past. Like their warmth his mother's presence permeated the house. Mrs Vannick was fastidious in the care she took not to interfere. Often Kim didn't see her for days together, and if Ettie saw her whilst he was at work he assumed that she chose to. Occasionally they would find touches added to their rooms, a silver jug left on their dining table, an embroidered footstool by Kim's chair. Never a bowl of flowers, nothing that could be construed as interference with Ettie's housekeeping or taste: just reminders of Mrs Vannick's invasive goodwill. Kim wondered whether the silver jug was hers to give or was in fact already his by inheritance. But he thanked her for it. You couldn't disentangle which possessions belonged to whom, you couldn't separate the needlework which was hers from the stool which was probably already his. Her desire to give permeated the house. Her humming kept the top upright on its axis. Bound as indissolubly to humming mother as to hummed-at wife his contending loyalties magnified the sound.

He entered the hall by a low oak door off the terrace. Sunshafts coloured the stone below high windows, whilst on an oak table in the cool watery dimness, amid the great space of the hall, light gleamed on silver and china. His mother's voice floated resonantly through the air:

'Apps wouldn't wait Kim darling so we began without you. Ettie says that you went to look at the kitchen-garden wall?'

'Tea's optional Mother, I don't come for the scones. How are you?' He took his tea cup and retreated to the stone-columned fireplace where he balanced on the kerb. 'Any news?' he asked.

'You surely don't mean to say that you come for the news.'

'Merely a conversational gambit.' He wondered what he did come for. To arrive perhaps. He felt no need to talk.

'Is Tom in Germany still?' Ettie asked.

The question set going Mrs Vannick's voice like a musical box when the lid is lifted: 'According to Clara he is behind the Iron Curtain if you please. Really, Tom's travels. Of course it is all factories and meetings I suppose ... still, it takes him away. And poor Clara left struggling. That wretched Hampshire house. Really, dry rot is too bad: it does rather take the gilt off the gingerbread for Clara, and poor Tom so keen that all should go swimmingly once he had persuaded her that Hampshire was not entirely stockbrokers. Which it is' she finished, her laugh touching a silver key of triumph.

'The penalty for looking for dry rot' Kim said 'is finding it. Typical of Tom—if he hadn't looked the house would have stood quite as long as he will. What's he trying to do? Found a dynasty?'

'I am sure he is trying to do what is best for them all.'

'It isn't best for anyone to make this tremendous fuss about houses' Kim said irritably. 'He's bought himself a house: fine: basta. His children won't want it so why bother with dry rot and stamping out beetles.'

'Why do you assume that the boys won't want it Kim?'

'Because no one's going to want houses like this—like that I mean, in twenty years' time' Kim said. 'Look I mean, what's the point cooking two chops in some vast kitchen and carrying them half a mile to the dining-room and then carrying the bones back again?'

'Theirs isn't a large house Kim' she said. They both knew he was talking about Larkford. 'I daresay they will eat in the kitchen. I would myself if it wasn't for Apps and Mrs Apps' she added.

'Then what's the point of having a dining-room? And paying people to dust rooms you never go in? And heating ten foot of air between your head and the ceiling? And spending your life slaving in a garden which was laid out for gentlemen to stroll through discussing Cicero's letters?'

'People have always gardened Kim, from houses such as this.'

'An occasional snip at the arbutus, yes; not double-digging the celery bed. Not the drudgery. The point I'm making is that you're forced to be your own servant if you live in a house that needs servants. I thought Tom was supposed to be

184

so practical, but it turns out he's mad as a hatter.'

'I am surprised you don't understand Clara's ambition to give her children some space to grow up in. A home with some freedom such as you and she had.'

'Why do you think I live in a caravan?'

'Why you spend the summer in a caravan my dear' his mother said 'is a mystery to me.'

Silence. Kim came to the table for more tea. 'We're a mystery to her' he told Ettie, 'she doesn't see the charm of life on wheels. To the call of the open road her ears are deaf.'

Neither Ettie nor his mother smiled. He retreated with his tea to the fireplace again.

'Bet this house has got dry rot' he said.

'Oh no Kim.' His mother looked up nervously at the coffered ceiling. He knew that she considered dry rot to be a judgement from above on Tom's house, on Tom for buying it. 'But if you have any reason to think so' she added 'we should get Mr Sowerby to make enquiries.'

'Why bother. I'm sick of people forever trying to prop things up. I'm sick of all the energy that used to go into building things being wasted in propping things up. This endless preservation of what ought to be ruins. No one's ever bothered before. You look at the people who built what we all admire so much, the Renaissance builders, they didn't care about old buildings they pulled them down. They saw the past for what it is, something you pull down if it gets in the way. Half the palaces in Rome were built with stone pinched from the Colosseum and places.'

'Rome had been destroyed by the Vandals a thousand years before that' Mrs Vannick pointed out. 'If Tom isn't exactly the Renaissance' she said 'thank heaven he is not a Vandal.'

'Not a Vandal? What do you call selling the Paradise Wood piecemeal to Rhinehart Cement?'

'Ah, so that is where the shoe pinches!'

'Tom's Vandalism doesn't pinch my feet Mother, because I live on wheels as you have remarked.'

'Tom's Vandalism as you call it provides you with your career Kim.'

'A career? In gravel?'

She pressed the edge of the table with her finger tips. 'Well Kim' she said quietly 'what else is there you want to do, if not that?'

'I don't care what I do. I don't care where I live.'

'I am beginning to be afraid that you don't. But you must allow that others may, others do. To suppose that the whole edifice is of no value to anyone just because you are not able to make use of it, that seems to me rather childish' she said,

He stepped down from where he had balanced on the hearth-kerb. 'All right then' he admitted 'I do care about the Paradise Wood.'

Her lips tightened. 'That is on the edge of things Kim, you cannot make that the centre. A wood.'

'Grandfather did.'

'Only latterly Kim. Besides, Grandfather by that time had become extremely eccentric—as one called people who were too rich to be shut away. Do you know, Ettie' she continued 'when first I came here Kim's grandfather used to spend a great deal of time solemnly swinging to and fro on a swing in the wood? He used to have it moved round so that one never knew where one would find him dangling next. Indeed as I have often told you Kim, he was on his swing when Father and I went to tell him that we were to be married. To and fro he went' her forefinger described an arc 'in cloth-topped boots and a wing collar I remember, his hat and stick against the tree. To and fro—it was like trying to break our news to a ping-pong ball. No' she went on 'he did hide himself away in that curious creation of his at the end. But he had made his way in the world remember. He had been an extremely successful man. That wood was a kind of folly he retreated into do you see.'

'So were King Ludwig's palaces' Kim said. 'Nobody pulls them down.'

'My dear, if you are going to compare yourself only with rich or royal eccentrics' she protested. 'And you say that what ought to be ruins shouldn't be preserved, surely of all things Burr Wood has outlasted its purpose. No one has touched it since before the war.'

'Not touching it improves it. That's the whole point, it doesn't need any preserving. And in fact I may tell you' he went on 'I met a man in the wood this morning who thought it was perfectly wonderful. He said it was exactly what he was looking for.'

Ettie spoke for the first time. 'Looking for for what purpose?' she asked.

'Oh purpose——' Kim regretted what he had revealed. 'None I should think.'

Ettie said firmly 'A man who makes films and has a Rolls-Royce you can be sure he's got a purpose.'

'He just happened to be passing.'

'His car is still there.'

There is one who remembers the way to your door.

'No no' Kim said 'he'll have gone back to Pinewood or somewhere by tomorrow.' *And the Stranger will depart and return to the desert.* 'It's like you say Mother, no one's interested in the place except me.'

'And your friend Swindells' she reminded him.

'Oh it'll take years for the cement people to move.'

'Years pass.'

'We've got our wheels.'

'Do you truly believe Kim dear' his mother said 'that that is any solution in the long run?'

'I'm not looking for a solution' he said. 'And as for believing—believe in my job in gravel? Some creed.'

'Who sweeps a room as for thy laws makes that and the action fine.'

'But I don't want what I do elevated into a mission. I want to remember it's just pointless drudgery. I know it leads nowhere. There is no heaven to espy.'

Silence. She gathered cups and plates onto the silver tray

187

as if one meal more had proved the futility of eating.

'Ah well my dear' she said 'there are always excuses to be found for giving up hope. If you convince yourself that the world is a very much more difficult place for you than it is for anyone else, then of course you will find excuses for caring for nothing and for assuming that the world is going to rack and ruin with you. Of course you will, and no one will prevent you. Ettie my dear' she continued 'I wonder would you mind just putting this tray through the door for Apps? And do just tell him if it suits you to stay to supper.'

'No we can't' Kim said. 'I mean sorry no, the point is we can't I'm afraid.'

Ettie carried out the tray. She had hardly spoken, only smiled. Of course she hated coming here. Like the Cheshire Cat she remained agreeable whilst being negated; the idea of a smile hung in the air after the door into the kitchen passage had closed behind her. Of course she resented the house, and he resented her exclusion. He had thought that marriage would bring her inside the enclosure, but instead the wall of the garden divided his heart in two. It was one of the many unexpected pains of marriage. No wonder he avoided action if he could, when its consequences were so complex. Even cutting the grass in the glade upset a balance and entailed drudgery without end. Better to do nothing. He balanced on the kerbstone and watched his mother sweep crumbs off the table into her hand. Next she would throw them into the hearth. Everything she did was familiar to him.

'Mrs Apps announced this morning' she said 'that for the weekend she had got a sirloin if you please. We could put it off until tomorrow if you two could come over for lunch and help me out.'

She approached the fireplace and threw the crumbs into the ash. Kim moved aside, walked away. 'I must get the oak that fell in the storm split up' he said.

'Don't wear yourself out now you are working all week Kim.' It was she who sounded weary. 'There is wood enough
188

here for all that I will burn. And I gather that you two are not planning to come back.'

'I'm not planning anything.'

Silence. On the table where she would dine alone she put a reading-stand to support her company, a book. Guilt, and sympathy he couldn't utter, made Kim turn away. 'I have no plans' he repeated.

She spoke, not looking at him, sadly: 'Kim, you are wasting your life. Is this house honestly a millstone to you? Because if it is I will walk out of it tomorrow.'

'No it's not that, it's not that.'

'What is it then?' Her eyes found his and held them.

'I don't know. Everything is so unreal/I do. But there's nothing else. Nothing more.'

'I have faith in you still' she said gravely, 'but you must not let yourself drift into such apathy that you no longer look for what you want. You must keep seeking, and recognize the chance when it comes—cost what it may. You remember Sir Gawain whom you used to dream of, how he kept the tryst? Don't fail.'

He turned away. Her will was a sword driving him on, not a hand held out to help him. No one would help him.

Then Ettie came back. 'I challenge you at croquet if you like' she said, her cheerful voice giving body to the agreeable idea of herself she had left with them. Mrs Vannick revived. She had elasticity, even gaiety, in her step and voice as she and Ettie took balls and mallets from the box against the wainscot and went out. From the shadowy stone hall Kim watched sunlight strike them both into life and colour as they passed through the door.

3.

THE NEXT DAY was Sunday and it rained. In a thousand runnels the trickling and purling of water carried rain down to the swollen stream. It was another world from yesterday,

189

the wood loud with rain pattering on leaves. The woodland resounded too with the blows of iron on iron. Sullen, sunken, they tolled like a bell-buoy marking a wreck. Tunc, tunc, tunc.

Their source was an oak which had gashed a clearing in the wood by its fall and which lay upon smashed boughs in the litter of its leaves. Branches had been shorn off the trunk and made a pile of arthritic fingers in the clearing. Upon these lopped fingers Kim worked with sledgehammer and wedges, splitting them into cordwood. The slow arc of the wheeling hammer, the dead beat as it struck the wedge; a grave picture in the rain. The fibres of the oak rent and cracked hollowly, a log split, was tossed on the heap; and then the labour began again.

Kim thought of nothing as he worked: his mind was empty. The rain had soaked through his father's old shooting coat, rain trickled from his hair onto his lips, the sweet soft rain, and his body ran with sweat. Beyond the weight and rhythm of the hammer, and the wedge driving, nothing existed. Work was the door into mindlessness. It was why he worked. He had entered an empty mind and shut the door.

Ettie's voice broke in like a finger on the doorbell. His rhythm broke, his stroke collapsed in mid-arc. He let the hammer fall and looked up. She was standing at the edge of the clearing with the stranger he had met yesterday.

'Kim' she said 'you met Jack. You didn't know who he was.'

Do I now? he wondered, wiping rain and sweat out of his eyes to look. Then he knew. 'Oh, Jack Peel. Oh I see. It was you I met.'

Jack and Ettie were standing close together, he in a trench coat, a tweed cap; she soaked and bedraggled, only her dark eyes shining as sloes gleam in a wet hedge.

'Jack didn't know you were married to me' she said.

Put in that order it made her central, Kim an appendage. He was only used to the idea that she was married to him. 'How did you find us?' he asked, leaning on his upended hammer.

Ettie looked quickly at Jack who replied 'I came on your village name on a signpost driving by. Thought someone told me Ettie lived at Larkford so I figured to stop by and take a look. Found the wood and you fishing.'

'Looking for me' Ettie asserted.

'Looking for all of this.' The gesture he made, embracing the whole wood and them in it, abolished her centrality. 'This is something wonderful. I stayed.'

'Jack has a plan' said Ettie, her face lighting, 'Jack wants to make a film about our wood.'

The purpose. It entered the field like a reaper into ripe corn.

'You mean a documentary?' Kim asked.

Jack stepped towards him. 'No a feature. A story set here. You know what? This is the only place I ever seen better than I could design for a set. I feel like was it Turner said when he looked around—Well done God.'

'What's the story?' Kim asked.

'You tell me.'

'What do you mean?'

'This is the wonderful idea' Ettie put in 'you think of the story Kim.'

'Me? I don't know any story.'

'But you do Kim' she insisted. 'What about—you're always telling me things about what happened, what about when you were children? You and Clara and the name she called the wood and the language you had to talk. And the dead lamb you found. And then what your mother told about your grandfather swinging. Oh he does know about the wood Jack' she appealed 'he does know and he can tell.'

None can do treason to us except one of us two. All he had told her was betrayed.

'For goodness sake Ettie no one wants to hear a lot of rubbish about my family.'

'You told it to me.'

'Maybe it's the raw material' Jack said 'needs shaping up to use maybe. But you have a beginning. Look' he said 'you imagine a couple of people living here. Why are they here? What do they do? What happens to them? What does the place mean to them? See? You have the raw material you can answer those questions and then we have a story.'

'If I could answer those questions I have a life' Kim said.

'You write me a movie you have a life.'

Silence. They heard the rain. 'But I can't write' Kim said.

'You ever try?'

'Kim you can, you showed me——'

'Please Ettie.' Betray no more.

'Look' Jack said 'the hard part is knowing, not telling. Telling's technique and its no problem. You come up with a ten-page synopsis and the screenplay we work on together.'

'I don't know what makes you think I know.'

'I told Jack how much the wood means to you' Ettie put in.

Jack shook his head. 'It isn't How much it's Why. You think Why.'

Why. Kim swung his hammer one-handed, knocking flakes of bark off the log at his feet. He longed to be back at the mindless work. 'You're a set designer aren't you?' he asked Jack.

'I was.' The voice was nonchalant. 'Now I'm into a situation that's kind of wild. I have this whole crowd of people tells me they'll make with the backing if I can find a subject I want to do. I just found the subject' he said simply.

Kim tapped a wedge.

'You want to get on with your work?' Jack asked.

'I should do a bit more.'

'It doesn't matter when you do this Kim' Ettie protested. 'It doesn't matter if you don't do it all.'

'I can waste Sunday if I want surely.'

'But this is such a chance darling.'

'A chance of what?' He looked at her. 'Of escape?'

She met his eye. 'Yes, of freedom, yes it is.'

The back of his mind was her prison. When he realized that, he could no longer accuse her of treachery.

192

'There isn't any hurry' Jack assured him 'time and money we have. You think, is all.'

Kim darted at the gap: 'No hurry?'

'I can come around tomorrow.'

No gap, no time. 'I can't think of a story in 24 hours.'

'You know what Whistler said, it wasn't a day's work he asked a thousand guineas for, it was a lifetime's experience. You got the lifetime's experience.'

'Anyway tomorrow's no good, it's Monday.'

Jack laughed. 'That make any difference in a trailer in the woods?'

Kim was aware of Ettie imploring him not to reveal that he worked in an office, was part of the subway crowd. He didn't betray her.

'Jack is coming to lunch Kim' she said, 'let's go and talk in the dry shall we?'

'If it's okay with you me stopping?' asked Jack.

Kim thought only of escape. 'The thing is' he said, 'yes you must stay to lunch of course. But Ettie the thing is, I didn't tell you but I promised to go to Larkford. They've got this sirloin you see.'

Into the silence the rain fell coldly.

Then Ettie said 'Well if you've told her we're going.'

'Only me. Honestly only me. I'll walk over the hill from here.'

Jack said 'And tomorrow morning we'll meet up?'

'In the evening's better tomorrow' said Ettie. 'Come on Jack, let's go and I'll make some lunch.'

'Listen, morning or evening or anytime it's no use' Kim said as they turned to go.

'You think' Jack told him.

'It would mean money Kim' Ettie added.

'Oh money!' It sounded like a curse on all currencies.

'Don't worry about money' said Jack fluently, like a man covering for his confederate's slip of the tongue, 'the money's easy. The money' he said 'is the easy part.'

Ettie had whistled up her dog. Slender, swift as a shadow,

the colour of a deer, he came slipping through the trees to join her. For a moment they stood on the edge of the clearing facing Kim, two hunters and their dog facing the trapped hare.

Then they walked away. It struck Kim how they suited one another, the stranger's easy stride, the slim rainy girl, the delicacy of the dog trotting at their heels; and it struck him how none of them suited the wood. They were like people in a film about the country. Even the dog was chic. When rain and the rustling leaves expunged their bright voices Kim went back to his work.

He took a wedge and with its point searched the grain of the timber until he found a weakness where the wood was splitting of itself. Here he set the iron and tapped it in. He lengthened his grip on the hammer's shaft. Then there recommenced the rhythm of heavy blows and heavier, the spoke of the hammer wheeling, the smitten iron sullen, sound in solid chips flying upward from each impact. Under the driven wedge the oak creaked and yielded, and under the weight and timing of the hammer-blows his mind began to empty once more. Cleave the wood and there am I.

Then the note of the struck wedge deadened. The split had fouled into a knot. However belaboured, the iron sank no deeper. The wedge bounced when it was hit. Then it flopped into the mud. Kim stooped wearily for it, sweat and rain trickling down his nose. The world rushed back into his head.

'God damn this bloody wood' he said. 'God damn you to hell.'

He leaned on his hammer. The father told his sons to dig the orchard and they would find treasure; they dug, and the harvest of fruit fell from above. But it was their own orchard that they dug, tricked it is true, but tricked into labouring at their true task. Kim knocked the other wedges loose and dropped them into his sack. For a woodman it was sufficient to split wood, but only for a woodman; there was no reward in it for Kim. It was not his orchard. He left the sack and the hammer and walked away into the wood.

The last phrase that Jack had used to him had stuck in his mind. 'Don't worry about the money, the money is the easy part.' To Kim the phrase meant that if once the restless striving towards material ends was stilled, then of itself came enough money, as peace follows grace. Work for work's sake, the phrase implied, but at your own work, your true task; and then, as upon the sons in their own orchard, the harvest falls from above. Only find the orchard. The money is the easy part.

Jack had stolen the phrase from Marco Roccaleone, on whose lips he had despised it. But recently in the film world Marco Roccaleone's attitude to money had become the one it was fashionable to adopt; as a pose it had come in with sneakers and army surplus clothes when the blue silk suits went out; now it was fashionable to pretend that money didn't matter, as you drove along in your Rolls-Royce. Kim didn't know it was a pretence. And nor did Jack know that the picture which Kim presented of himself, up a tree fishing in gypsy clothes, was a pretence too. Neither saw through the mask of the other.

But a truth is no less true in the mouth of a liar, as the father's advice to his sons to dig the orchard was no less sound for being a trick, and what Kim thought he heard in Jack's words worked no less powerfully on his mind for being insincerely spoken. As birds sow seeds with their excrement so what Jack said to Kim was seminal. Find the orchard and dig: the harvest is the easy part. Kim walked about the wood in the rain. He had nowhere to go, not Larkford, not the caravan. There was only the wood, the wet trees, himself, tomorrow and tomorrow. There was no orchard but himself. That stubborn and compacted earth defied the spade. Hard as that concrete garden in London. He walked about the wood and found nowhere to hide from himself, no little pointless tasks, no little tubs of soil to dabble in. Solus ad solum he could bear himself no longer and went at last down through the trees to the caravan.

Débris of lunch littered the table. Above the two coffee cups, the two wine glasses, hung the smell of French cigarettes. He had not smelt it since Ettie gave up smoking in the winter. It reminded him of Rome, and freedom. Next door the bed creaked.

Kim stood absolutely still, willing himself to vanish.

He hoped that she had betrayed him: in this way and no other. If she had, he was no longer responsible. More; if they were in bed together then it was for Ettie that the stranger had come, and not for him. He would be free. He backed with great caution down the steps.

'Kim?' Her voice. 'Kim?'

'Yes it's me.' He climbed the steps again. Hope only finally faded when he opened the bedroom door and saw Ettie lying alone fondling her dog's ears. Rain slithered down the window pane. It was not in that easy way that she had betrayed him. He was not free.

'You look awful' she said. 'Orfool' she pronounced it, annoying him.

Then she got up and walked past him as if she would have walked through him if she could. The dog watched, his paws still on the bed, uncertain of his rights to the furniture now that Ettie had gone. Kim stared at him with considerable dislike. Ettie and her dog's relationship was a secret injury which he could not with any dignity complain about. 'You get on the bed if you want' he said 'you're no bloody use to anyone you stupid animal.'

Next door Ettie was clearing the table. He did not help her because she was smoking a Gauloise, keeping it in her mouth as she worked, as French people do, her eyes creased against the smoke and the cigarette very fat and white between her lips. Why it annoyed him so much he did not know. He felt her animosity. The room, the whole caravan, was too small for the mood of one to be isolated from the other. Yet he felt detached, uninvolved in the work he watched. So this is what our life looks like, he said to himself. Drudgery. He might have been in a train passing a lit window, pitying the interior scene. He looked away. But there was nowhere else to look.

'I wish to God it would stop raining' he said.

Pressure escaped: 'So that you can go on splitting stupid wood?' He watched the cigarette bobbing as she spat the words at him. She returned to her drudging. 'You won't even try' she said. 'Even when it's offered you won't even pull your fucking finger out.' An American intonation.

'You sound absurd talking American' he said.

'I learned it before I learned your English. A whole year I learned it. Anyway' she said 'you talk it too.'

'Not with a French accent I don't.'

'I always told you a foreign accent would annoy you in the end. But if you won't talk French any more.'

'Talking French in the middle of a wood in England would be even more absurd than talking like the movies' he said.

'Whatever I do is absurd to you.'

'Whatever *I* do is absurd to me.'

She washed up miserably. He watched miserably. Not long ago misery would have brought them together. But it was too late, it severed them. He went out, trying not to creep but feeling rather small, like a man at fault.

His footsteps led him towards the river as they had done all his life when everything else had failed him or betrayed him or shown itself indifferent. The vaster indifference of water flowing he could bear. The rain had ceased: in the glade his dingy hummocks of hay steamed, and the woodland was full of the smell of wetness, leaves glistening as the light grew stronger. Singularly clear fell raindrops dripping from eave to eave of the wood's roof. The sky had hollowed, and into misty blue the birdsong mounted ardently again. The wood wakened after rain. A phrase came into his mind: 'Woe to him who saith unto the wood, Awake'. Ever since words had had any meaning to him Kim had attached these words to this wood. His tongue had called it Burr Wood or Rub Doow or whatever other name Clara had told him it was to be called; but in his heart he had known it by that phrase, its secret name. So too he had known summer and winter as messages conveyed secretly in the sound of the word, spells profounder than spelling, the word 'winter' as resonant as a stone sent skimming across the frozen lake ... 'Woe to him who saith unto the wood, Awake'. In echoes like the long sob of the stone across the ice that phrase spoke to him.

He had never known what it really meant. But by repeating it to himself he could be sure that he had described the wood and left out nothing, as a pentangle described in the dust contains magic. Everything he knew about woods was there: the winter's morning he had found blood in the snow, scarlet holes blood burns in snow, that knowledge, that the woods drank blood each night, was contained in the phrase: and the berry he had eaten, the bitter fruit of the thorny tree: and the lamb dying: and the whetting of the Green Knight's axe by the frosty stream: the phrase was a spell spelling meaning in another language, the language which the trees spoke in the wind outside the night-nursery window. What did it mean? Somewhere in the stubborn earth of himself, trampled so hard that its crust deflected the spade, meaning was buried.

As he made his way down the steepening slope towards the river he remembered a little boy waiting alone just here one summer morning long ago, chivvying ants with a stalk of grass, day dreaming, waiting where he had been told to wait by Clara for one of the games she invented which he didn't understand. Startling him out of his day dream something stirred the bracken. The shivering fronds set up a shiver in his mind; the sound of the river came nearer, flowed in his ears like his own blood pounding. But he had to look. He crept towards the source of his fear. In bracken and brambles a lamb was entangled, matted in filth, froth bubbling from its mouth. He knew by its frightened eye that it was dying. From the steep above came Clara's voice, clear as a cuckoo, calling his name in her mirror language. Let the lamb be dead before Clara came and stared. Die! Die! he screamed at it silently; and as if his panic struck it blows the lamb kicked and struggled free of the brambles' grasp. But it had no strength, and the slope was steep. It fell, and he watched. Over and over it tumbled, slack, its limbs broken spokes loosening stones, tumbling towards the waiting river. In it pitched, and was gone. The river flowed on smooth and dark. Black as a window at dusk the river concealed what it held. Death. The lamb. The fish. He had never hooked a fish in that river that he had not thought of the lamb.

'You think why.'

To answer that question was the work. The money is the easy part. Think why. *You shall not deny the Stranger.*

4.

ON MONDAY MORNING Jack drove along the lane in his damaged car to pick up Ettie at the wicket gate as they had arranged the previous day. He was depressed. Yesterday he had invented a rôle for himself, the man with money and time looking for a project, but today he couldn't believe in it. When he had come back to the village pub from lunching with Ettie the landlord had accosted him. 'Someone phoned, said to phone back.' Sol Wenkel: Sol's grip was clamped on his satraps as if telephone wires were his tentacles. Willing victims, the whole gang making his movies rang in and left a number when they were out of town. That way they stayed plugged-in to the power grid. Smoothing the moustache he had grown because Sol had grown one Jack dialled London.

'Hey what happened?' growled Sol's voice affably 'you playing hookey?' After listening to Jack's excuses he said 'Look Jack, you check in tomorrow night can you.'

'They're still fixing the car Sol.'

'You mean I have to invent trains for you?'

'Okay Sol. Someway I'll try and make it tomorrow.'

'No hurry man. You get to the club in time we eat is all. Take care.'

The line went dead, and the rôle Jack had invented for himself went out like a light you switch off. Sol had reached out and annexed the pub, and annexed it stayed, a remote point controlled from London. Sol made it remote, and Sol made it dingy. The attic room where Jack lay awake worrying on Sunday night smelled of failure. A cheap room: the fall from grace. Jack needed to move fast. So long as he was working for Sol that gave him prestige, a little leverage, and if he moved fast he could try and put a deal together to set up a movie on his own. You knock around town with the Pope, you get to paint the Sistine chapel. You fall from favour and you fall fast, you find yourself boiling eggs in the kettle in a cheap lodging like this attic, and saying Excuse me on stairs smelling of cabbage to other lodgers on their way to bed because they have nowhere else to go. Jack hated the night, when no man can work. He lay awake worrying. He must use that wood where he had believed in his own power to take the big step and make a movie. Whilst in the wood, he had believed; so he believed in the wood.

He waited in his car by the wicket gate. Ettie was the way into Kim, that was all she meant to him. Finding her had been like finding the one door he could push open. Sunday morning he had been walking in the wood in the rain trying to imagine a story into the place. But it stayed dead. All he could picture was how it would be to film a wet day in a wood, how the paper cups they brought you coffee in would dissolve in the rain; he couldn't hear dialogue or see action, all he could hear was the hum of generators burning money and the voices of technicians asking him what shot he meant to take next. He saw a setting but no story. And then he came on the figure in the landscape, Ettie swinging on the swing. He had forgotten that it was she who had brought him to Larkford in the first place; but meeting her was like getting a pay-off from the one-armed bandit he'd been feeding food and sex all that year in Spain. She was the way into Kim, the split in the wood's grain he could open with a wedge. So he waited for her on Monday morning. The field gate his car had wrecked had been cobbled across the gap with wire. But it didn't plug the hole. Waiting, he heard behind the wood an uneasy sound, giant footsteps trampling on shingle, which had been silent at the weekend. In the hazy sky only a stain showed where the sun was. No birds sang.

Ettie appeared under the firs. She slipped into the car beside him quickly as if she had decided to act dishonourably. 'You go on a bit and you see the drive' she said, leaning forward in her haste to get on.

Jack asked 'What's that noise you can hear?'

'That? Oh the gravel works. They own the wood.'

'Own the wood? I thought Kim owned it.'

'Well they have an option or something, I don't know. Come on.'

'Christ.' His mind flicked over it. You'd need to shut the works down and pay lost production if you wanted live sound—no one is about to believe in a paradise which has that kind of racket going on. On the other hand another owner of the wood could give him more leverage with Kim.

'Come on Jack.'

'Okay.' The car surged forward. 'Kim around someplace is he?'

'No he's out. He goes off' she said vaguely.

'I can't be too long today, I have to be back in London tonight.'

'Tonight?' She looked crestfallen. Then she said sarcastically 'Sol being strict is he?'

'No' he lied, irritated, 'it's not Sol. This is something else.'

Mutual dishonesty engendered silence. The Rolls turned in at the Larkford gates and swept up the drive scattering gravel in its wake. The stone front of the house came in view, as well-seated in its park as an outcrop of rock, gleaming in the misty light. It grew larger and larger until Jack drew up the car and stopped, diminished, between its enfolding wings. Neither doors nor windows acknowledged their existence.

'Now remember' Ettie said, her hand on the car door, 'she's the one who can make him do things.'

'He doesn't look like he'd do what anyone said.'

'I don't mean that. I mean she knows. Knows what he'll do. For instance she knew he would marry me' Ettie said. 'She's like a dictionary he looks himself up in to see what he means. Come on' she said, getting out, 'she'll be in the garden I expect.'

Between stone piers they descended stone steps onto a paved walk which lime trees overarched. The sky was shut out: Jack felt the garden close over his head. Ettie walked ahead, searching for Mrs Vannick, and Jack's sense of distance or direction was soon confused by the turns they took, now looking into a deserted roundel where a stone figure, as if playing Grandmother's Footsteps, stood more still than stone; now crossing a sunken lawn crowded with clipped yews which evidently formed a pattern if one could have looked down upon the architecture of the garden from above. But Jack was not above, he submerged deeper in the garden at each turn; losing all sense of its plan he could only follow where Ettie led. They seemed to be moving inward, by mossy paths and screened walks, through one enclosure after another, towards a maze's centre. Behind them successive gates closed, separating him from the world outside, each gate clipping off part of what he had arrived with, as the dog's jaws in the legend are said to have bitten off the hare's tail. At length a mellow wall rose before them, and by a final door they entered the kitchen garden. At last there was open sky above. Although enclosed, and filled with fruit and flowers and vegetables, its paths lanes between espaliers, hothouses glittering in the misty light, it seemed to Jack the open space you find at the centre of the labyrinth.

Because sparrows fluttered off seed beds, and a pigeon or two clattered up at their entry, he thought the walled garden too was deserted. But the clink of a trowel betrayed that it was not. He looked for the source of the sound. At the foot of a newly-planted tree, as if it was a child whose shoe she latched, Mrs Vannick kneeled weeding. He understood at once why the birds were not frightened away by her presence in the garden.

'Mother' Ettie called 'I've brought someone to see you.'

She rose and shaded her eyes with her trowel. Then she came towards them between the espaliers. Jack, with the image of the old house still in his mind, saw that same calm assurance in her countenance. They were introduced. She might not frighten the sparrows, but he found the grip of her hand very resolute.

'Mother, Mr Peel designs films' Ettie said 'very good ones and he's got this idea for another and I thought could he see your garden. Our garden' she amended. 'You see he might want a garden in the film.'

'Splendid' said Mrs Vannick. 'Come, we will have some elevenses shall we, and then we can walk round. If you are really interested' she added, looking keenly into Jack's face.

'Yes I am' he claimed. His moustache, his long hair, all the pretence of fashion felt like seedling weeds her eyes rooted out to discover what of permanent worth grew beneath.

'What are you making Mother?' asked Ettie, looking towards the part of the garden where Mrs Vannick had been working, which was hidden from their view by the espalier.

'What indeed! Come and see' she said, walking ahead of them. 'A designer's advice is just what I should have liked before I started on this business. You see part of our poor old wall tumbled down in the winter Mr Peel? Of course before the war we would have rebuilt, but now Mr Sowerby tells me we can't, or mayn't, so I thought I would turn the gap into a "vista"' she said, pronouncing the word as if mocking its pretension. She went on to describe her plan as they approached the axis of paths quartering the walled garden. Listening to her voice Jack could imagine the avenue of tall grave cypresses she described, the sun-steeped grass between yew hedges, the maquis-scented steps over the wall's

203

ruins, the cool of the shade in the shrubbery beyond...

'What do you think Mr Peel?'

He looked up. In place of what she had described to his imagination his eyes saw all that as yet existed. Baby yews, spindly cypresses two feet high, bare earth leading towards the rubble of the collapsed wall.

'It may take a little time' he suggested.

'There is plenty of time' she said 'if the design is right. What do you think?'

He looked; he could feel the shadows of her cypresses fall across his mind. 'It's right' he said with conviction.

'Ah, I am so glad you see it as I do.'

'But I don't know' he added 'I never designed anything that grows. On the movie we just done everything I built they came along and bombed next day. It's a war movie' he explained.

'Well, that has happened to me too' she said.

'In the war they bombed your garden?'

'No' she said 'not the garden.' Then she added 'Still, a bomb here and there teaches one not to set too much store by one's plans I suppose.'

'Should do, but don't you set store by your garden plans just the same?'

'Yes I do' she admitted 'but in my imagination chiefly, where it is reasonably bomb-proof. Do you know I think nothing makes you live in your own mind—in your intentions so to speak—quite as gardening does. You see in the winter, when one does all the hard work, one must imagine the summer: and year in year out one must keep in mind a future one will never see. You work away and the only reward is in your imagination. Alas' she said, turning away from her infant vista, 'the reward for imagination is only cashable in the imagination's account. When you step back and look you only see what is. Still, not much harm can be done to what is. Tell me Mr Peel, is your next film to be about war and bombs too?'

'No it'll be about peace and quiet' he decided, 'nothing'll

get bombed in my picture.' As they walked between the espaliers his mind filled with the kind of film he would make as his head filled with the scent of unseen flowers. At the door in the wall he turned back for a last look across the kitchen garden. He saw the vista she imagined: the wall had fallen not as a ruin falls but as a seed might fall, to grow in time into something wonderful. 'Your plan'll be a knockout when Kim is 100 years old' he said.

She laughed, unlatching the door into the walled rose garden. 'I hope so. I thought, Kim so loved Italy do you see; he might one day rather care to have the sketch of an Italian garden here. Next' she said to Ettie 'next my dear we must lay out a French parterre for your old age.'

She took Ettie's arm. Her affection—even her affection—hampered the freedom of the girl's stride as they walked between the roses. 'But Mother this is what you made for yourself, isn't it, this rose garden?'

'Oh, rose gardens are very much a thing of the past' said Mrs Vannick with scarcely a glance at her creation before opening the gate in the further wall. 'When I was young I wanted quick results you know. Roses, herbaceous borders, any plant I could put in one year that would flower the next. As I get old I realize that the things you can complete in your own lifetime are not really the most worthwhile. All there is time for is setting things going. If you have reaped the rewards of the past you have to try and sow some rewards for the future.' She led them to the house, to the refectory table in the hall where they sat down.

Everything Jack saw, everything he heard said, seemed to him part of the film he would like to make. But it was all in a language he could not quite understand, which cast only shadows of meaning, like the shadows of those cypresses which had as yet no substance. The ineffability of it attracted him: he wanted to make a film he didn't quite understand, for he was always dogged by a suspicion that what he himself understood must be banal to subtler minds. He wanted to be thought subtler than he was. He wanted to talk in riddles because that way people looked for meaning in what you said. For the first time in his life his ambition was vague. In the hall, between the high stone windows, their coffee was brought to them. This was all a scene from the film. All the waste space between their heads and the shadowy ceiling gave to what was said the resonance of a Lesson read in church. People would wonder how he had designed such a set. People would think it a stroke of genius to have the old butler whistle all the time. People would wonder what the hell it all meant.

As Ettie poured out coffee for them she said 'Mother Mr Peel was driving looking for a place to make his film and he found the Paradise Wood and Kim fishing he found. And he thinks Kim could be the one who could write this film. But Mother what do you think?'

'The Paradise Wood!' She laughed. 'Do you know, I cannot think of it except as Burr Wood.'

'Why Burr Wood?' asked Jack catching at the clue.

'You know those horrid clinging burdocks? The children once came back from that wood with their coats covered in them. Thick. I was so disappointed, such nice little tweed coats, and one needed clothing coupons at the time. Hours it took us, pulling them all off. It was called Burr Wood after that.'

'Burr Wood.' Jack tried the name. Yes, he saw now that The Paradise Wood was too obvious, Burr Wood much subtler.

'Did Kim say anything when he came to lunch yesterday?' Ettie asked.

'When he came to lunch?' enquired Mrs Vannick cautiously. 'What about my dear?'

'About Jack's film.'

'Jack?'

'Mr Peel I mean.'

'Ah, Mr Peel.' Her eyes pierced Ettie's pretence that Jack was a stranger to her. 'No' she said carefully 'Kim said nothing at all at lunch yesterday.' St Alfonso da Liguori would have allowed this statement to pass as truth. 'But why do you think Kim should write your film Mr Peel?'

Jack searched his combat jacket unsuccessfully for cigarettes. 'Because I want the film to centre on the wood' he said 'and seems to me Kim really loves that wood.'

'I don't know that love is what he feels for it' she said.

Ettie asked 'What would you say then?'

'Nostalgia?' she suggested. 'Or—what is that word for going back beyond history to something older? For leaving history out?'

'Atavism' Jack supplied. He knew a lot of words which categorized concepts and saved him the trouble of grappling with ideas.

'Atavism perhaps. I would say panic if panic still had its old sense, to do with Pan ... there are several stories which have always fascinated Kim' she went on.

'Such as?' He leaned eagerly forward.

Too eagerly: she withdrew. 'Ah, I don't remember their names' she said. 'Just old stories we used to read.'

He knew that she did remember, and that she was protecting a trust. 'Do you have a cigarette Ettie?' he asked. No use pretending he and Ettie didn't know one another.

She put her hand in her bag to take out the crocodile case which he had given back to her. But she changed her mind. 'I don't smoke' she said. 'Mother listen, do you think Kim ever would try and write a story Jack could use?'

Mrs Vannick regarded them both thoughtfully. Jack had the impression that she was not debating what to say but debating whether or not to say it to them. Not the question but the questioner made her pause.

'If ever Kim did write anything' she replied at length 'you may be sure that woods and trees in some shape or form would figure in the story. How much use what he wrote would be to Mr Peel I do not know. I believe it is always said that creative people are trying to understand the mysteries in themselves by their work. The knowledge in themselves, but just beyond their grasp. Is that not so Mr Peel?'

Jack realized in that moment that he understood himself

only too plainly. The shadows in his mind were always cast by other people's ideas not by his own. 'I guess so' he said 'I guess they do try and work out their own problems.'

'Yes it is guesswork for the rest of us' she agreed. 'He who knows doesn't tell, and he who tells doesn't know.'

'Zen' said Jack. Bang! He shot the quotation dead without thinking what it meant. Everyone in movies was into Zen like they were into army surplus and moustaches.

Mrs Vannick looked at him. Then she said to Ettie 'But to answer your question my dear yes, I have always believed that Kim would produce something in the end, and if I were you I would make him try. He won't like it' she warned 'and nor will you.'

'Oh I'd love him to write!'

'You would like him to have written' she said. 'That is rather different. Now my dear, are you and Mr Peel going to look round the garden and then come in to luncheon?'

'Look I have to rush' Jack said, giving his watch a couple of winds, 'I have to pack up and get to London. But we saw the garden looking for you.'

'Ah you miss the point, looking for something.'

'Maybe I'll be down again if we get a deal on the movie.'

She rose and came with them to the porch. 'Yes, the garden is always here' she said. 'People are forever telling one that their garden was at its peak last week, as if they were training up a horse which had lost its race, but really one can judge a garden best in midwinter. Flowers only hush up mistakes in design. You should come again in winter, if you are interested in design. Goodbye Mr Peel. I hope your plans work out for the best.'

She closed the door. Jack had an abrupt sense of exclusion. London seemed remote. When it came to making her surroundings seem like the fulcrum of the universe, he thought, Sol Wenkel had a rival in that lady.

'You going to come and have lunch in the pub?' he said to Ettie as the car turned out of the drive gates. He wanted to be free of her, believing that he had a great deal to think about, but he must keep open his door into Kim.

She wouldn't look at him. 'No, you're in a hurry you have to get to London.'

The tone of her reply dropped him back into the world of transparent motivation which he understood, and it wearied him. 'Come on sweetheart' he said, dropping a hand onto her knee, 'it's only lunch.'

Now she looked at him. 'I shouldn't. After that time we had lunch in Paris I really shouldn't.'

He said nothing. He thought of the dismal attic, the narrow bed. Why did girls always think there was a bed in the middle of your mind? Just because they have no other furniture in their heads? His hand lay on her leg like an empty glove, though the soft-sprung rocking and heeling of the car as it sped too fast along the lane put enough life in the glove to make believe it caressed her. She covered his hand with hers.

'It's what you want isn't it?' she asked in her throat. 'Why you really came?'

'Yes.' To let his hand do the lying was easy. Harder to lie with his voice. 'I don't know.'

'Don't know? Don't know what you want? You always told me that was the first thing to know. I know.' She dragged his hand up her thigh. Now he couldn't stop his fingers straying, his sex stirring.

'So I thought' he said. 'I thought so, but this thing I'm into now this is something else. You know what you want, you limit your objective. To what you know you can get. You limit the possibilities to what you have already.'

She pushed his hand away. 'You don't have me already.'

He looked at her as if she was a burden. 'Don't I sweetheart? Don't I? It was you sent for me remember.'

The car stopped in the pub yard. His impetus stopped with it.

'Lunch?' he suggested.

'I'll help you pack first.' She opened the door.

'Okay you go up. Left at the top of the stairs. I'll pay the check and follow you.'

He watched her slip into the pub. Yes, he thought wearily, this is real life. This is the way people act in the movies everyone makes. People act, and cast no shadows. Because the door his side wouldn't open he followed Ettie through hers and entered the pub. He accepted what he had always known, but had never before experienced from the losing side; that vague ambitions in one person are always at the mercy of concrete desires in another.

5.

THAT MONDAY MORNING Kim's body, like a hat left in token occupation of a seat on a train, occupied his office chair. He had next to nothing to do. They had created room for him in the building by partitioning the typing pool with hardboard but they had not troubled to create a job. Time passed very slowly. He sat reading the newspapers, which had never interested him, and listened to the typists giggling next door.

When the giggles hushed, and a chorus of 'Good morning sir' formed a guard of honour to his door, he was warned to expect a superior. The door opened and there entered Mr Swindells, local manager for the parent company, a London man.

Kim caught deference like an infection from the typists. Restraining his impulse to stand up he watched his visitor staring out of the window. 'Rotten morning' he said accusingly.

Swindells turned. 'Rush visit' he said 'dropped in. Remember Wally Stroud, Blewston? As I daresay you know I fixed him up with a cottage down Hampshire way when he retired Christmas time. Just come from there now. Terrible shock.'

'Murdered?'

'Terrible shock' insisted Swindells, 'heart attack. Out mowing his lawn, dropped down dead. Postman found him stiff and stark by his front gate this morning he told me. Bird messes all over him poor old chap. Beastly birds. And do you know a funny thing? Well I say funny—touching. Cup of tea stone cold on the blessed silver salver I gave him, all engraved with the names of chaps I got to subscribe to the presentation. Makes you think.'

Kim said nothing. In his mind a tyrant was overthrown. The scene at the cottage gate, the big rumpled corpse splashed with bird-lime like a washed-up walrus, and the mower and the tea cup on the half-cut grass, were extraordinarily vivid to him, and suggestive to his imagination.

Swindells strutted about the room talking. 'Funny the things you think of at a time like this isn't it? When a great character passes on. Little thing, silly really, example I'll give you: had a garden I did, won the prize most years, well the boy next door grew weeds in his, hell of a mess, seeded all over mine. I was a bit of a piratical character I suppose, anyway I pulled 'em up lock stock and barrel this kid's weeds, wild flowers as he called them. And I showed Wally in a book where it said they were all weeds. Do you know Wally accepted that? Saw he was wrong to tell me off. Never be above learning, that's a thing he taught me. Humble.'

'I don't remember him being humble' Kim said. 'Crusty old bugger. Bad tempered. Remember the way his head wobbled around when he got angry?'

'War wound' said Swindells briefly, straightening his shoulders.

'Yes the first war.'

'Doesn't matter what war you're wounded in old boy.'

'It matters how out of date your trauma is if you want to teach people.'

'You never did your National Service did you? Let me tell you' Swindells said 'those of us who did our bit had cause to be grateful to Wally Stroud when it came to showing a bit of spunk.' Here he tapped his broken front tooth significantly and said 'Wasn't all beer and skittles in Cyprus I can tell you.'

'You didn't break that tooth in Cyprus' Kim protested at

last against this reconstructed past, 'you got it bust at Blewston.'

Like a curtain dropped to cover a mishap on stage Swindell's lip shut rapidly over the tooth. A look of pure misery fled through his eyes. In that moment Kim recognized the boy he had known at Blewston. Then that starved unhappy child was pushed off stage with his unwelcome truth, and Swindells as he had created his own image repossessed his place. He punched the air so as to consult his watch, a straight left knocking Time into shape. 'Must rush' he said, 'the point is I'll fix up a little memorial service I think: you just jot down some sort of appreciation I could spout will you? You know the kind of thing I'd want to say.'

Kim was not as world-weary as he thought: he was still outraged that people do not listen to what you say. 'But I don't think our views on Mr Stroud are quite the same' he said.

'Oh I think you'll find they are. Anyway you wrote advertisements didn't you before you came to us? Take you ten minutes. Of the company's time' he added heavily, allowing his eye to dwell upon Kim's newspapers. Then he opened the door. 'All going well here? Fitting in all right are you? Splendid. Don't bother to move, I know my way. Let you know about the memorial service and we can go together.'

He was gone. The typing pool hushed, rippling once more with giggles as the further door clapped to. At his desk Kim felt like a piece of scenery from Swindells' life stowed back in the prop box. Yes he was fitting in. Like Mr Stroud—like everyone Swindells had ever known—he was being made to fit in with Swindells' view of the way the world should have been arranged. With those straight lefts of a determined will Swindells cuffed history into submission. The facts of the past, even his physical appearance, had been manipulated by his willpower: conjured away was the rabbit-toothed and jug-eared object of contempt at Blewston, and in its place was substituted 'a bit of a piratical character'. Foursquare on his new foundations Swindells faced the world. The achievement went beyond mere lying and became creative fiction. When he appreciated this, it was the creativity of the operation which most impressed Kim.

For he remembered the gardening incident. Yet the facts he remembered were inadequate to contest Swindells' fiction. Only another fiction as lively as Swindells' could establish Kim's own view of the truth. Supposing he had been the boy gardening in the next plot to Swindells, who grew field flowers which seeded amongst Swindells' asters; supposing Swindells complained to Mr Stroud, backing his complaint with a book which categorized Vannick's wild flowers as weeds: how would the Mr Stroud whom Kim remembered have reacted?

... weeds were of course forbidden, so it was a ticklish point whether or not this anarchic garden should be allowed to flourish amongst the other boys' utilitarian plots. Mr Stroud issues vague warnings. Then one afternoon he finds Swindells and Vannick wrestling over an uprooted plant. Seizing Swindells by an enormous ear he cries 'Did you pull up this cow-parsley you donkey?'

'Oh sir but it says in my book sir——!'

'I don't give a rap for your book!'

'Oh sir but it's hemlock sir, it's dangerous' squeals Swindells.

Letting go his ear Mr Stroud picks up the plant. Hemlock sure enough. Because he should have recognized the sinister growth flowering under his aegis he turns angrily upon Vannick: 'That's caput to your gardening my lad! Get a barrow, dig all these weeds up, burn the lot.'

'All my garden sir?'

'You heard what I said!' Although already regretting his irascibility there is no going back on a decision in front of boys. 'Get a barrow, off you go.' Swindells stands smirking with his book under his arm.

Away Vannick darts. His lightness of foot, which looks like lightness of heart, makes Mr Stroud aware of the weight of his years. He looks sadly down at the condemned garden at his feet. If these weeds are Vannick's idea of flowers then the whole of nature is his garden, a pleasaunce of which neither Swindells with his book nor any man's irascibility can deprive him...

It had not happened so, but it might have done. Facts are liquid, the liquescent raw material of creativity: this was the perception which came to Kim. Poured into any mould, in that shape the facts will set. Designing the mould is the act of will; the facts then serve your purpose as Swindells made even his broken tooth serve his purpose. You can make what you like out of mere events. Hitherto they had been in Kim's mind intransigent ruins cluttering the landscape of the past. Now he realized that he could steal stones from those ruins and build what he liked, as in the Renaissance they had built with the stones of Rome's ruins.

He walked about his office. In his imagination Mr Stroud, like the bronze statue of a Victorian governor in a remote province of empire, and similarly splashed with bird-lime, fell from its plinth and became the meltable raw material of creativity. What he himself conceived to be the truth about Mr Stroud, that was the mould; into it could be poured molten facts, just as Swindells had poured them. The die of what did happen must be broken, for the infinite possibilities of what might have happened to be set free. 'Those who will not crack the shell of history will never get at the kernel.'

Yes, he would write an appreciation of Mr Stroud's work at Blewston. It would be fiction, as Swindells' view of Blewston was fictional; it would re-present truth. It would be a story relating events. Vividly he saw the great hulk of Mr Stroud's corpse splashed with starlings' messes by his garden gate. Flux coalesced into shape, a shape he felt in his mind which communicated its strength to him like the salmon's take in the flowing river. Fattened on nuts fallen from the nine hazels the legendary fish showed him its silver flank. The

214

piece of paper he pulled towards him seemed covered with the shadows of meaning like a child's magic-writing book where he had only to scribble for order to emerge.

But he feared to begin, in case it did not. You cannot make a bold stroke or two, as a painter can, you have to begin at the beginning and form the first letter. The whole landscape of the past liquefied into flux awaiting the word.

He got up and sharpened his pencil and then wished he hadn't; the paper now looked emptier than before, the word-shadows fading. Without form, a void. His head too. He wished he had a pen. He wished he had a typewriter. He knew he was capable of scratching down letters, words, sentences; but the Word, could he catch that, the word which was in the beginning, and created order, could he catch that with the overused pothooks of the proper languages he had learned, pothooks bent out of shape by catching rubbish?

Fish there be that neither hook nor line
Nor snare nor net nor engine can make thine;
They must be grop't for, and be tickled too,
Or they will not be catch't, whate'er you do.

It was a pity to spoil the magic paper by beginning wrong. He was too restless to begin. He would begin again another time. It was too near lunch time to be worth beginning now. He stood up. And back into his mind sank the image of Mr Stroud's rumpled corpse like a washed-up sea creature reclaimed by the tide, like a lost salmon sinking back into the river, like a lamb plunging into the stream. He was glad to be rid of the weight.

Instead of eating in his usual café he got out his car and drove towards Larkford. Towards Jack Peel, whom he needed to tell—he didn't know what. He needed help. You couldn't do it alone. He wouldn't begin with the story about Mr Stroud, it was too difficult; he would begin with the story about the wood and Jack would tell him what to write.

The Rolls was where Jack and Ettie had left it a few minutes earlier in the pub yard. Kim entered the pub and looked in the bar. Jack was pacing to and fro under the low beams, the foam of his stout whitening his moustache. At the sight of Kim a startled look fled sideways out of his eyes.

'Ah, caught you' Kim said.

'Caught me? What do you mean?'

'I thought you might be at the caravan with Ettie.'

'Oh. No. No I'm just waiting for the bill then I'm off.'

'Off? But we were going to meet this evening.'

'I told Ettie. I let Ettie know.'

'You've lost interest?'

'In what?' Jack asked.

'In making a film here.'

'Soon as there's a story I'm interested.'

'That's what I came to talk about' Kim said, 'what sort of story do you think it ought to be?'

'That's the question I asked you.'

'Yes but I mean should it be ... or ...' The blank page. The void.

Silence.

All Jack could focus on was the man's wife waiting for him upstairs. This was a movie already, the kind of movie he understood. This you could point a camera at.

'Look Kim' he said 'listen: what a movie is about, it's about the way people behave is all. It isn't contriving, it isn't fancy motivation, it's watching what people do. You put them in a situation, you point the camera at how they behave.'

'But yesterday you said ... You asked Why. You said that was the question. You asked What's the idea behind the wood.'

'I think maybe it's only books are about Why. You can't put cameras inside people's heads.'

He looked disenchanted. Kim felt lonely. 'Maybe if I made some notes we could ... discuss ...'

'You write a story. There has to be a story nailed on the page we can point a camera at. What happens? That's the question you have to answer.'

There was no help. No accomplices. The page was empty and he had to fill it: the flux and he had to divide it: the orchard and he had to dig it. There was no help. He was alone.

Then Ettie entered the bar. Seeing Jack she said angrily 'What happened to you?' Seeing Kim she said no less angrily 'What are you doing here?'

Jack thought That is the way people behave. Ettie was alive, angry, charging the air with life and anger. Now we have a real scene coming, he thought. First real scene since he hit the mail van.

But it all went vague on him. What happened? Nothing. Kim explained, Ettie lied, they talked, nothing happened. People didn't collide. Why? After all it was Why that mattered. The ideas behind the people. The part he didn't see. Their shadows.

'Kim's going to rough out a treatment' he said.

'Are you Kim?'

'I can try. Yes, I'm going to try.'

'So ... so you'll be back again Jack? Or we'll come to London.'

'Soon as Kim nails some words on paper.'

'Kim you must start.'

The landlord came in with the bill and Jack wrote a cheque. The man turned it dubiously in his hands. 'Gent a friend of yours?' he asked Kim.

'Yes it's all right' Kim said.

Angrily Jack asked 'You want cash, dollars, gold bars—what you want?'

'Cheque'll do sir, with Mr Vannick's word. Inn belongs to Mr Vannick.' He left them.

'I never knew that' Ettie said. 'Does it Kim?'

'Yes I suppose it's mine.'

Jack thought, Kim's word: by Kim's word he was permitted to exist, pay his bill, look in the wood—all by Kim's word. 'I must pack up and get on' he said.

Upstairs in the room owned by Kim, where Kim's wife

had waited for him on the bed Kim owned, Jack threw his possessions into his bag. It was as though everything that happened happened inside Kim's head. As if Kim knew everything. When he came downstairs they were standing on the step of the pub arm in arm. What had they been talking about? And what language did they speak together? As they walked towards the cars Kim asked him,

'When do you need to have a treatment by?'

'No rush.' Jack chucked his bag into the Rolls, got in and slid across to the driving seat. 'Don't feel you have to turn in your four pages a day like some Hollywood hack' he said. He wanted to recreate the simple concept he had first found, a man up a tree fishing, a man splitting wood in the rain. 'You take it nice and slow' he said 'after you finish fishing. Then you call me. Take care the two of you.'

They stood one either side of the car as it slid away. When it had gone they did not close the gap which the car had left between them. Indeed Kim backed away towards his own car.

'Come back for lunch darling' Ettie said. 'Then you can stay like sometimes.'

'I really can't today.'

'You never have anything to do there.'

'Now there is. Now I must. Shall I drop you at the gate?'

'No I'll walk.' She slung her tote bag on her shoulder, faced the road which led to the wood. 'I might as well walk.'

He heard the appeal in her voice but he could not sacrifice what he needed, to be alone, merely to save her from being alone. There was no help. He must begin at the beginning, alone.

His car too slid away from her. In the dust of farmyards which opened into the hamlet's street hens pecked and dogs lay asleep on steps in the empty afternoon. That scene, and her forlorn figure diminishing in the midst of it, disappeared behind him. Before him stretched the empty pages. An immense and empty beach upon which he could see only the shape of Mr Stroud's corpse, splashed with bird-lime, which he must reach and rescue before the flowing tide again reclaimed it.

6.

KIM WROTE HIS story about Mr Stroud during the office hours of the next week. It absorbed him totally: he emerged at the end into the world of actuality blinking and blind as an owl in sunlight. He showed it to Ettie. She read it but didn't bother to give it back to him. As she washed up supper one evening she said 'Did you really think you were going to be a writer like you told Mr Stroud?'

'Told Mr Stroud?'

'In your story.'

Kim scarcely identified himself with the boy called Vannick in the story. 'I don't know' he said. Had he put the pattern in, or had the pattern emerged? Life must be lived forwards (he remembered reading somewhere) but can only be understood backwards, in retrospect.

'What are you planning to do with it, the thing you wrote?' she asked presently.

Her tone with this question was unfriendly. He said 'I'm not planning to do anything with it.'

'Then what's it for?'

Use—French bourgeois practicality! He watched her busy hands in the sink. He wished that he hadn't given her the story to read, now that he had to justify it. 'It started because Swindells asked me to write something for the old master's memorial service' he explained, drying up a glass.

'They can't read out that stuff at a memorial service.'

'I know that. It went beyond what I meant. Swindells annoyed me.'

She washed up with rapid efficiency, outpacing his slow and careful drying. 'You think just mocking is enough' she said, 'just refusing to take part.'

'I don't mean to mock. I don't mean the story to mock

anyone, I mean it to try and explain' he said.

Evidently she didn't think the story worth discussing. 'Well I hope what you write for Jack won't turn out to be no use' she said, tipping the water out of the bowl. 'Viens Aiuto! Allons-y!' she called, and slipped out into the dusk with her dog. Recently she had taken to going for walks at dark: Kim, his mind so full of his story that he had been like a man intent upon carrying an overfilled pitcher from the well, had hardly noticed that she was gone.

Now he did. When he had finished the drying-up there was nothing to do. He would have liked to have read his story again, but he couldn't ask her to return what she set such small store by. The empty caravan was lonely. He mooned at the window, its dark pane reflecting his face, and wished that he could go on thinking about Blewston.

But he could not. It was finished: he had built something new from the stones of the ruin, and the ruin itself no longer darkened the landscape of his mind. All that existed now was the form which he had created. It was complete.

Yet there was no peace. Life can only be understood backwards, by the retrospective eye which penetrates the opacity of action and fixes upon the motivation behind action—by pouring the fluidity of what happens into the mould of the perfect tense—but life must still be lived forwards. You can't stop the water flowing. He dredged up office work with which to busy himself for several days, and pretended to himself that he hadn't time to attempt to build something new from those other ruins, larger than Blewston and haunted by vampires grimmer than Mr Stroud, which had menaced the landscape of his mind, had rimmed that landscape with forest, since first he had read of the tryst at the Green Chapel and had heard the whetting of the axe across the stream.

As they sat over their supper one night Ettie said 'It's next week your holiday starts isn't it?'

'Yes. Next week. My annual vacation.' Holidays built in to work made holidays a duty too. He sighed. 'Have you told your mother when we're getting to Paris?'

'No I haven't. Kim I've been——'

'Well you better had I should think. The entire thing'll be wasted if they're away or something.'

'Kim I've been thinking maybe why don't we stay here? For one of the weeks anyway and you could write this thing for Jack. Do you think?' When Kim said nothing she continued 'I give up my time, being with my family I mean, so you can do this. Do you think?'

He understood her logic. In his holiday time which he owed her he was to exchange one duty towards her for another. Between them she and Swindells owned all his time. He felt pressure rushing in upon him. 'Why are you so set on me doing this thing?' he appealed.

'If you can you should.'

'We've got all we need. Why try and take more than we need?'

'Have we? All you need? In gravel?'

He tried to avoid the question. 'You mean you haven't all you want.'

'Nor have you.'

'You can't know about me.'

'Kim I can know about us. Us' she said 'is all I've got.'

He saw Jack's car sliding away from between them. 'And us isn't enough?'

She bowed her head miserably.

'You want this film' he accused her, 'you want it to bring you back in touch with that whole world. Don't you?'

Her eyes flared at him through the sparkle of tears. 'Yes, with life, yes I do.'

'You call that life?'

'You call this life?'

He saw her forlorn figure left alone in the village street after he too had driven away. It was he who had brought her out of her own country to that empty street. And abandoned her there. He scraped back his chair and stood up. But there was no escape. The room was too cramped to be evasive in. He trod on the dog's foot and helplessly sat down again.

She dabbed away her tears. 'You don't know how lonely I feel' she said.

'Ettie' he said gently 'I remember you saying once no one was a good enough liar not to have to face the truth in the end. Well this is the truth in the end, people are alone. Solus ad solum.'

'Kim talk a language I understand.'

'I tell you what someone once said: "Except a man say in his heart I alone and my maker are in this world, he shall not find peace". It's true.'

'But Kim I don't want peace.'

He was silenced by that strange cry. It was a revelation to him, that there were people in the world who didn't want peace. That such an opposite should share his life, should live inside his head with him, opened a chasm in his mind. He could stare at himself from both sides of the abyss. To see clearly from opposed points of view gave him the detachment which appreciates not the distinction between opposites, which is crude, but the residue of each which is in the other, in which intermingled spring is the source of all stories. He had assumed for so long that all he wanted was peace that he had forgotten that he knew and understood what it was like not to want to peace. He felt that he had been given back half his own self. He saw his way. Yes, he acquired through that insight another I, another eye, which doubled his point of view. Solus ad solum; yes, he saw in his own soul thus confronted the primordial pair of opposites whose conflict is the warfare which all fiction reports upon. He saw his way. He went out of the caravan without a word and carried those spillable ideas in his head carefully, as a child carries a full cup.

He walked as far as the path led him. Where the path ended, at the brink of a stream, he stopped. It was dark, the luminous June dark. Across that stream, shadows he made out, ruled holly and oak. Robin and wren too, winter and summer, the inseparable opposites. He saw, he heard: a barbarous sound clattered amid the wood fit to cleave it apart.

The sound inside his head of that game which the inseparable opposites play: the beheading game. He stepped across the brook which set the limit on his grandfather's creation, and was alone in that ancient flowerless forest where no paths had been made.

7.

MORE THAN A week later Ettie lay on the bed which almost filled the little bedroom. She listened to the rain pattering on the caravan's roof, watched it stream down the windowpane. Another shadow in the room, her form made so slight a hummock under the quilt that she scarcely seemed to be there, even to herself. Only Aiuto's nose, peeping up onto the pillow beside her, was the cold touch linking her fitfully to existence. The dog knew that all could not be well in a world which allowed him to spend the day in bed; if Kim's chair scraped next door he struggled to leap out. But Ettie clasped him tight. She listened to the hesitant chat-chat of Kim's typewriter as though it was the voice of a girl seducing him, and kept her arms tight round Aiuto.

All week it had rained from a sorrowful low sky. Kim was totally abstracted from her. Physically he filled their living space, bodily he was difficult to circumnavigate: yet so abstracted was his mind that she was utterly alone. Far more lonely than if he had not been there, for he looked through her body and listened through her voice; she felt that she was standing in front of something he wanted to see. And all the time the tap-tap of the typewriter, Morse-keys sending out messages she couldn't decipher. He told her nothing. He watched and listened and wrote.

What could he be writing about except themselves? What else did he know about? The Kim she knew could only write about herself and him, for her Kim knew nothing else. This suspicion of betrayal undermined her like finding microphones hidden in the walls. When he went out, and she heard the tune he whistled, 'The Holly and the Ivy', receding into the sunken woods, he left typed pages face down on the table. She laid meals round them: she wouldn't show her jealousy by prying. Upon one sheet face-up were written three lines with the formality of an epigraph:

Bizonde þe broke, in a bonk, a wonder breme noyse
Quat! hit clattered in þe clyff, as hit cleue schulde
As one vpon a gryndelston hade grounden a syþe

It meant nothing to her. She had lost Kim as if he had vanished, had faded into the trees whistling that carol as out of place in the summer wood as the hollies themselves, those thickets of winter waiting under the oaks like creditors under summer's windows, awaiting the tryst in their green armour till winter should strip the oak's limbs bare. He had faded into the trees and she couldn't follow.

What desolated her was that only so long as his mind had been empty had she been allowed to live in it; now that it had filled with his own purpose there was no room for her. His need for her had been a token of his despair. But she without him was as incomplete as if she had been beheaded. Clack-clack-clack mocked the typewriter next door. She hated the big old black machine which she had herself brought from an attic at Larkford to entice Kim to work. She had set it like a mantrap which had caught him in iron jaws, and into it leaked his time, his holidays, his life's blood which was hers. If she had trapped him surely she could release him? She sprang out of bed and barged into the living-room.

There sat Kim bowed in front of the typewriter. He looked lonelier even than herself, like a boy who can't answer an exam.

'Kim?' she said.

His eyes slowly focused on her.

'Kim would you catch two fish for our supper?'

He rubbed his eyes. 'Two fish. You know what ages it

takes.' He looked at the rainy window. 'I expect the river's in flood.'

Summer was bankrupt, the river washed away. Winter waited. She watched him counting the pages he had written. 'Kim give it up, please give it up and let's go away' she begged. 'We needn't go to France, couldn't we go to Italy? To Rome?' she tempted.

'Rome' he repeated as if wondering where it was. 'No I must go on now I've begun.'

'You only began because I asked. Kim stop now I ask you.'

'It's beyond asking' he said. He got up and went to the window, his hands in the back pockets of his cords. 'It's way beyond asking' he repeated.

'Kim it's only a film. I didn't think it would be so hard.'

'It's not only a film to me.' He returned to his chair and sat down. 'There's no point having waited all this time and then writing some rubbish' he said. 'Useful rubbish.'

She pitied him at the typewriter, Sisyphus at his stone and the hill so steep. 'It might help to go fishing' she suggested.

'Nothing helps.'

'It would help me.'

'I can't help you' he told her. 'Oh I can be useful to you yes. To save you going shopping I can bring you dead fish. But for anything better than useful there's no help. You're alone. I'm alone.'

'But Kim you're not alone, we're married, there's me too.'

He looked at her as though she were the stone he must push up the hill. Then he looked through her. 'No' he said 'there isn't you too, not when it matters. Huddling together doesn't help.'

Alone at the typewriter lonely he might be, but he looked to her complete. She was on the fringe of the light cast by his conviction of what mattered, inadequate in her loneliness, a sickle of moon.

'In the end it's all pretence' he went on, 'all the huddling together people do. In offices, marriages, everything. In the end all there is is what's left when everything is taken away.'

225

She moved restlessly. 'Kim don't play riddles.'

'Riddles are the only serious questions' he said, 'asking riddles is the only way you can make people aware of all you might mean. Riddles put all the possible answers into people's minds. They make people wonder, and there's no other language does that. There's no other language tells people what's truer than facts, it's why mythology is full of riddles.' Evidently it was the subject on his mind; perhaps the matter of his story.

She only clung to what seemed to concern herself. 'So what's the answer then? What is left when everything is taken away?'

'I wonder.'

'You mean you don't know the answer?'

'Not your answer. How would I know what you'd be left with if everything I know you've got was taken away?'

'I'd be left with nothing.'

'Then that's the answer.'

Silence.

'At least it's the answer unless you think for yourself' he said. 'Unless you wonder.'

She closed her mind like a door into the dark. 'Kim I wish you'd go fishing' she repeated, returning to the starting point.

'It's no good. It's too late.' He had returned to an earlier point, was reading what he had written before she came into the room.

'It was you thought we had enough, before' she reminded him.

He didn't look up. 'Adam had enough before Eve came along with the apple' he said 'but he ate it.'

'You mean it's my fault.'

But he wouldn't even allow her centrality as a cause. 'No' he said 'it was the snake's fault. Eve was only trying to be useful.'

He shifted the carriage of his typewriter to begin a new line.

She went back into the bedroom and crept under the quilt.

To need for her very existence what was not hers, as he was not hers—as Jack, as England, as nothing was hers—was to wonder what she had left. She lay clasping Aiuto and gazing through her jampots of herbs on the windowsill, through them and through the wet windows to the melted shapes of trees beyond. She hardly knew that she was crying until the dog moved his muzzle away from her cheek to avoid the trickling tears.

8.

JACK PEEL WALKED through Mayfair towards Sol Wenkel's house wearing the fishing jacket he had bought to direct the movie in. It was as like as he could find to the jacket Kim had worn the day he had split logs in the rain, except that unfortunately his was new, a rather bright green, the material hissing and rustling as he walked. It was a problem with the kind of clothes that were fashionable, how you aged them before they went out of style, and he wondered how Kim had contrived to get his jacket looking so old. He was on his way to collect Kim's story from Sol. A day or two earlier Kim had rung up his service flat.

'Look I've finished a story of sorts' the remote voice had said.

'Terrific, that's terrific Kim.' Jack couldn't help feeling that he had been rung up by a character he had invented himself. It was the protagonist in the film he meant to make who had rung him up. 'A story about the wood?'

'Well—yes. About woods in general you could say. I've tried to get at the answer but ...' The voice failed, though Jack pressed his ear to the receiver to hear more.

'You want to outline the story?'

'You fall in pretty deep' Kim's voice warned. 'I couldn't find another way.'

'I want to fall in deep' Jack encouraged him.

Silence. Then 'I've put it in the post to the address Ettie

gave me. You'll see. Or you may see' he added.

'I'll read it and get back to you.' Then, focusing on the character he had discovered—had invented—that first day in the wood, he asked 'How's the fishing going down there?'

'Fishing? Oh I'm not at Larkford I'm in Paris.'

By this news the image which Jack had invented of Kim was cracked in half. The man in his film had no business in Paris. He ought to be up a tree fishing the way he'd been invented. This character stepping out of character made Jack uneasy about the story. He allowed a couple of days for the post and then set out to collect it from Sol's office.

Not having seen Sol for a week or more he was glad to have an excuse for dropping in. Though still under contract for another couple of months his work on the war movie—which publicity in its mirror-language now described as an anti-war movie—was finished, and nobody talked about the next Sol Wenkel movie to him. The gang which had made the present picture behaved like shipmates nearing port, ostensibly rejoicing at journey's end but in their hearts looking forward to the next voyage together; and Jack suspected that he wasn't going to be signed on again. In self-defence he had started talking about his own film. That people questioned him politely about his project made their solicitude sound to him like condolence. He told them he was going to make a movie about an individual for once, not some bullshit about a crowd of actors pretending to be a crowd of heroes. Everyone thought individuals were terrific. They all wore sneakers to work nowadays, even the associate producer, who was a banker, wore a moustache and National Health spectacles like everyone else. Whether people believed in his film or not the idea that he was going to make one began to have a kind of reality in their minds: you tell people you're going to have a baby, they start in and knit. In this mood of pregnancy he had bought himself the fishing jacket, a prop to convince himself he had conceived a film. It looked rather like a maternity garment the way it billowed around him as he walked.

228

Sol's house with its diamond lattices, its window boxes, its bay trees on the step, resembled a cottage ornée set down in the Mayfair mews. However, as Jack knew, a photo-cell scanned you on the step so that the door sprang open without you pushing the fake bell. Through wreaths of marijuana smoke he could hear Sol talking in a room off the hall. He went in. Sol's large shaggy figure pushed one hand through grizzled hair as he grumbled into the telephone, sunk in a chair in the panelled room, his flying boots crossed on a club fender. The strong-featured face, heavily seamed and furrowed, was made melancholy by solemn eyes. Remarkable eyes, big jewels pouched in the leather face. When he blinked it was with the quickness of a gunfighter.

What Jack noticed was that he had shaved off his moustache. Sol's shaven lip turned his own moustache into fancy dress. 'You junked the tache' he said when Sol clapped down the telephone.

'Didn't fit the new picture.' He held out his cigarette. 'You want a drag of this garbage?'

Jack drew on the joint. So there was a new picture, and he wasn't in it. The impact emptied his gut. He felt as if he just fell out of an aeroplane. Was this how it was being an individual?

'I have your mail in the office' Sol said.

He led the way into a low, crooked, black-beamed room which Jack had copied for him from a farmhouse kitchen they had once used on location. It was all false: beams, fireplace, flagstones, everything. Yet the man himself was real, Jack thought as he followed him; moustache, flying boots, whatever he wore or wherever he lived were external to him, all camouflage like the stripes which disguise the tiger's weight and power in the jungle. He was an individual trying to look like everyone else; the rest of them copied him to try and look like individuals.

'Here's your story' said Sol, handing him Kim's envelope. 'You're on your way Jack. Hope it all works out for you.'

Although dismissed Jack hung on—he hung onto the false

lintel over the hearth as though a real fire burned there, and snow lay on the ground outside. It was winter, facing the future alone.

'You want to tell me a little about the project?' Sol suggested. By dropping into a chair he imposed stillness on the room.

In the stillness of this room Jack saw through the pretence of interest which other people asking him questions had shown in his film. Sol didn't pretend anything. Here what you said echoed, if it was true. Superficially false, this room was the power-house. As in Sol's unswerving eyes, here there was no pretence, no pity, only reality. In reality there was very little to tell about his project. Kim's story was a featherweight in his hand. He tried to break up the stillness by walking around.

'I don't have too much on paper yet' he said. 'I have a lot of notes of stuff I want to use. Images I want in.'

Stillness. No echo.

'Thing strikes me' said Sol's slow voice deep in the wing chair. 'Writer thinks a movie's about words. Designer thinks it's about images. Hell, you even get wardrobe thinks it's about clothes. So on. It isn't. You get to make your own whole movie you realize it isn't about any one of those things. It's about relating them. Relating, narrating—same thing. Proportion. Balance. Vital. You know the Gestalt theory of perception? You read that. You ever think why Apollo has a pair of dividers in his hand? Because fixing the proportion of the figure to its ground is what art is. Relating relationships. You got something good to relate there?'

'This is more like it's a situation I have Sol' Jack said, 'this guy I told you I found, he's really inside of that place. He knows. And he's into the names of trees and flowers and stuff, he's really in deep. And into fishing like he was part of the rod.' It still didn't echo; like wedges in a fouled split the words didn't cleave the wood.

'That's all of it background Jack' came the voice from the chair. 'You think in Oshkosh Nebraska they line up around

230

the block for a botany class? If you want to tell them about trees, first you have to keep them in their seats by relating what you want to say to what they want to know. What they want to hear is more crap like they heard already: you have to relate to their ground. You read the parables, the lesson's related to what those AD 20 mouthbreathers had in their heads already, like it's farming or it's fishing. Right? But you re-make the Bible now, those parables don't relate to any damn thing the subway crowd has in its head anymore. You think J. Christ is about to stand up at Hyde Park Corner and spitball a lot of stuff about the sower going forth to sow? He did, and he wouldn't have the catering problem he had with the 5,000 that time. Look Jack, guy comes to me the other week says How about we make David and Goliath as a Western. I said Fine, break it down, re-relate it. You know all he done? All he done, he wrote a treatment where Goliath is this ten-foot Red Indian. Now related to King David's context okay, Goliath was a giant because people were scared of giants. But if you want the ultimate enemy for cowboy David in Dakota in 1879, no giant Indian is about to scare him. The cowboy's biggest enemy was the man who invented barbed wire: there's your Goliath 1879, it's a creep in a suit is running barbed wire across the cattle ranges. Then you're relating. You follow me? Break the raw material down, relate it to what the mouthbreathers have in their heads already. They don't have trees in their heads anymore and you can't put them there. But if a story's got a meaning when it's related in a wood, then it's still got meaning when you re-relate it to the city they built where the woods was. But you want to find the meaning first and then the setting. The point is Jack, I never liked the way you found the location first, because movies aren't about locations. It's only designers think they are. You could fall in a heap of shit there Jack.'

Jack leaned on the fake lintel. What he had, what he thought he had, disintegrated. He had nothing. In the void he glimpsed how fundamental creativity must be: it wasn't a

231

question of moving existing furniture around, you had to start by making the furniture. You had to go back to the wood and make the furniture. Here the stillness, the grey light, the resonance of Sol's words, reminded him of the hall at Larkford, that other point of equilibrium. If he could only make the shadows of Mrs Vannick's cypresses fall across Sol's mind.

'Hell' he said 'this picture's more of a mood the way I see it.'

'Mood is a bad smell in the front office Jack. You know that.'

'You look at Federico's movies the business they do.'

'You look at the way he got to make those movies he does now' Sol said. 'You don't want to ape the way people act at the top of the tree Jack, you want to ape the way they climbed to get there. Sure Federico talks about moods. Now he has the leverage he can talk riddles if he wants. Shit, he even made a movie about a guy who couldn't make a movie, but don't you copy that without you copy the eight movies he already made which all of the eight made money.'

Money. Oh, money! 'You remember that guy in Rome, the one we had trouble with over the score, remember what he said? The money is the easy part. This writer I found, he's the same type—you know he never even asked about the bread?'

'Jack for the writer maybe the money is the easy part, like getting handed the cup is the easy part after you won the race. But for the producer it's the prerequisite. You know that. You got any money?'

'I plan on looking outside the industry for the pre-production. Like Nick did for his picture.'

'The place Nick looked was his wife's pocket. Jack you can't act like exceptions were rules. I tell you the rule now, rule is if you can't raise the bread inside the industry there's something wrong with the project.'

'Or something wrong with the industry.'

'It's the only industry we have. They got your balls in nutcrackers. They only distribute what they finance. Jack you have to relate to the way things are. This writer you found' he asked next 'he have any track-record?'

'You mean screenplaywise?' said Jack cautiously. Sol was demolishing him piecemeal, stripping him of illusions one by one. Kim's unread story, the featherweight envelope in his hand, was all he had left. 'I don't think he wrote a screen-play yet.'

'What he wrote then?'

'Wrote?' Jack cursed Kim for not being a heavyweight he could flatten Sol with. 'Oh, books and stuff I guess.'

'Any the industry bought?'

'He's not some Hollywood hack Sol. He's something else again. I don't know what he wrote. Maybe what he done been wrong for movies yet.'

'Listen Jack there's no right and wrong, a book sells enough copies it can be a time-table and for some stumble-ass on the Coast it's a movie already for the reason it has leverage. I'm looking for the leverage to get you off the ground and I don't see it. I don't see it in what you tell me you have.'

'What you trying to do to me Sol?' asked Jack, suddenly angry, 'you trying to destroy me?'

'I'm trying to make you relate to the facts Jack. That only destroys your illusions. If I've took away your illusions what you left with?'

'A film I want to make. I want to make a film.'

He spoke with purpose, conviction. His feet were on rock bottom.

'Okay.' Sol's large slow hands were rubbing the tobacco out of a filter cigarette. 'Okay, you go ahead. You remember your objective though—a film. Not some masterpiece but a movie, any movie you can get to make. Throw out everything that doesn't relate to that. Right?'

'Right Sol. Well, I should be on my way.'

'Wait.' He carefully tapped marijuana into the empty cigarette paper. 'I'll pick up your pre-production exes Jack. You pay this writer you found for a draft delivered in two months. I have approval, I take five per cent of the gross if I elect to go ahead. If I want out, you buy the turnaround.'

Money! The bread of life. 'Why, Sol?'

Sol lit his reefer. 'If you're convinced you can make a movie maybe you can.'

Jack walked to the lattice window. 'How much you put up?'

'Five.'

Jack saw the five fingers held up. The bait in the trap. He turned back to the window. He knew its glazing bars, simulated lead, were in fact a steel lattice wired to a burglar alarm. You didn't break into Sol's house easy. But you didn't break out any easier: the house was a steel strap. He took the bait.

'It's a deal' he said.

9.

'You're very rude to Clara' Ettie said to Kim when his sister left them alone in her sitting-room. They were staying the night in London on their way back from Paris.

'I can't stand this house' replied Kim from behind the evening paper.

She looked round. 'What's wrong with it?'

'Everything. Everything I don't want. Tom's life. What's waiting if you fail.' He too looked round the fussy, plushy room. 'Limbo' he concluded.

'It's very comfortable I think.'

'That's the bait. This is the trap.' The newspaper didn't hold his attention. 'I know about that, I took the bait with the job they got me in advertising.'

'What bait? You weren't comfortable.'

'Security. Burglar alarms. Keeping your seat at all costs. And the waste of what you might be if you weren't so busy being useful like Clara is. Being efficient about rubbish that doesn't matter. No I wasn't comfortable thank God' he said 'I'd still be there if I'd made myself comfortable.'

'I thought you rather admired Clara.'

'I thought I had to. I thought I had to learn to.'

'You've still got a job Tom got you' she reminded him. 'However much you mock.'

If she expected to needle him he was unperturbed. 'Yes but it isn't the middle of my life any more.' He read the paper.

'What is then?' she asked presently, someone on tiptoe trying to look over a high wall.

He did not reply.

In a moment or two Clara came bustling into the room with the coffee tray, setting it ready now, at seven o'clock, so that it would be at hand after dinner. It was her latest improvement for running things smoothly. Ettie jumped up to help, admiring the electric percolator.

'Yes they're so little trouble' Clara said, 'I'll give you the name of the shop.'

'I should wait till we taste the coffee' said Kim from behind the paper, 'the question is not Is it no trouble? The question is What's the coffee like?'

Clara looked at him. Kim felt his sister's animadversion, but it came now from so great a distance, she was so remote, that it didn't trouble him. They were divided; it was a relief to acknowledge the severance. What had hurt hitherto like a rift in himself, this division from his sister which it had seemed essential from childhood to reconcile, had now become the separation, the freedom, of himself from an alien. He had eliminated what he was not.

But it irritated him that Ettie had admired the percolator. In France, hearing her speak her own language again, he had been struck by the observation that in French her vocabulary contained fewer of the conciliatory politenesses which her English persona mouthed. In French her views, her whole identity, was in sharper focus; to France she was related, both by blood and as a figure to its ground. He had realized that the porter who carried her bag off the boat onto French soil was related to her more nearly than he was himself. She was a foreigner, which he had begun to overlook. The recognition

235

strengthened both her identity and, in consequence, her separateness, as a line drawn round a figure both contains what it is and excludes what it is not. Because of the sense of his own non-attachment, of his freedom, which had come to him since finishing the film treatment, he had welcomed this strengthened, separated identity at his side. Her independence made him less responsible for her. But now she had started admiring English coffee pots again.

Clara rushed in and out of the room, making one preparation or another, her final pose for Tom's homecoming being to sit down and stitch at her tapestry as though she wasn't busy at all. Behind his paper Kim listened to the conversation between his sister and his wife as if their voices were sound waves squeaking from a distant planet. In the wooded country of his own mind, however isolated, he was no longer unhappy.

At last the front door slammed and the house shook under ascending footsteps. Tom strode through the door, strode through Clara and Ettie's kisses like a hero through a ticker-tape welcome, crossed the room and picked up the telephone. 'Sorry' he said, dialling, 'just remembered something vital. Hallo there Kim. Good holiday?'

'Yes thanks.'

'Paris fun?'

'Yes we——' He stopped, for Tom held up a traffic policeman's hand.

'Hello, Rhineharts?' Tom said into the telephone. 'Get me Mr Swindells will you if he's still in his office.'

Kim returned to his paper. Since finding him employment Tom's manner towards him had become brusque. Before, whilst Kim was at Cambridge or abroad, Tom had dealt warily with him, as with a stranger whom he disapproved but could not measure. Now that Kim had a position within the hierarchy the balance of their relationship had altered; the job was the man, for Tom whose whole life was work, and for a job as humble as Kim's he had no deference. There was no need to deal warily with a clerk. Just as Clara's tireless effi-

236

ciency in matters of no importance irritated Kim, so did Tom's yardstick for measuring men. He listened to the telephone conversation. Meetings. Money. Plans. *We all dwell together to make money from each other. And the Stranger will depart and return to the desert.* Tom's voice: 'Yes, got him with me now, fresh from gay Paree ... what? He doesn't need us to tell him that old boy, he married one. Right you are, I'll see he's delivered back to you safe for Monday morning. Bye old boy, bye.'

Tom hung up, sat rubbing tired eyes with the heels of his palms.

'Darling.' Clara put a Martini in his hand. 'Good day?'

'So so. Well Kim.' He fished out a smile for them all. 'Old Bob says you're fitting in all right, slowly but surely.'

'Actually I'm fitting out. I've decided to chuck it.'

'To chuck it?'

'To give up your job?'

If he had shot himself he wouldn't have shocked them more. Kim too was surprised. Was this a decision?—this sudden explosion? He continued to hide behind the paper.

'You don't want to go chucking too many jobs' Tom commented in a careful voice.

'Tom's not an employment agency you know' Clara warned.

Kim waited for Ettie to speak. She said nothing. He loved her for that silence which was on his side, as if she had shared his decision: he forgot that it was her separateness not her compliancy that he esteemed when he didn't need her support. To his sister he said 'I don't want employment Clara. I've already got something else I want to do.'

But Clara knew how to poke her needle into his head: 'Not this writing surely?'

'What writing?' Tom asked.

'Oh' she said scathingly 'some man asked Kim to try and write some film.'

Tom looked at Kim, still hidden behind the paper. 'If I were you I would look before I leaped' he said.

Decisions had gone to Kim's head. He took another. 'We've

237

decided not to sell the Paradise Wood either' he announced, including Ettie for her loyalty. You said 'decide' and people believed you. He was amazed.

Tom put his Martini carefully on one of Clara's little coasters. 'How far has this film got?' he enquired.

'Nowhere.'

Then Ettie spoke up; 'But it will, it is a very well-known film person doing it. It's not just "some man" Clara.'

Clara smiled coldly and made another stab with her needle. 'You were friendly with some man in films Ettie weren't you? Not him by any chance?'

'Yes but——' Ettie began. Then she sat back. 'Yes, him' she said.

'I see' said Clara.

Kim knew what Clara saw. She saw the figure she feared herself, the configuration she guarded against with her tireless formulae of domesticity but whose outline she saw nonetheless everywhere, emergent wherever she looked, threatening her security, sketched in the dirt on the windowpane as a frame for all the relationships she saw, and framing her own frightened reflection in the dirty glass: in the proper language she spoke, the looking-glass tongue she had learned from magazines, the configuration was called The Eternal Triangle. Amongst people who huddled together in the timekept city the figure stalked and destroyed: out of their very need to huddle together, their fear of isolation and of the Stranger who knew the way to their door, jealousy destroyed them. Kim knew what his sister saw, and he did not fear that.

And Tom saw only money. Kim watched him rub his work-dulled eyes so as to focus upon the goal of his work. 'Kim' he said 'it's all very fine reneging on our contract with Rhineharts but how do you propose to finance Larkford if you won't capitalize the disposable assets?'

'Look Tom, don't try and blind me with money-jargon.'

'You blind yourself with emotional jargon. Calling it the Paradise Wood is emotional jargon.'

238

Kim saw the truth of that. Maybe he didn't need the wood. Maybe it had served its purpose. But Clara said 'Yes exactly Kim. Only Grandfather ever called it the Paradise Wood, and we all know he was mad. You never even knew him.'

'Typical!' Kim cried, throwing aside his paper at last, 'so typical of you. You think he was just an old booby eating muffins because that's all you could see. All right I never went to tea with him: but I know what he was like. I know what was in his mind when he created the wood.'

Clara raised her eyebrows, went on stitching.

Tom said 'You may not find it possible to break our contract with Rhineharts you know. Have you looked at the terms?'

'All they need is money. It's all you want out of it too isn't it, you and Clara?'

Tom looked uncomfortable. 'You say "all"; I don't know where you'll get it quite.'

'I'll sell things I don't want. The rubbish.'

'You won't get much for rubbish.'

'What I don't want is rubbish. The house is full of things I don't want any more.'

To Tom Clara said 'I didn't think the contents of Larkford would last long once Father was gone.'

'Clara it's a question of elimination' Kim told her. 'If you can have everything, like Grandfather had, or if you just keep hoping for a lucky break like Father did, you never have to choose. But need makes you eliminate. The last thing you're left with when everything is taken away is all you need.'

'There is Mother to be considered. It's her home.'

'The pictures and stuff aren't holding up the walls you know. The house won't fall down. So long as we don't start looking for dry rot' he added.

'Oh' sighed Clara, in her agitation getting up and plumping the cushion she had been sitting on, 'and just when everything seemed to be going so well at last, with you settled in a job.'

'Not well Clara' Kim said. 'Just neatly.'

'And what's wrong with neatness?' she flared at him.

'Just that it doesn't exist. It's the pattern nobody fits.'

'Well people should try at least' she asserted. 'And Mother deserves to be left in peace I should say.'

'Oh for God's sake Clara' he cried 'don't keep wheeling Mother onstage like the blind flower girl in a weepie.'

'Kim how dare you!'

'Well it's true you do. You try and use her. And she doesn't need phoney pity, or wheeling anywhere by you or me or anyone. Whatever anyone takes away from her she'll keep all she needs.'

'That is true darling' Tom said, 'your mother is well able to look after her own interésts.'

Clara grabbed up their martini glasses. 'Do you want to eat?' she demanded fiercely.

'You already ate the guests' Kim said.

When they laughed he wondered if they thought that the stand he had taken was a joke too; if he had after all decided nothing, never would. But on the way downstairs Tom said 'If you've made up your mind, well and good. We know where we are. You'd better get a pal of mine in Sotheby's down to value what you don't want.'

'Yes I will.' The pace at which he felt the water flowing convinced him that he had jumped in. 'It won't affect your Hampshire house, you'll get Clara's share I promise.'

'Oh that. If Larkford's there for certain I wonder if we really need it, the Hampshire place. Might leave her money in Larkford ... anyway I'll talk to her.' Then he chuckled, looked sideways at Kim: 'Blow for old Bob Swindells.'

Surprised, Kim asked 'Are you secretly anti-Swindells?'

'Don't tell him that. He has his uses.'

'He wouldn't believe me anyway' Kim said.

'No he wouldn't I suppose. He simply ignores the fact that nobody likes him.' Tom paused, his hand on the dining-room door, considering Swindells. 'He makes his own world' he said 'really rather a wonderful feat, to make a world where it doesn't matter if no one likes you.'

'He's unassailable' Kim agreed. 'He'll convince himself there isn't any gravel under our land, you see if he doesn't. It won't be a blow at all. Nothing will ever be a blow to Swindells.'

'Until he gets the news that he can't take it with him, this world he's constructed.'

They went into the dining-room together, where Clara had already lit the candles from a box of matches she kept handy for that purpose.

10.

KIM AND ETTIE arrived back at their caravan on Saturday, but Kim would not go to Larkford to see his mother until he had been to the office on Monday and resigned. Ettie was glad of this independence, in which she felt that she shared; even the fact that he had not consulted her before taking his decision seemed to her to increase their self-sufficiency as a unit, Kim counting upon her agreement as though upon part of himself. Like the ivy and its host they met the axe together. Their trip to France, the awkwardness of her parents, had made it plain to her that France was no longer her home. At last she accepted that. But the more she eliminated of what she was not, the larger grew Kim's share of what remained. She was reconciled to the fact that half her proper name, and all her context, was now Kim's.

The only thing that was not Kim's, and she guarded her possession the more jealously because it was so small an illusion to keep out of all the illusions she had given up, was her dog Aiuto. With him she shared that melting ice-floe, the kingdom of childishness.

On Monday evening she walked over to collect Aiuto from Larkford, where she had left him whilst they were in Paris; it did not seem like a homecoming until she and he were reunited, so she chanced meeting Mrs Vannick and called his name stealthily through the empty house. She found him in her mother-in-law's upstairs sitting-room, relaxing on a sofa from which he arose slowly, yawning, stretching his delicate frame, a smile in his velvet eyes. By her own love and need she was able to excite him into staging a welcome. Then she scribbled a note, put on his collar and took him away. Walking back across the fields, watching him range the valley swift and free as a sunshaft, her spirits rose. That uncatchable swiftness was hers.

She came upon the Rolls-Royce where she had first seen it, parked by the gate into the wood, as if it had never really gone away. Sleek, black, predatory, it waited like a cat at a mousehole. It had come for her. The full penalty for her actions had not yet been exacted. As if she saw her own executioner, she was frightened. There is one who remembers the way to your door.

She whistled up her dog and entered the wood with him at her heel. She knew where Jack would be if he wasn't already at the caravan. When she saw him, before he saw her, she hesitated. Apprehension clubbed her stomach—that same sensation which once she had thought was excitement. The free fall. He was pushing the swing to and fro in a dangling arc. Against the trunk of the tree leaned a long thin parcel. A present: she wouldn't accept it. She stepped into the clearing.

'Hello Jack. Did Kim know you were coming?'

'He knew I'd come. He around?' Jack had let her approach close to him; now he turned and picked up his parcel, avoiding contact with her.

'No he's at work' she said. So the present was for Kim. It was not for her after all that he had come. Was she jealous or relieved? 'He'll be back before long.'

'At work? Cutting wood you mean?'

'No at his office. He works for the gravel company.' It seemed trivial to her now, what Kim pretended to do. The time for truth had come.

The news evidently disconcerted Jack. But, committed to

his own pretence that you took things as they came and nothing surprised you, he asked no questions. He hesitated, energy leaking to waste in fussy strokes of his clean-shaven upper lip. Copying the casualness of powerful men, he lacked their repose. Ettie remembered the first time she had gone out with him, how upset he had been to find the restaurant closed; he had not progressed since then. She had. She began to relax.

'We might meet him coming home if we walk up' she suggested.

'Okay fine.' He tucked the parcel under his arm.

Midsummer roofed their path with unvaried green. The flowers had fallen. The quintessence of the wood had withdrawn into the imagination of those who knew it.

'Happy to be back?' Jack asked.

'Paris was awful' she admitted.

'You never did like Paris when you finally got there, did you? Remember the Christmas with me you kept on wanting to get to Paris?'

'You never stopped me wanting to go back there.'

'Can anyone?'

'Yes' she said. 'Yes, now I stopped wanting to go back.'

'Now you just going to stick around here?'

'Now I just don't mind much where.'

He looked up at the leaden foliage in the heat of the evening. She knew that he couldn't see the point of the place, and she was glad. What he had come for had evaded him.

'Dull here all of the time isn't it?' he suggested.

'You need the dull parts' she replied.

She, or the wood, irritated him. 'Not in the movie I don't.'

'Then you won't get the whole wood in your film. Or the whole anything.'

'I'll get what I need' he said. They walked side by side under the stale trees until he went on: 'The spring is all I need. What was here when I first come, all flowers and ... But Christ, you know what?' he asked, suddenly aggrieved, 'in this story of Kim's the whole time it's winter. He threw out the

243

flowers. The whole point, and he threw it out. Christ, in winter it could be any wood.'

She saw. She heard the carol Kim had whistled, the barbarous counterpoint of winter underlying summer's flowers. Only the stripped frame of the oak met the green-armed holly by the frosty stream in winter. She saw what Kim saw, as the ivy sees through its host's branches, and said nothing.

'How about this movie Ettie?' asked Jack presently, 'you want Kim to do it do you?' He waited. 'Because I tell you, as it stands his story won't work. For one thing it's unfilmable. For another I can't understand what the hell it's about.'

She smiled. 'I doubt if he'll change it' she said, 'I doubt if he'll put the flowers back in for you.'

'So you don't care either way, right?'

'What he decides.'

'Sweetheart, it's me does the deciding.'

'What he accepts then.'

Irritably he said 'You talk like accepting's as good as deciding. Deciding you impose, right?—you choose and impose. Remember I told you that way back in Rome? Accepting, why, you just knuckle under with the other schlmiels.'

'People who try and impose' she said, and shook her head. 'It's people who can't accept who try and impose.'

'You only parrot this kind of stuff from Kim' he said. 'That kind of thinking is the way the schlmiels try and justify the way they are.'

'Yes' she admitted 'I only copy what someone says. I only ever will.'

They had reached the caravan. The sun's fire still burned in the highest trees but beneath them the wood was dark, burnt out. Call it choosing, she thought, call it what you like; maybe it was just an age she had reached, ossification, but she was certain that she would remain as she was. In this mould her fluidity had set. She sat down on the step with her arm round her dog, and did not invite Jack into the caravan.

She had forgotten how mean his mouth looked without a moustache.

By the time Kim appeared they were both glad to see him. His long stumbling stride which Ettie loved hardly hesitated when he saw Jack, but carried him towards them between the rotten haycocks he had never burned.

Jack sprang up and greeted him. 'Brought you a present' he said, putting it into Kim's hand.

'A present?' Kim weighed the long thin parcel cautiously.

'Well?' Ettie enquired. She was anxious to be certain that he had given up his job, expected a sign.

Kim gave none. He busied himself opening paper and box. From a canvas cover he drew the two pieces of a trout rod which he fitted together. When he sprang the cane to and fro the rod lay so naturally in his hand, as a tool fits the hand of a craftsman, that it appeared to have belonged to him before he accepted it. Yet he didn't seem to want it: he gave it to Ettie. 'It's lovely' he said 'you feel.'

'Lovely' she agreed, and leaned it against the caravan.

'It's in place of the one you broke' Jack said. They were as polite as two children with a present they mistrusted. He didn't mind that: his object had not been to please Kim but to introduce coinage, the idea of payment, indebtedness. Once Kim had accepted this thin end of the wedge he would accept money; and for money Jack would make him work in the direction Jack chose. 'How about we take it down to the river and try it out' he suggested, 'we can talk while you fish.'

He knew that Kim's manners would make him accept. He wanted to set up the scene he had first found, Kim fishing, so as to start over again; and this time he would dictate the proceedings, on his own terms. When Kim had found a reel and some flies they set off together through the dusk of the wood. He waited for Kim to speak.

'You read the story I sent?' Kim asked.

Jack left silence like an antechamber Kim had to wait in. He was determined to keep control over the direction of the conversation, and in his head was a synopsis of what Sol had said to him—now reworked and scaled down so it fitted inside his narrower comprehension—with which he planned to annex Kim the way Sol had annexed him. He put it in order and began: 'Kim I tell you what we have to think about. The lines we have to think along is how we relate to this background we have in the wood here. The whole trick is you have to relate. You know the Gestalt theory of perception?'

'Never heard of it.'

'Look and I'll show you.' He plucked a pad from his denim shirt, leaned it against a tree and sketched on it with a gold pencil: he copied the figure he had found in an encyclopedia when he had looked up Gestalt after Sol used the name. If you looked at the image one way you saw two profiles face to face; if you looked again you saw the outline of a chalice contained between the two profiles. 'See here' he said.

Kim took the pad. 'Yes it's fascinating' he said.

'Get the trick? You can see it two ways.'

'Yes I know the idea. It isn't a trick' Kim said 'it's a question of keeping two things in balance in your mind at the same time. The eye can't do it but the brain can. Like the eye can't see the wood for the trees, only the brain can. It's your brain you have to look with, to see ... But it isn't a trick' he repeated, studying the drawing, 'it's true, it's the way things are.'

It was a trick to Jack. 'You said you didn't know the theory' he said.

'I said I didn't know what it was called.'

'Gestalt. It's called Gestalt.' Jack had shot the idea dead and put its name on file in his mind. But Kim's absorption was with the live idea. It made Jack jealous—did the figure mean so much? To him it was a trick his magpie brain picked up and stored for its glitter. He didn't see its application to reality. Did anyone? Maybe Sol did, and now he had given it to Kim maybe Kim did. Like the carrier of a disease, he was immune himself but able to pick up the germ and pass it on; the crippling disease of understanding, which he could not catch. He took his pad away from Kim: he had to keep control.

'Now Kim I tell you' he said 'what I wanted from you was a story fits the ground we have. A story to fit with the background we already have.' He discarded Gestalt, which had bent in his hand, and drew another of Sol's weapons: 'Listen, guy came to me the other day said how about we make David and Goliath as a cowboy picture. So I told him "Okay, but remember Goliath isn't no ten-foot Red Indian to a cowboy, Goliath is the man who invented barbed wire". You follow? Same way in our movie——'

'But that's a marvellous idea' Kim said. 'Are you going to do it?'

'It's one of the things I might do if this wood project screws up' Jack said. He saw he'd have to keep Kim and Sol apart: with the way they'd understand each other there'd be no go-between needed. He went back to what he wanted himself and left Sol out of it. 'All I needed from you Kim was a story we could film in this wood' he repeated in plain terms.

'You could film my story in any wood' Kim said.

'I know!—now give me the good news. Where's all the flowers and stuff that makes this wood special? Where's the whole point of it being this wood?'

'It's there' Kim said, 'it's there if you look.'

'You could have fooled me.'

'The winter fools people. But the flowers are there . . . in the wood, in the sap. Is immanent the word? But leaves and flowers come and go, if you want a story related to the wood itself it has to be about what doesn't come and go. It has to be about what's behind the flowers. Look' he said 'look, if you saw a Western about the man who invented barbed wire you wouldn't recognize him as Goliath would you? The idea behind him is what he shares with Goliath, you have to look through appearances to see ideas. You have to look through the leaves to see the trees, and through the wood to see what it means. I agree about relating' he said, 'it's making the archetypal figure wear everyday clothes, like the mediaeval painters dressed Christ in the clothes they wore themselves.

That's relating. The deceptive figure like a riddle which means more than the eye understands at one glance—look at the image you drew.'

He reached out for the notepad but Jack wouldn't surrender it. 'Kim that Gestalt crap is only some professor's theory. This movie——'

'Don't call it names that don't matter, look at it! You talk about it but you won't look! You can't see the truth in what you draw yourself' he said 'how can you see it in what I've written?'

Silence. Night approached under the trees.

'We better get on down to the river if you're going to fish' Jack said.

As they walked on he shifted his ground; by elimination of what he did not understand the ground that was left to him defined itself. 'Kim you listen' he began again 'okay you and me know all of that stuff that's behind your story, but how about the customers Kim? No one told the mouthbreathers about mediaeval painters and stuff, right?' His voice strengthened. 'Look, I'll give it you bad: that stuff we know about is the lead balloon. You think in Oshkosh Nebraska they're about to line up around the block for our views on the Gestalt theory of perception? No way. And it's those mouthbreathers we have to relate to Kim. Christ' he said 'you talk about context, let's have a look at this thing in the context of the movie business shall we? That's what it has to relate to: to filling a movie house. This isn't some deathless fucking poem we're constructing right now, it's a movie it's supposed to be. Okay later maybe we put the subtlety in. Right now our problem is we have to knock up a script I can show the front office they'll understand. Look, those guys in the drip-dry suits don't know if they're making movies or wheaties half time, you ever think what kind of crap they understand?' Kim was silenced. Jack went on 'So let's look what we got already we can sell. We got this wood the way it was first time I come here, right? A great setting. So let's not throw that out the window. All you need more is some girl-boy stuff, couple
248

living in the wood maybe, happy, no money, then you have another guy come along, guy in a big car comes busting in— I'm only spitballing to show you how damn easy it could be if you don't do it the hard way. Sure it'd need working up, need a writer. But stuff I can point a camera at. See what I'm getting at.'

'Certainly I see what you're getting at. Yes I do.'

Encouraged, Jack explained 'People like to be taken out of themselves at the movies Kim, given a treat: soon as the lights dim the subway crowd want to quit worrying about their mortgage and say to themselves There's a couple don't even have a house, wish I could dump the wife and live out in the woods with a movie actress and squirrels and things all around. See?' he said, peering into Kim's face in the shade of the trees. He could not make out its expression.

They had almost reached the river before Kim spoke. 'I didn't think you just wanted to make a TV commercial for the Garden of Eden' he said. He sighed. 'I know why ad agencies make rubbish like that, the formulae take over from the people and just churn it out. What I don't understand' he said 'is anyone going into films especially to make rubbish.'

'I'm not going in I'm in already' Jack replied 'and I tell you, first off I aim to make a movie. Just a movie. Okay postpone the masterpiece, we'll make that next. What I need now is a script I can sell a backer on. You can write it—anyone could write it. Then next when we have leverage we make the masterpiece. Listen Kim; there's bread in this. I can get you probably a thousand advance and you'd wind up with five six grand maybe—see, look, I'll show you how I figure it.'

He snatched out his notepad again and began scribbling sums over the chalice or silhouettes he had drawn earlier. Holding up the pad to catch the failing light he explained the figures to Kim: pre-production, below-the-line, turnaround and the rest of the jargon of the trade. Kim peered at the sums like a boy called up to the master's desk.

'How did you get this much money without a script?' he asked.

Jack paused. 'I'll be straight with you Kim, I know why I got the bread' he said. 'I have this bread promised to keep me quiet a couple of months till Sol has his anti-war picture in the can and my contract runs out. Sol, he hates to have people croak on a movie, it's bad vibes, so what he's done he gives me money like it was a Monopoly set he lent me to play with. He doesn't care if I set up a movie or if I fall in a bucket of shit so long as I stay out of his hair for two months. No script and he'll sue me for his money back. But the two months I have, and the money.'

'It seems to me you've got the frame and no picture still. Which you told me the first time we met—when you said the money was the easy part' Kim reminded him.

'Yes but now I really have the money I see it different' Jack replied. 'We spitball a picture you and I. Any picture that'll fit the frame we already have. Look Kim' he said 'there may be good films and bad films, but there's one kind is definitely the lead balloon, is the kind you can't get off the ground. Whatever the hell masterpiece the writer thinks it is. The movie business Kim, it's a whole nother context from books and stuff. Christ, you hear Sol talk you think he painted the "Mona Lisa", you go to a movie he made you think What happened to the genius? I tell you what happened, the genius is out to lunch planning the next picture. While the tradesman makes this one to pay for the genius's lunch. That's the film industry if you want to work in it.'

They had come to the liquid darkness of the river too late to fish. Kim said nothing, watched the water flowing. It's opacity, the withdrawal of light and translucence, made the idea that it held fish unimaginable.

Jack turned his wrist to read his watch by the sky's glow. 'I must get back to London' he said 'you call me when you think about it.'

'Why me?' Kim asked.

'Why you? It's your wood.'

'You can use the wood. I think I've finished with it' Kim said.

'Listen Kim, you hang on. Next we'll make the master-piece.'

'People don't make masterpieces next.'

'Being about to is what keeps them happy. That they don't keeps the audience happy. You think, and you call me to-morrow. Now I have to get out of the wood before I miss my way again. Take care.'

He crackled away through the wood like a flame spitting along a powder train, and was gone.

Kim wondered what he would do. Take Jack's offer? What was the difference between working for Peel or Swindells? None. Both meant surrender. What urged him to surrender was recognition that the question his story had tried to answer had been asked him by a liar.

Perhaps it didn't much matter what happened. They could film in the wood or not, as they chose. They could either of them, Swindells or Peel, put the place into a wheelbarrow and burn it, as Mr Stroud had done with his garden at Blewston. But he was the flame as well as what the flame consumed. Not what happened, but what he made of whatever happened, might count for something. That was what he understood by the glistening water which, it now seemed to him, might hold Leviathan. He had answered the question, and it didn't matter who had asked it.

He heard Ettie's voice, clear as his sister's had once sounded in her secret language, calling Aiuto from the steeps above. Help! Help! she called. But not for him. He heard the Rolls start in the lane, saw its tiger eyes peer among the trees, hunting. But not for him. He was alone in the midst of the wood, as he had always been. His spirits rose.

Ann Oakley

The Men's Room

Charity Walton has everything she could want. A husband, four children, a successful career, *and* a lover. To say nothing of a more adventurous sex life.

But if Charity knows what she wants, the same cannot be said of the men in her life. Sexually spellbound by the exuberant Mark Carleton, she finds herself in thrall to a relationship that makes her feel both claustrophobic and abandoned. For Mark is energetically unfaithful, and the slow, tortured disintegration of their lives together is poignantly both sad and funny, a love story of a different kind.

'Devastating.' *Sunday Times*

'Ann Oakley knows her habitat well . . . she displays an unfailing generosity in allowing each of her New Bohemians, even the women, to take a turn as the butt of her jokes . . . a touching, bitter story.'   *Observer*

'What keeps one reading is Ann Oakley's straightforward narrative skill, her ability to make one want to know what happens next . . . *The Men's Room* is a guide to what both men and women want . . . I have never read a book quite like it.'   Anthony Thwaite, *New Statesman & Society*

Flamingo

Alice Thomas Ellis

Home Life Three

In this third collection of weekly articles from the *Spectator*, Alice Thomas Ellis once again brings inexhaustible wit and profound sagacity to her commentary on the ups and downs and inside-outness of daily life in town and country.

Pondering on life's little ironies as she fields minor crises from the perverse behaviour of domestic appliances to the accidents befalling Loved Ones – be they pets or people – she quips and cusses her way through the year with a mixture of jeu d'esprit and despair. Musing sanguinely or with a measure of hysteria on the cast of friends, family and other creatures who embroider and beleager her life, and on matters of concern from conifers to cardboard boxes, she amuses and enlightens us as ever with those irrepressible secret-of-the-universe-type insights.

'A wonderful mixture of classical education and homespun philosophy.' Robert Harris, *Observer*

'There are people who buy the *Spectator* purely to read Alice Thomas Ellis, in the same way diners willingly confront the fried eye and thorny dampness of *truite aux amandes* simply to eat the nuts off the top.' Clare Boylan, *Sunday Times*

Flamingo

E. Annie Proulx

Heart Songs and Other Stories

The nine stories in *Heart Songs* introduce a unique, new voice in contemporary American fiction. The settings are small New England blue-collar towns; the characters are the dispossessed working class confronted by an influx of Yuppies from New England cities; and the themes are the traps people set for one another, out of malice or naiveté, premeditation or misunderstanding. The stories in *Heart Songs* play on all keys – loneliness and lunacy, dead-end humour, country music, and the saving grace of trout fishing. E. Annie Proulx writes of her New Englanders' pinched lives with the understanding and irony of a northern Faulkner.

'A new writer of such unarguable talent that it is not a question of "promise" but of performance.'
Vermont Sunday Magazine

Flamingo

Flamingo

Flamingo is a quality imprint publishing both fiction and non-fiction. Below are some recent titles.

Fiction
- [ ] Rich in Love *Josephine Humphreys* £3.99
- [ ] City of Blok *Simon Louvish* £3.99
- [ ] Deep Diving *Stephanie Conybeare* £3.99
- [ ] States of Emergency *André Brink* £3.95
- [ ] Rock Springs *Richard Ford* £3.95
- [ ] The Silence of the Sirens *Adelaida Morales* £3.95
- [ ] Playing Foxes *Helen Dixon* £3.95
- [ ] Blue Eyes, Black Hair *Marguerite Duras* £3.50

Non-fiction
- [ ] A Pike in the Basement *Simon Loftus* £3.95
- [ ] Solitude *Anthony Storr* £3.95
- [ ] A Leaf in the Wind *Peter Hudson* £3.99
- [ ] In the Land of Israel *Amos Oz* £3.99
- [ ] Taking it Like a Woman *Ann Oakley* £3.95
- [ ] Feeding the Rat *Al Alvarez* £3.95
- [ ] Uncommon Wisdom *Fritjof Capra* £4.95

You can buy Flamingo paperbacks at your local bookshop or newsagent. Or you can order them from Fontana Paperbacks, Cash Sales Department, Box 29, Douglas, Isle of Man. Please send a cheque, postal or money order (not currency) worth the purchase price plus 22p per book (or plus 22p per book if outside the UK).

NAME (Block letters) _____

ADDRESS_____

_____

_____